Praise for Sara Read's *Johanna Porter Is Not Sorry*

"Laugh out loud funny and poignant, this debut novel gem has it all, a messy soccer mom on the run, an art heist, dubious choices, and a heartwarming love story. I loved it! Sara Read is a writer to watch."

—Lori Foster, *New York Times* bestselling author

"*Johanna Porter Is Not Sorry* is a story of one woman's excavation of identity, and the inevitable mess before the beauty happens. Debut author Sara Read's prose is agile and evocative in this nuanced exploration of human imperfection, reminding us how sometimes the transformation we seek can only happen when we get out of our own way. Vivid, visceral, and sexy—I loved it."

—Jen Devon, author of *Bend Toward the Sun*

"Debut novelist Read has created a thoroughly sympathetic character in this witty, quick, and emotionally turbulent tale that will have readers cheering for Johanna well after the last page."

—*Booklist*

"*Johanna Porter Is Not Sorry* is...a fast read with a strong message about women learning to stand on their own, and powerful men who do as they please."

—*Star Tribune*

"I could gush about so many things in this book. I do want to point out the writing—it is brilliant! The plot is clever, mixing an art heist with payback, art, addiction, self-discovery, and even romance. I loved Johanna for her spunk and spirit."

—Susan Ballard, *Subakka Bookstuff*

Also by Sara Read

Johanna Porter Is Not Sorry

To learn more about Sara Read,
visit her website, sararead.net.

PRINCIPLES
OF
(E)MOTION

SARA
READ

GRAYDON
HOUSE

**GRAYDON
HOUSE®**

Recycling programs
for this product may
not exist in your area.

ISBN-13: 978-1-525-83665-7

Principles of (E)motion

Graydon House
22 Adelaide St. West, 41st Floor
Toronto, Ontario M5H 4E3, Canada
www.GraydonHouseBooks.com
www.BookClubbish.com

Printed in U.S.A.

To Morgan and Mia

Logic moves in one direction, the direction of clarity, coherence and structure. Ambiguity moves in the other direction, that of fluidity, openness, and release.

—William Byers, *How Mathematicians Think*,
Princeton University Press, 2007

PROLOGUE

On the day that felt like the end, I arrived at my grandmother's house having survived a transcontinental nonstop flight on nothing more than benzodiazepines and the kindness of a flight attendant named Parthy. I was all of twenty-three years old.

My cab pulled up behind a motorcycle parked on the street, and I got out and climbed the steps to the yard. Nestled at the bottom of a hill near a bend of Rock Creek in swampy DC, the grand, wooden structure had a reserved manner, set back amid four giant oaks and an acre of overgrown garden. A porch wrapped around three sides, and at the corner rose a matronly tower.

My grandmother lived there alone. It's no wonder a person would want company in a place that big.

As I reached the porch, a man wearing a tool belt came to the front door, and my heart rate spiked. I wasn't expecting anyone but Lila. But it only took a second to see that he was just as startled as I, which was oddly calming.

He was younger than me, but not by a lot. Taut and wiry

with close-cut brown hair and a long, bony nose. He held the door open for me, and I stepped inside.

Lila's voice carried from the back of the house. "Meggie—finally. Isaac, could you help with her bags before you go?"

I had that feeling when you have to talk to someone and you're not ready. The sudden exposure. And I think he felt it too. He looked up, his expression flat and opaque.

His eyes were an unusual color. Reddish-brown, like cinnamon. I must have looked too close, and for a split second his defense slipped. Suddenly we really saw each other, and it surprised us both.

"This is all I have." I motioned to my carry-on. "The rest is being shipped."

"Yes, ma'am," he said, clearly relieved.

I watched Lila approach through the big center hall with her slow, limping gait, a tiny, birdlike woman in wire-rimmed glasses, white braid hanging over her shoulder, peasant dress swirling around her ankles. She kissed my cheek and turned to Isaac.

"This is Meg. Remember I said she was coming? Meg, this is Isaac Wells." She gave him a fond look. "He's the only reason this old place is still standing."

He managed a polite smile—he couldn't have been more than twenty—looking like all he wanted in the world was to make his exit. I knew what that was like.

"So next week?" Lila said to Isaac.

"Yes, ma'am." He nodded as he stepped out and closed the big door behind him.

When I graduated college at sixteen, the *Washington Post* wrote it up. *Newsweek* magazine ran a profile when I cracked the Karvonen Hypothesis at twenty. But no one—not the news or the gray eminences of mathematics—would be interested in this phase of my career, where I left the validating structure of academia and went into the wilderness. Where I became unaffiliated and therefore "unserious."

Leaving my academic life behind and coming here felt like the first decision I ever made entirely for myself, but it hadn't been exactly voluntary. The panic attacks were getting worse, and more than once I had had to cancel class. I left before I broke, though not by much.

But though I earned disapprobation with my hasty departure, I gained a single, key freedom. I could now work on Frieholdt's Conjecture uninterrupted and without the oblique digs and outright scorn of my peers.

My father himself introduced me to Frieholdt's when I was fifteen years old, and ever since it had been my guiding star. A fine riddle for a gifted teenager, Frieholdt's was not considered solvable. For two hundred years it had withstood every attempt. Veteran math professors had nicknamed it the Impossible.

But not impossible for me.

As I stood in Lila's foyer, it was as though a dry, dusty shell fractured and fell from my body. As fragile and exposed as I felt underneath, I was safe here, and finally I could breathe. No one to perform for. No one's expectations to fulfill. Only a big, quiet house and my wisp of a grandmother. My relief was both immense and exhausting.

Lila patted my arm, her palm soft as ancient flannel. "I'm so glad you're here. How long can you stay?"

Turns out I could stay for fifteen years.

1

The night before Lila's funeral, I rose from my nest on the couch in my study on the third floor of the tower. I had not been sleeping well. Across the room, a damp wind blew through the open window. With both hands, I wrestled it down. The windowpanes and sashes were curved to match the walls of the tower, and they tended to stick. This one wouldn't shut the last inch, so I gave it up, turned off the lamps, and returned to my couch, pulling a throw blanket over my legs. Outside, bluish beams of streetlight illuminated the top limbs of the trees as they swayed in the wind.

Since Lila's death, I had felt so unmoored that it was almost a physical sense of drift. After spending nearly every hour of every day spooning applesauce off her chin, drawing her ancient arms through threadbare sleeves, bathing and changing her, waking up when she cried out in the night, I felt her absence like a missing chamber of my own heart. So I went where I always went when I needed an anchor. Back to Frieholdt's.

My family thought I was in denial, spending the days and

nights after her death closed in my study, but it wasn't denial. It was comfort. As Lila's needs had increased, I'd had less and less time for Frieholdt's Conjecture, and now after all that time away, I had new perspective, like seeing it for the first time. I could feel the answer just at the extremity of my understanding.

I was also exhausted. I tugged the blanket toward my chin. Past the rain-rippled windows, the air, water, and trees all moved in apparent entropy—so much turbulence against the unmoving light—and as a mathematician's mind tends to do, mine searched for patterns. They were always present, and always changing.

I must have slept, because I woke to dark and stillness. The fitful rain had stopped. A single cicada chirped in the top of a tree. As I ascended into a sleep-loosened consciousness, a light glinted—a bright, inner North Star—and in less than an instant I was on my feet, as awake as I had ever been in my life.

Comprehension cannot be predicted. It may come when bidden, one may struggle after it for a lifetime, or it may wait two hundred years to send its bright ray through the darkness. That night, comprehension picked me. It picked four in the morning, after a week of relentless, grief-driven focus. But it found me ready. I knew from a lifetime of training that when the ray of light appeared, I had to keep my eyes on it and not look away, no matter the consequences.

Though the rest of the third floor was a glorified attic with sloping roof and dormer windows, the tower room maintained the grandeur of the rest of the house. I paced the floor, eyes closed, head tilted up.

I forgot the emptiness of the bedroom below my feet where Lila had breathed her last breath. I followed the bright rail of my thoughts as they plunged through the darkness, skimming along, light and swift, to the very center of Frieholdt's Conjecture where I could finally see the last remaining knot. It lay within the Gault function, itself contained within the Wang-Hickman method, a central tool used to predict the motion of noncompressible fluids. The threads grew clear, loosening, almost floating.

From a bent bit of gutter, a single rivulet of water tap-tapped onto the balcony. The pattern began to form.

Turbulence: resistance. Constraint pulling inward. And in parallel, release: spooling out. The opposite of friction. Twin forces, intertwined, dancing.

Math is logic purified to its essence. And logic seeks order and sequence. Deep within that last tangle, I separated the radiant strands. I restrung them and laid them straight, end to end, and at last—*at last*—they formed a jetway to the center of the universe.

Feet barely touching the floor, I went to my board—five feet tall and twelve feet wide, built to fit the curved wall, with a hand-carved ledge at the bottom—and lifted a cool piece of chalk between my fingers.

Daylight shone through the windows when I woke, still clutching the nub of chalk.

There on my board were a series of functions and shapes in green, white, and yellow. A dimensional representation. A kind of mathematical shorthand.

At that moment, it was not something I could have presented even to another mind such as my own. Still more a small pot holder than a perfectly woven tapestry, but it was all there. So much simpler than I had imaged. As if it had been there all along—which, like all math, it had.

Done.

Twenty-three years of study. Done.

My hands trembled. I blinked, sure that it would disappear or dissolve into nonsense as it had done so many times before. I turned my back, crossed the room, and looked at it from a distance.

Still there.

I opened the window and looked out. Back in the early spring, a work crew had started a renovation on the big house across the street. Men. Trucks. Lumber. The damp smell of oak and grass wafted in. It made me think of Isaac.

I wished I could tell him *I did it. I really did it.* He always believed I could, if for no other reason than I believed it myself.

There's a feeling when you meet someone, that somehow you've known them all your life. And not even all *your* life. Like you've known them all of some other life where you are completely yourself. Not the one you're living, where you are who people expect you to be, but some better life. The one you should have been living all along. That's how it was with Isaac.

No one in my family had known him except Lila, and now the memory was mine alone. And perhaps even Lila didn't know what we became to one another.

I turned and looked at my board again. It still seemed impossible, but there it was, and the afterglow of epiphany was heaven. Breathless astonishment. A floaty, weightless feeling in my chest. I had done it. At last. And after so many years, it came in such a sudden burst of light.

This would vindicate me. It would prove that Dr. Margaret Brightwood was not a batshit-crazy recluse after all. This would vindicate the little girl who people read about in the news, who had so much power and so much promise.

A soft creak from the third-floor stairs startled me, and I jumped to my feet. No one ever came up here.

"Who is it?" I pressed a hand over my racing heart.

"Meg? Are you all right?"

The door opened, and my panic melted, replaced by that fullness of heart which so often ends in tears. Sweet Lizzie. More sister than cousin. The Sun to my Moon. Her golden hair was tied up, but a fallen strand stuck to her black dress.

I plucked the loose hair off. "What are you doing here?"

"Are you okay?" She looked at me, then scanned the room for—what? "They sent me to look for you."

"Oh my god." The funeral. I spun around. "Oh my god. What time is it?"

My clothes. They weren't even pressed. I had barely slept. I ran past Lizzie and headed for my bedroom. They would all be waiting. My father. My sister. The pastor.

"Meg, you look pale." Lizzie followed me. "First tell me if you're okay."

"Yes, I was—" I stabbed my arms into a black shirt. Legs into slacks. "I was working."

They would be waiting. Expecting me to drop everything. To run and fulfill my part in this ritual obligation. I sat on the floor to pull on my boots.

But why?

Funerals are for the living. For people who want or need to grieve together. Here's the truth. As tiny as Lila was, and as hard as she tried not to be a burden, the last years of her life had been a constant struggle, and grief had been my daily companion. I was spent.

My father had visited occasionally. The minister dropped by for a few minutes each week. And my older sister—had she even seen the inside of the house in five years? In the last months, caring for Lila had consumed everything. I slept next to her so she wouldn't be alone.

My obligations were done. I didn't need a funeral. I didn't need to weep and hug a bunch of strangers dressed in black. I only wanted some time to walk the house before the sense of her presence was gone forever.

Lizzie examined me with her gentle eyes. "So…are you done? Working?"

Strong emotions competed for dominance, and extreme exultation was the first to break through.

"Yes, I'm done. I'm finally done." But laughter gave way quickly to defensiveness. "I have been care-giving twenty-four seven. I swear to god, I haven't had an uninterrupted hour in I don't remember how long. And now I finally, finally have the space to think, and you know what? I did it. I did it. And I just want a few fucking minutes to enjoy it."

By the end I was almost yelling. Then, of course, I wanted to cry. Lizzie didn't deserve to be yelled at.

She dropped to the floor and put her arms around me. Lizzie was small, slim, and fit. Five years my junior and un-fazed by my moods.

"You did what?" she said.

"Frieholdt's. I solved it."

"Meg, that's amazing."

"I miss her," I said. "I miss her so much, but it's been so long since I've been able to focus."

"It's all right, sweetheart." Lizzie held tighter.

"I'm not going. I can't." I leaned into her embrace. "Maybe Dad's mad that I'm not there, but he'll see. They'll all see that my whole fucking life was worth something."

Lizzie kissed my cheek. "You were already worth some-thing."

Then she got out her phone and sent a text, leaning her shoulder firmly against mine like a mare to a skittish foal. "They can finish without us."

"Lila wouldn't mind. She never wanted a church funeral or a grave."

"Plus it's hot, and the pastor is so boring." Lizzie put her arms around me again. "Remember when he came over and Grandma would be like, 'Oh here comes Mr. Finkley, *bless his heart*.'"

I laughed, so grateful they sent Lizzie. With Lila gone, she was the one person on god's green earth I could be myself with.

We spent the rest of the morning with photo albums, cross-legged on Lila's big bed.

"Oh, remember this?" Lizzie held up a picture of the two of us. We were maybe eight and thirteen, standing arm in arm on a rock, a broad shining river behind us. Lizzie had been a sturdy reed of a girl, whereas I had grown curves early and stood as if I were trying to hide them. But we were both smiling and squinting in the sun.

"Harpers Ferry," Lizzie said. "Lila walked that entire trail with us."

"Dad didn't want to let me go." I took the picture and looked at it close. "But Lila made him."

Lizzie wept, and I held her in my arms feeling only a hollowness in my throat.

I had wept when Lila started struggling after words for everyday things. When she asked me to stop the crying of a baby only she could hear. When she forgot my name.

I had nothing left.

At that moment I grieved not for the old woman, but for

the young, strong Lila who hiked with me and Lizzie to the Shenandoah that day. The last and only person who could get my father off my back.

Dad let himself in without knocking.

He called my name from the bottom of the stairs. A summons which I answered. There was no point in fighting it. My joints creaked as I got up, usually the first harbinger of an attack, so I stopped at the bathroom, took out the bottle of Klonopin, and split one in half with my fingernail. I let the little pill dissolve on my tongue as Lizzie and I descended the stairs. As depleted as I felt, I wasn't taking any chances.

"Where the hell were you?" he said.

What my father, Henry Brightwood, didn't have on me in height he made up for in presence. Middle seventies with gray hair only slightly thinning, he occupied every space like he owned it.

"She was working," Lizzie said and breezed past him toward the kitchen. "It was just for us, anyway. Lila wouldn't have cared."

I followed her, as did he. He opened the refrigerator, closed it, and scanned the counters until he found the wine.

Dad shook his head in mock amazement as he poured a generous glass. "Well, you must have had a goddamn epiphany, to *work* through your grandmother's funeral."

My sister, Sharon, broke the impasse, clip-clopping in on her hard-heeled shoes. She looked untouched and untouchable, as always. Her two sons followed. Lanky teenagers, all long limbs and shaggy hair.

"Hey, Aunt Meg," Colin said. I nodded to him and his brother and managed a half smile. They beat a quick retreat to the back porch.

"I'm sorry," I said. "I couldn't make it."

Sharon looked skeptically at my half-finished outfit.

Dad turned to her. "Dr. Brightwood was *inspired* this morning. She found it impossible to tear herself away from her work."

"Give it a rest, Uncle Henry," Lizzie said. "I think after everything she's done, Meg gets to decide whether she goes to the funeral or not."

Dad ignored her. He crossed his arms. "So let me see."

"See what?" Sharon said, looking for cream in the refrigerator.

"The Impossible Theorem. Did you crack it when you missed the funeral?" He swept his arm out. "The discovery of the century."

The kitchen in Lila's enormous house had never been renovated. It retained its initial dimensions, from back when kitchens were built for work, not for show. We squared off in that small room.

Had he shown even the smallest bit of empathy or understanding, let alone gratitude, I would have told him everything. It was one thing to tell Lizzie, who loved whatever I did, big or small, but she wasn't Dr. Henry Brightwood. It *was* the discovery of the century. I craved the relief of sharing it with a mind that could truly comprehend.

But empathy or no, I knew that the second he actually believed I solved Frieholdt's, it would cease being mine and become *ours*. I would not give him the satisfaction.

"I was just working."

He leaned in. It was possible he was already drunk. "It was embarrassing. Everyone was asking about you. You couldn't just tough it out this one time? Take a break from *work*."

He even went as far as air quotes.

"Dad—" Sharon held up her hands. An effort at de-escalation. My voice cracked. "This one time? *This one time?* I have toughed it out a million times."

I bitterly envied my nephews on the porch, laughing at something on Colin's phone, blissfully disconnected from the family drama.

"This wasn't optional, Meg. It was a funeral," Dad said. "You don't 'work late' and miss a funeral."

"Just leave me alone." Tears. I hated that he could bring me to tears. "What difference does it make if I was there or not?"

"Dad?" Sharon put a hand on his shoulder. This time she had a tone of conciliation, but also of warning.

Lizzie scowled at him. Dad swallowed most of his wine in one go and left his glass on the counter.

"Oh, hell with it. Can't win when all the women are against me," he said and walked down the back hall to the side door which led to the garage and the driveway.

"Dad, stop." Sharon started to follow him, but he closed the door and was gone without so much as a wave goodbye.

I had to get out of that cramped room or the anger would bury me. The floorboards creaked under my feet through the butler's pantry to the dining room, then the parlor. Through the foyer to the library. Then I turned and walked back again. On my third circuit, I found Sharon standing at the French doors which opened from the dining room to the back porch. Lizzie sat at the dining table, legs crossed. Sun filtered through the high branches of the oaks.

My breath still wouldn't travel past my sternum, but the urge to move abated.

Sharon turned to face me, hand on her narrow hip. She looked more like Lila than anyone else in the family.

"He'll get over it." Her blond bob barely moved next to

her expensively youthful skin. She had switched from coffee to wine, and the sun flashed off her glass.

"I don't care if he does or not."

She sighed and shook her head. "Anyway, are you okay?"

"I'm fine."

"It was pretty boring. You didn't miss much." She took a swallow of her wine. Something had loosened in her since Dad left. "Listen, since we seem to be dispensing with all the small talk… Are you really going to live here by yourself two more years?"

It was in the will. I could live here for two years before Dad and his brother were allowed to sell.

"Of course I am," I said.

"We'll pay you fifty thousand dollars to move out."

Lizzie sat up. "Sharon, what the fuck?"

I shook my head. "What? No. I've got— No."

"How much do you think this house is worth?" Sharon said.

"I don't know. A lot?"

"Nine million."

Sharon went for deadpan, but she got our attention, as I'm sure she knew she would.

Lizzie laughed out loud. "No way. In this condition?"

But Sharon was no fool. If she said nine million, I believed it.

"The house isn't where the money is. It's the land it's sitting on. There's a buildable lot, and I know a developer who's ready to make an offer."

Lizzie's face darkened. "Sharon, we *just* buried her."

"I'm aware of that." Sharon went into the kitchen and returned with the wine bottle.

She filled all our glasses, and up close I could see the ef-

fort it took to look as cool as she did. We all grieve differ-
ently, I supposed.

"It's not like you think," she said. "These are the people
I do business with. They know me. They know our family.
I've been getting offers on this house for years."

"What do you care about selling the house?" Lizzie said.
"The money's going to your dad and mine, anyway. Not to
us."

Sharon sighed. "I'm the messenger."

"What does that mean?"

But I understood. "It means Dad didn't want to ask me
himself, and Sharon's doing him a favor."

I pulled a chair from the dining table and sat at a right angle
to Lizzie. My hands felt limp in my lap. "I can't move."

"Yes, you can," Sharon said. "Why can't you?"

"I have an illness, if you'll recall? When Mom had to take
me to the emergency room?" My first panic attack. Age eight.
"As inconvenient as it might be for you and Dad, it hasn't just
gone away. I'm safe here. I'll move eventually, but I need time.
And I'm at a—an important point with my work."

I knew as I said the words. *Work. Safe.* She didn't know
those words the way I did. Sharon was twelve years my elder.
We had not grown up together but she had known me all my
life. And yet she still didn't understand that there were days
I couldn't even leave the house. Days I could barely leave my
room.

Sharon believed that if a person tried hard enough, they
could overcome. And that if a person didn't overcome, it had
to be because they didn't try. I saw it on her face, and it pissed
me off that, after all these years, she couldn't stretch out just
a little, to understand something beyond herself.

"You're not a kid anymore," Sharon said. "You'd be fine in an apartment."

Lizzie stood up. "You can't be fucking serious."

Sharon always thought Lizzie was a lightweight. She was wrong, of course, but believing it gave Sharon an advantage.

"Yes, I am *fucking* serious," Sharon said. "You've been living off Lila for fifteen years. And besides, it's ridiculous for one person to live in a house this big."

"If you had spent a single night in this house in the last five years, you'd know she wasn't *living off* Lila," Lizzie said. "You should be grateful. You know what a nursing home costs."

"I know. But still."

She didn't know. She didn't have any idea how hard the work of caregiving had been.

Sharon looked at me, without much understanding, but not without compassion. "It's going to happen sooner or later, Meg. You've got to figure out what you're going to do."

There were six bedrooms on the second floor with big beds and fireplaces, but Lizzie and I slept up in my room that night—the smallest bedroom at the top of the house, just as we had since we were little girls visiting Grandma's. The room held two twin beds separated by a nightstand, a dresser with a set of ivory combs on a tarnished silver tray, and a small armoire.

The morning's defiance had worn off with the remaining hours of the day, and now I lay awake.

"Sharon's not wrong. I do need to figure out what to do."

I spoke quietly. Lizzie was the midwife on call for her practice that night. If she had already fallen asleep, I didn't want to wake her.

She rolled over. "True. But she didn't have to be such a bitch about it."

My cousin had grown up with plenty of money and very little hardship, but in her case chance had bestowed these gifts on a person immune to their pitfalls. A life of ease that would have made others discontented and obsessed with nothings instead grew Lizzie into a hardworking woman and a generous, purposeful friend. A person who could both afford to and wanted to give time and love where they were so badly needed.

"I really can't move out," I said. "Not right now."

"But how long can you afford to stay?"

"Probably not for two years." In her will, Lila had left me fifty thousand dollars and two years to stay in the house. Whether the money would last that long, I wasn't at all sure. One cold winter and heat alone could break the bank.

Lizzie tucked the blanket against her cheek. "Maybe you could negotiate with Sharon about the house."

I laughed. "Negotiate? Sharon would wipe the floor with me."

Moonlight poured in through a window in the dormer. A tiny white moth flapped in a current of air.

What was I going to do? Sharon had meant something altogether different by that question than I did when I asked it of myself.

I was going to write Frieholdt's into a full proof that other scientists could understand, and that proof would explain turbulence. Make it predictable. Engineers would use it to create efficiencies that could only be dreamed of. Trucks and ships that ran on a tenth of the fuel. Carbon emissions would plummet. Someday an airplane would cross the country on a gallon of sunflower oil. It would stop climate change in its tracks, and my name would go down in history.

That's what I was going to do.

2

The Impossible was comprehensible by me, but turning it into a proof that could be understood by others meant writing it out, step by logical step, no shortcuts, no shorthand, formatted and edited and clean. It was a painstaking process, and one for which my skills were only barely adequate. I longed for help, but help would only create different problems.

Attired in work clothes, which is to say the oldest, softest, grayest garments I owned, I opened a fresh, spiral-bound notebook and focused into the soft, lined pages.

I have spent a lot of time alone in my life, and sometimes I am lonely, but when I am at work—really at work—I am not alone at all. Mathematics is a conversation hundreds of years long, between minds famous and unknown. Minds that moved and built and grew the understanding of truth. They were all with me. Pythagoras, Einstein, Ramanujan, Nash. And the unknowns, Grisman, Xi-Ling, and Fenty. Bonnie Fenty in her whalebone stays, who published as a man because a woman of that era couldn't possibly have *that kind of a mind*.

I sharpened my pencil. Frieholdt's needed a path to become

public, but after being unaffiliated with any university for so long, none of the academic journals would touch me, let alone with a proof like this. It would be like the *New York Times* running a front-page story on Bigfoot sightings. My proof would not—could not—be traditionally published.

There was *arXiv.org*, where all manner of people, academic and non, posted work to be read and reviewed, but it was the Wild West on there. I'd had my work "borrowed" enough times that I wasn't about to take the work of a lifetime and throw it to the coyotes.

The best way would be to present. It was the best protection against plagiarism—to speak it for the first time to the public from my own mouth. But presenting was torment.

I had the misfortune, as a mathematician, of being pretty— a very conventional kind of pretty, nothing jaw-dropping— and in the bastion of wise and serious scholars who plumb the depths of knowledge, there was no place for *pretty*. It was considered a "distraction." If I appeared in person, men would stare, and they would talk. And of course the possibility of a panic attack was always there.

But I had done it before, and I could do it again. I could muscle through. An hour of searching online yielded a small, regional conference at a college in Connecticut in September. There were openings. I registered to present on an obscure but acceptable subject called the Loading Hypothesis. Not much had been published on it, and it had a small cadre of devoted fans in the math community. An hour later the organizers sent me an acceptance. Done.

Now they would see just what this pretty girl could do.

Three months passed, and I did not venture farther from the house than the back garden wall. I had my groceries delivered and kept the first-floor windows locked. I watched the yard go another summer without pruning and clearing. And I worked.

In the thick notebook with its heavy-duty plastic cover, using a vanishingly sharp pencil, I wrote out the proof. It was harder than I had anticipated, and more than once I wished for a living, breathing colleague, or even a student to help me. Mathematics was a collaborative field. It wasn't natural to work in isolation like I did.

Lizzie brought me food and got me to go outside a couple of times. But she was busy. She had her own life. I lost sleep, lost weight, nearly jumped for joy, and huddled on the floor pressing my head between my fists. I wore a path from my desk to the front windows.

I followed that path again, pacing my study, but now my notebook rested, closed, on my desk. A complete proof of Frieholdt's Conjecture with Linear Partition Inequalities, by Margaret Brightwood, PhD. Impossible no more. After the presentation, once it was provably mine, I would have graduate students begging me to let them edit it and type it up.

A ray of sunlight reflected on the floor where there was still some varnish left, and a curl of paint that had fallen from the ceiling lay in my path. I left it undisturbed.

When that bit of paint had fallen, it disturbed the air around it. Atoms moved around its edges, and then around each other, in seemingly random formation. But their movement was not random. It was an ordered and predictable response to the variables of shape, size, medium, and movement. Stepping carefully over the curl of paint again, I leaned on the windowsill and looked out.

The big house across the street was known as the General's because someone or other important in the Union Army had signed something or other important in the library during the Civil War. It was older than Lila's house. Three stories of brick-work, built into the hill like an elegant bunker. The renovation was progressing fast, and the place had been busy and noisy.

I settled in the armchair by the window. Watching them work on the General's was a kind of vacation for the mind. Simpler and slower than television. It was a long way away, looking down from my third-floor window, and much of their work was obscured by trees, but there was a guy who had a saw of some kind set up near the corner of the porch where I could see. Always in a hat and sunglasses, he seemed to work separately from the others and on smaller pieces of wood. Lots of measuring, walking in and out, measuring again, and shaving another sliver off a board.

A breeze fluttered the dark green leaves in the tops of the oaks. This was the time of morning when he usually arrived, and he appeared as usual in the passenger seat of a black truck.

The original drawing for Frieholdt's was still on my board surrounded by notes and diagrams written, erased, written-over, washed, and written-out again. The closed notebook didn't carry the same sense of elation as that drawing. Instead, it gave a sense of finality. It grounded me. With the Impossible done and documented, my mind could stop spinning through its patterns, checking and rechecking.

So I looked out the window and watched the carpenter work.

Back when I first arrived at Lila's, the wall that would later hold my giant chalkboard was bare. My belongings took two weeks to be shipped from California. I didn't have much that I couldn't carry with me. A desk. A rug. A couple of pictures. And my first board. It was an antique, small and green, mounted to an iron stand with hinges so it could be flipped.

In those two weeks, I did not leave the house. I left my study only to eat and help Lila, but back then she didn't need much help. It was a desperately needed rest. And though the tremor of anxiety clung close around me, I never felt the clench at my heart when it verged into panic. I had walked away from a crowning achievement—a professorship at Halberstam, the MIT of the west—prestige I had been groomed for my entire life. My father was not happy. Nor was my dean. Even I was not exactly happy, but at last I was not miserably *un*happy.

The day my antique board arrived, I spent a quiet hour with my thoughts. Finally free from all the bullshit and judgment of my professorship, I could devote myself to the Impossible Theorem again. Every so often a shard of anxiety would cut through—about tomorrow's lecture, a meeting with an advisee or the dean—then the blessed relief as that shard melted away. There were no more lectures. No more meetings. Just me and my thoughts. I flipped the board on its hinges, ran my fingertips down its smooth surface, then flipped it again.

Footsteps approached from down the hall. They paused outside the door for long enough to signal uncertainty. Then someone knocked. I opened the door. It was Isaac Wells, toolbox in hand.

"I'm sorry. Lila asked me to come up here and look at the balcony door. She said it doesn't open." He had a soft Southern drawl that took the edge off my nervousness.

There was a curved door that led out to the smallest, most secret balcony of the entire house, tucked behind the tower, looking down the hill toward the park. From the front, you couldn't even see it was there. He was right, the door didn't open. And I wished it did.

"You can come in." I stepped aside.

He crossed the room, looking at my board as he passed. I had learned a few things by that point. He was nineteen. A high-school dropout, living in a tiny apartment with his sister in a cheap part of town. Sometimes the motorcycle he rode to Lila's worked. Sometimes it didn't. By class and education, we couldn't have been more different, and a four-year age difference wasn't nothing.

Finding ourselves alone together, I sensed we both had our guard up. But his weren't the fresh, bristling defenses of a person who doesn't use them much. They were like earthen berms built high and heavy, and long since grown over in grass. Like mine.

"Somebody painted it shut," he said, running his hand down the doorjamb. He got a razor knife out of his box and cut through the paint at the seams.

I sat on the sagging couch by the back wall with a book, but really I was watching. He had a self-contained way of being in someone else's space, an easy presence to be around, and there was something about him that made me feel safe. Like it was okay to just be as I was.

Mumbling a bit as he worked, he cut through layers of paint, testing, then cutting through some more. Slowly the door began to move. He oiled the hinges and the latch. He pried at the edges with a bar to loosen them. And finally with a screech, the door opened an inch.

"It must be nice to do something actual. You know, that you can look at when you're done." I waved at my board. "What I do is so abstract."

He nodded and smiled a little, as if letting me in on a joke. "It is. But if it all falls apart, I have to look at that too."

With more prying and coaxing, he got the door open the

rest of the way. I stood up. I had always wanted to go out on the balcony.

Isaac went through first, testing the floorboards. It could have been ten years since anyone had walked on them.

"It's safe," he said. "Just avoid that spot right there. And I wouldn't rely on the rail just yet."

It felt like a bird's nest, up there level with the top branches of the trees. I stepped out, crossed my arms, and hung close to the door. Midday sun reflected off his face. He was pale. In need of a haircut. Arched eyebrows gave him an exacting expression, and a groove was already beginning to form between them, as though he had done a lot of hard thinking for a man so young.

I ventured two more steps out.

"I like your board." He nodded toward the open door where we could see it standing in the center of the room. "Is it an antique?"

"Early 1800s, I think. The university was selling off some old stuff."

"That frame is handmade."

"How can you tell?"

He walked back in, and I followed.

"See here, this decorative part. And where the frame is attached to the casters, you can tell." He crouched down and pointed to the details near the floor. "This is wrought iron. Not cast."

"I love it," I said. "Only, I'd like to have a bigger one too."

He walked over and examined the concave expanse of the tower wall. "Well, you've certainly got the space."

Every inch of my big board was now covered in chalk. The full proof in my notebook was much, much longer, of course, but I had put as much of it on the board as I could. All that space had been crucial to working out the problem.

With the proof complete, I finally called Sharon and Dad and allowed them to come over. I had custody of the house for a little less than two years, but my father had been ready to divvy up its contents since the funeral. I sat in the breakfast nook as they did a preliminary walk-through. They couldn't actually tag the stuff until Lizzie's dad, my uncle Stuart, came down from New York, but they were still itching to inventory the thousands of old things that had been liberated by Lila's passing.

I made coffee, but that's all. They could come find their own mugs and spoons.

They roamed around the house for an hour, talking in businesslike voices while I sipped my coffee and stared at the garden. Dad returned to the kitchen first. He was doing his version of ultracasual, which meant his polo shirt was not tucked in to his khakis. Sharon followed.

"It's not safe to go in the library," she said. She was dressed for work, not a speck on her cream-white pencil skirt or her sharp, red shirt. It always struck me how comfortable Sharon looked in clothes that seemed so stiff.

"What's wrong with it?" Dad said.

I stood in the corner, hugging my mug to my chest. "The floor is rotten from when the bathroom flooded before I moved in. It was always too expensive to repair. I could have told you that."

"I almost put my foot through it," Sharon said.

Dad poured himself a cup of coffee. "You're not really still working on Frieholdt's, are you?"

"Of course I am. You knew that."

"You mean after the funeral?" He waved off the idea. "I

was just angry. I didn't think you were still at it. I mean, after all this time."

Something didn't feel true—either his quasiapology or his thinking I wasn't working on Frieholdt's, but he carried it off with enough confidence that I couldn't tell. I handed him the cream from the refrigerator.

"Thanks," he said. "I hear you're presenting at the NES conference."

My chest flashed hot. No. No. I wanted to throw something. To stamp my foot like a child. He was not supposed to know. No one was supposed to know. NES was the conference in Connecticut. It was tiny. Not something Dr. Henry Brightwood would care about. I was going to sneak up there, make a presentation, and that would be it. The Impossible would be out with my name on it. I would make history, and the rest of the business could be conducted from the privacy of my study.

I nodded, lips pressed tight.

He patted my shoulder approvingly. "Good going, Meggie. Do you have something new on the Loading Hypothesis?"

I nodded again. That look in his eyes, the smile. When he called me Meggie—that was my father's approval, and it was powerful.

"Yes." It wasn't exactly a lie. What I had was definitely new.

"A presentation, Meg?" Sharon said, with a discerning look. "I thought you hated those."

"I know. I don't like it, but…" I immediately wanted to inhale the words back into my mouth and leave them there.

Henry rolled his eyes. "It doesn't matter if you like it. That's the only thing that ever held you back, this idea that you have to *like* it."

For god's sake, how many times did I need to hear that?

You'll never be great if you keep trying to make things easy on your-self. A person with your abilities doesn't get to be comfortable.

"Say, what if we go up to the NES together?" my father said. "Are you taking the train? I've got friends there I'd like to see, and I want to be there if you make a comeback."

If.

It was as if some total stranger were standing next to me, because if he had half a clue about his own daughter, he would have known I always traveled alone.

And if he had three-quarters of a clue, he would know that Henry Brightwood was the last person I wanted in that audi-torium. Even the idea of a comeback was his. Not mine. All I wanted was to stand up and present my proof, leaving no doubt in anyone's mind as to its veracity or its authorship. The idea that there was any glory around it was his. Glory for him.

I didn't care about a *comeback*, but that one other word got under my skin.

If.

Defiance had a momentary victory over doubt. Not *if*. *When.*

3

So many times, I had wished to look unremarkable. To blend in. To disappear. Hence the closet full of black, brown, and gray. I slid the hangers right to left, looking for the best presentation outfit. The strongest armor.

The fourteen-hour days of writing were behind me. Now it was polishing and preparation. I would read from a script as I always did, and my voice would carry. That had never been a problem. I might have been anxious, I might have been young and awkward, moving through the field on a different curve without any peers, but when it came to my research, I had zero trouble making a point.

Black was my favorite for armor, but it had its vulnerabilities. Lint. Fading. And one discovers quickly the things that leave white smudges: cereal, milk, makeup. I had a perfectly serviceable cardigan sweater set, but with a body like mine, a sweater had to be the size of a grain sack or half the room would be staring at my tits.

So I got out my phone and ordered the same shirt I had been wearing since my first day of graduate school—the black

Brooks Brothers button-up. Brand-new so it would stand rigid around the body. The quintessential serious shirt.

Yes, there would be a bit of chalk dust on the sleeve when it was all done, but it wasn't meant to be perfect. It was meant to be ignored.

The next day, with a week to go before the presentation, I started practicing out loud. Having spent so long with the proof, explaining it to an empty space was easy, but all my weapons would come with me to this battle because the proof wasn't the problem. The room was the problem. I printed a script and taped it to index cards, and standing in front of my big board, I spoke clearly to the faded couch, the desk, the windows that listened from the far side of the tower, trying to imagine I was speaking to a lecture hall full of strangers.

The presentation itself would take an hour. The conference had allotted me forty-five minutes, but I wasn't worried about going over. By the time I hit that mark they would be hanging on my every word.

When I finished my practice, I leaned against the board, unsettled in body, exhausted in mind. As long as I could focus on the pure clarity of Frieholdt's, it was as if nothing else existed. But the moment I stopped, I felt the weight of anxiety hovering close.

I slid to the floor and put my head in my hands. Breakdown was a very real possibility. I might not even make it to the auditorium. Twenty years of work, a historic breakthrough, and I faced a bottleneck. This one hour. If I could only force myself through that tiny space, then there was freedom on the other side.

On the morning of September 14, the sun rose just like it always did, and I wanted to throw open the window and shout, *Stop it. Slow down. Don't you know the world is about to change?* But that would have been unreasonable.

Instead, I zipped my new shirt and my good pair of slacks into a garment bag. Hardly aware of my own body, I put on my makeup. I had done it so many times. Hundreds. Thousands, even. I could have done it in my sleep. Then a light gray long-sleeve and jeans. Protection enough for traveling. If I was lucky, I wouldn't see anyone until I had to check in to the hotel. I snapped the lid on my makeup box and fitted it into the corner of my suitcase. That suitcase had not left the house since it arrived fifteen years ago. Neither had my leather shoulder bag. The one I used to bring to class. Then to my office. Then under the seat on the airplane home. It was stiff and creased from its long residence in the closet.

Into that bag went the notebook, the index cards, and a Ziploc bag of chalk. My own chalk from the rail under my board in my own room. I wasn't above a little magical thinking to get me through.

It was time. With sure steps I descended, bags in hand, face forward. Nothing was forgotten. Something akin to hope welled in my chest.

Morning light sparkled through the old, rippled glass of the front door. I stepped through and turned the key in the lock.

Driving always settled my mind, and I made it to Connecticut, to the hotel, through the lobby, and to my room without incident. I even got a decent night's sleep. In the morning, I brushed my hair smooth and got dressed. With the wide bathroom mirror before me, ready to start the makeup routine, I paused. Took a sip of coffee.

That was when I felt the first visceral fear. I had known it would come, and I was not unprepared, yet its sharp point in my chest was more sudden and stronger than I expected.

Too pretty, it said.

Nine-tenths of that room would be men. Old, young, all shapes, sizes, colors. But all men. And nine-tenths of those men would look at me, and the very first thing they would see was *pretty*. I remembered it too well. The whispers and smiles. The awkward flirting. Even, on two occasions, the hands.

And then, of course, the excuses.

He didn't know any better. He's socially awkward. He didn't mean any harm. Don't make a big deal out of it. Do you want to ruin his career?

A cold tooth of anxiety mixed with anger drilled through my chest, stinging the center of my diaphragm. It didn't matter what I looked like. I was living with the body and the face I was born with, just like every old white dude that ever stood in front of a room with chalk in his hand.

Too pretty.

But my looks did matter, no matter how much I fought the fact, if only because I knew that people would be looking, and I needed them not to look but to listen. I needed any relief I could get from being so glaringly visible. I pulled my hair tighter. Buttoned the top button of my shirt. But it was no use. I couldn't turn myself into a different person, and if I skipped the makeup, it would only be worse. They would look at me like a curiosity. *Are those really freckles? I've never seen freckles like that.*

So I began. Primer. Concealer. Foundation, applied heavy with a sponge.

You can back out. There's still time.

Eyebrows. Narrow them and diminish the arch. The mask was not to accentuate, it was to suppress.

It will go badly.
The tiniest bit of blush. No contour. Neutral eyes.
You'll pay for this. Remember. Remember the time in California?
I was sixteen.

"I don't know if I can do it," I had said to my father as we stood outside the doors to that auditorium. I remember the dry breeze that blew through the hall.

He had been so proud. All the royalty of mathematics in attendance. Everyone gawking at a girl my age graduating from college, with a doctorate ahead.

He'd scoffed at me. "Of course you can."

This back-and-forth had been going on all morning. I felt sick with anxiety. I had tried obstinance, begging. Nothing worked. He waved it all off. "You're fine, Meg. You're just winding yourself up."

I longed for the slightest understanding. The slightest sympathy. Finally, minutes before my presentation, a hot wave surged through my gut. I crouched down.

"I think I'm going to throw up."

My father crouched down next to me. "Do we need to go to the hospital?"

"What do you mean?" I looked up. Something wasn't right about the way he said it. I didn't understand.

"Are you that sick?" he said in a whisper, his face close to mine. "Do I need to drive you to the hospital and admit you to the emergency room? Because if you are so sick that you can't do a presentation that has been planned for months. That the national news showed up for. That Dr. Kovalyev of Berkeley showed up for. If you are that sick, then we better go to the hospital."

No, I was not that sick. I made it through. I clenched my jaw so hard I cracked a tooth. I stammered and sweated, but I was sixteen. The audience expected nerves. When I finished, my father was the first to stand and applaud. He was proud, Dr. Kovalyev was impressed, and the press was adoring. Then I barely ate for a month.

It's different now, I told myself, putting on lipstick the exact color of my lips. I can do this. I'm older.

Fuck them. Fuck all of them. I had solved Frieholdt's Conjecture. This would be the end of debate. I would write QED— *quod erat demonstrandum, the proof is complete*—at the end of the board, and I would enter the history books.

I knew it would be a fight, so I gathered my things and went to war.

The room was full to capacity. It held sixty, and every seat was taken with several people standing along the sides and in the back. My neck and back grew stiff and immobile as I stood at the entrance to the side of the stage. This was not supposed to happen. It was a small conference. It was supposed to be half-full.

Turn back.

Anxiety could not stop me from walking into that room, but it could wrap its talons around my chest. My breath grew tight.

I am Dr. Brightwood, I told myself. *I am smarter than everyone in this room. Including my father.*

Scattered around the room were faces I knew, and faces that knew me.

You don't own me. You don't control me.

I stepped out of the doorway and walked to the center of the low stage. The rumble of conversation in the room subsided, and all eyes turned toward me. I was used to breathing in the tiny top corners of my lungs. I was used to the creaking in my joints and feeling hot like I was standing in front of a fire. This would be like every presentation I had ever done.

The chairs in the auditorium rose steeply up from a concrete arc of floor. Three vertical columns of green chalkboard were mounted on sliding rails so one could be written on, then moved up to continue on the one below. I would need them all.

I scanned the room. And there was my father, seated in the middle by the aisle. I gripped the piece of chalk in my hand. My own chalk from my own board. My father smiled and nodded.

I took a deep breath. "Good morning."

I got through the introduction without incident. The room looked on with interest and attention.

I stood straight and went to the board.

"Let r be an odd prime…"

The beginning went reasonably well. I glanced over my shoulder to a room full of quizzical faces. They knew. This wasn't about the Loading Hypothesis. Many mathematicians had attempted a proof with this opening. They knew where I was going.

"…the tensor gradient, del u, assumes a fourth-order constant of proportionality…"

My chest felt tight, but I could still breathe. So far, I was winning.

I glanced at the room again. Henry leaned to whisper something to the man on his left. Then he smiled.

Watch this. That's what he said to that man on his left. I knew it. It's what he always said. *Watch this*. When I was about to do something that would astound the room. At five. At twelve. At twenty. He loved it.

I turned back to the board and lifted my right arm, starting into the main body of the proof.

"...global representability implies local representability. However, the converse does not apply..."

I would blow their minds. Exceed all expectations. I had to, or I could never come back.

My father leaned back in his chair and crossed his arms. There was no halfway, and failure was death.

"...again, the Galilean invariant..."

I couldn't get a breath. I tried to lift my chalk to the board. My heart lurched. The air shuddered, muffling sound. Shooting pain ran down my left arm, and my chest squeezed, heavy, tight.

No. Please, no.

A heart attack.

No, it's not. Jesus Christ. How many times have you thought it was a heart attack? It's not. It's a panic attack. Push through, goddamn it. Push through. This is your one chance.

My hand felt cold as ice. I couldn't speak. The murmuring in the room filtered through a dense block in my ears. The crushing weight bore down on my chest, like a black hole where my heart should have been, the most immense gravity field pulling my ribs, my muscles, even my skin inward.

Palm to my chest, I stopped.

No. For god's sake, no. It's not a heart attack. Push through it.

The room swayed under my feet, and an overwhelming ache bloomed inside my ribs.

It's real this time. Oh my god, it's real.

4

I had to get out. Out of that room. But the bag. My proof. If I left it, I would lose it. Someone in the front row stood. Said something. Barely able to see or hear, I felt for my leather bag, closed my icy fingers around the handle, and staggered into the hall.

"Are you all right, Dr. Brightwood?" It was the grad student assigned to the room. A guy, smooth-skinned, blond-haired, twentysomething.

I strapped the bag across my body, notebook safe inside, and I leaned my back against the wall, palm pressed to my breastbone.

"Should I call someone?" he said.

Other voices and faces blurred around me. A crowd. Watching. I wanted to say, *I'm fine. I'm fine.* But I couldn't speak.

I wasn't fine. My body screamed at me to escape, but I had to finish. I had to get back in that room.

The hall swayed, and I slid down the wall to my knees. Pain shot through my chest again, and I clutched at my shirt, unbuttoned the top button, tried to stand but failed and dropped to my knees again. It didn't matter if I dropped dead, if I could finish—if I could only, only finish.

The graduate student crouched at my side. "Should I call an ambulance?"

"No," I wheezed. "Just give me a minute. I'm not done."

He stayed close, but he didn't make contact. If only he would. A hand on my arm or my shoulder, a lift up. I saw it in his eyes. He was afraid of me, like they always are.

"You'll be all right," he said. "Let's get you some help."

"There's no all right here. Nothing's *all right*."

Why wouldn't he make contact? Just a moment of human contact. But I couldn't reach out. I shifted away from him, sliding along the floor.

He stayed still, watching me. Just like everyone else. Everyone except my father, who was nowhere to be seen.

I wanted something real. A feeling. Anything. Even anger, if that's all I could get.

"Just go away." I forced my voice through the smallest of spaces. "I can't fucking breathe."

"It's okay. There's an ambulance coming. You need—"

"How do you know what I need? I need to finish this presentation. I need to get on my fucking feet." I forced myself up, but the hall lurched again. The reality began to break through. It was over. Dr. Brightwood was beaten like any animal in a fight, slinking off to lick its wounds. The pain exploded in my chest again.

Someone in a uniform caught me.

Nothing made sense. Why couldn't I just think? Why wouldn't this claw let go of my chest?

Despite the nurse's assurances of its safety, I would not let go of my bag. My forearm burned, and my hand felt like a steel clamp rusted shut around the leather handle, but this was my life's work. There was nothing else I could do. Nothing else I was good for. If I dropped dead from a heart attack, it would be with this bag in my hand, and there would be no doubt whose proof it was.

The nurse unbuttoned my black shirt. They stuck leads on my chest and a needle in my arm. For a few minutes the cubicle was so full that people nearly bumped into each other. All eyes were on the EKG, and as the paper crept out of the machine inch by inch, the urgency in the room fell several notches. The doctors peered at the readout.

Someone said, "It looks normal."

I fought it, but finally the strong medications they gave me pulled me under.

I woke to a doctor sitting beside my stretcher. The overhead light reflected in his glasses.

"There isn't anything wrong with your heart."

Sleep cloyed at me, and I probably sounded drunk. "So it was a panic attack."

"Yes."

I rolled my eyes. Same old shit. *Manage your stress*, the doctor said. *Get some exercise.*

Eminently reasonable, all of it. And eminently doable, the way he made it sound. But that's how doctors are, I thought. Solutions-oriented, actionable steps. I thanked him, and he unfolded himself from the chair and left. He meant well, but he didn't have to live my life. Then a nurse came in. I collected myself and sat up, and she gave me a thick stack of papers stapled together. I was being discharged. A sudden shock blew through the haze of whatever medications they had given me.

"Where's my bag?" I looked around the tiny room. "I had a bag. Where is it?"

The nurse smiled. And patted the bag, which rested in my lap.

When I emerged into the waiting room, my father rose to meet me. He was the last person I wanted to see at a time like

this, but if Henry Brightwood didn't go to the hospital to collect his daughter, it would look bad, and Henry Brightwood
did not like to look bad.

I stayed silent as we walked to the car. Silent as he drove. It
wasn't until we were parked at the hotel that either of us spoke.

"It was going to be a proof of Frieholdt's, wasn't it?" he said.

I stared straight ahead but acknowledged the question with
a twitch of my eyes.

With the wipers off, a drizzle obscured the windshield, and
the lights in the parking lot softened and refracted.

I reached for the door, but my father said, "Wait."

"For what?"

"You really did it this time, didn't you? You wouldn't have
tried to get in front of that auditorium if you didn't have it."

The drugs were wearing off, and I was tired. Thoroughly
tired in body and mind, I didn't have it in me to fight or to
flee, so I froze. I sat and said nothing.

"I know things haven't been so good between us." His
voice should have been soothing, when he used it like that.
The gravelly, fatherly voice. I remembered it. *Good job, Meggie. Nicely done.* But I didn't trust it. Not this time. I had failed,
and he didn't use that voice when I failed.

"This is important," he said. "I want to help you. Let's work
on this together. I can do the heavy lifting when it comes to,
you know—people."

I crossed my arms around my bag and looked away out the
window into the rain.

"It will change the world," he said. "You know that."

Of course I knew. The sooner it was out there, the sooner
engineers could get their hands on it. Operationalize it. The
sooner the potential would become real and tip the balance by
making fuel efficiency profitable. It wasn't a figure of speech.

This proof would literally change the world. Not to mention the sooner I would win the Beckett Prize and the money to live somewhere when I moved out of Lila's house.

I was unreasonable. That's what he was thinking. My whole career, that's what everyone thought of me. I should collaborate. Use someone else's strength to complement where I was weak. I should accept help.

But I knew what *help* meant. *Help* meant the name of my adviser appeared first on work that never would have existed without me. *Help* meant that everyone assumed the men had done the work, and no one asked me about the papers I supposedly *co*authored. *Help* meant that I was pretty window dressing. Not serious. Not a real mathematician.

This was different, though. This was my own father. Once my mentor. The one person who had understood me when everyone else looked at me like a creature in a zoo. A fascinating, nine-year-old freak.

In, out. My breath felt mechanical. The body doing what was necessary to survive despite the treachery of the mind. The car hummed. I stared at the pinpoints of the dashboard lights, which still split and wandered a bit from the residue of medication.

Henry rested a hand on the steering wheel. "It's not fair for you to keep this to yourself. This belongs to humanity."

I hated him for that. He didn't care about humanity. He only wanted his name on the proof. But he was also right. The Impossible needed to be out in the world, and soon.

I could just say *yes*. *Yes*. You take the reins. You guide this thing through. *Yes*. I'll step back. I'll hide out in my study and let my name be the only thing that needs to make a public appearance. *Yes*.

"Only my name," I said.

And my father hesitated.

Clarity swept the haze from my mind, and I looked directly at him. There was the look. The impatience. And I knew exactly what he was thinking.

"Only my name," I said. "This is mine. You didn't do it. No one else did it."

"Meg, you're going to need editorial help at least."

"No. There's no second author on this. You had nothing to do with it." I gripped my bag as if he would snatch it from my hands.

"Nothing? Meg, be reasonable. No one publishes something like this by themselves."

My eyes prickled, and my throat clenched. On another day, this would have meant tears, but a fire in my chest burned them dry before they came anywhere near the surface.

"You have everything. Nice car. Nice house. An emeritus. You've got friends and kids and money and a mind that works and doesn't betray you." I stabbed my finger at the bag clutched against my chest. "I have *this*."

"Calm down. You were just in the hospital." He said it louder than he had been speaking before. Not much, but enough, and it was all the escalation I needed.

"No," I shouted. "I have this one amazing thing. I can't do anything else, but I did this, and no one's name is going on it but mine."

I threw open the car door. Rain soaked my hair as I wrapped my arms around the bag and ran for the hotel entrance.

Men in slouchy sweaters and faded jackets were gathered in the lobby, drinking and talking on couches and chairs. They stood as I entered.

"Dr. Brightwood—"

"Dr. Brightwood, are you all right?"

I crossed the lobby at a run, nearly slipping in my wet shoes.

"Was it Frieholdt's?"

"Will you present it tomorrow?"

"Dr. Brightwood—"

They would surround me at the elevator, so I headed for the stairs. I ran up the first two flights, heart pounding, but once the door banged closed behind me in the echoing stairwell, no one followed. Finally alone, I leaned against the cool, cinder-block wall and caught my breath.

5

Lila's heavy front door closed behind me with a click. I leaned against it and slid to the floor, stretching my legs out on the woolen carpet. I was home. Outside, a dense drizzle grayed out the sky and dripped off the leaves, and inside the house was dim and cool. I pressed my palms on the floor. Rough. Dry.

Sharon wasn't wrong. One person didn't need this much house. But once it becomes *your* house it's different. Especially when you don't fit in anywhere else.

I checked my phone. There was a text from Lizzie.

How did it go?

I stared at the screen for what felt like a long time, trying to think of what to say. Then gave up and simply wrote, It didn't.

I rose to my feet and hefted my suitcase up to the third floor. My phone had filled up with notifications on the drive home. Calls. Emails. Texts. WhatsApp messages. How people got my number, I have no idea. I powered it off. All I wanted was to go to bed and stay there until I was good and ready to get up again, which might not be for days. A panic attack like that is exhausting. Like running a marathon with a rabid dog at your heels.

I left my suitcase in my bedroom and pulled the comforter off the bed. Carrying it in my arms, I dragged my feet down the narrow hall into the tower room, dropped my notebook on the desk, and collapsed in the armchair by the window.

But I didn't sleep. I tried, but I couldn't. I lay there beyond exhausted, yet wound-up with useless energy, my brain ticking through an endless set of cogs, winding its way through half a rotation, then catching on a new wheel and rotating the other way, and again and again. An endless, meaningless path that led nowhere.

But after ruminating over a hundred other things, the path led me to a little girl, and there I stayed, circling that one wheel. My one friend. There were barely any friends in my world, and Lizzie hadn't lived nearby when we were little. But when I was ten there was one. Her name was Cheryl Hertzberg. She lived down the block in a big house with a pool.

Cheryl Hertzberg had a pink bedroom with a bunk bed, and she wore barrettes with ribbons in her blond hair. She was the kind of kid who could befriend anyone, and given that I was four houses up and by far the closest and most convenient candidate, Cheryl took me in hand. I was surely one—and a forgettable one at that—in a long series of best girlfriends for Cheryl. But for me, the memory stood out like a room where someone has finally turned on the lights.

Cheryl showed me how to put on mascara. She pronounced my freckles *fascinating*. But best of all, Cheryl Hertzberg had a pony, and she took me to the stables to see him.

I remembered the smell of straw and horse. The rumbling huff of his breath. His velvety nose and my own damp palm after feeding him half an apple. He was glossy brown with a white stripe down his face. I almost laughed to myself at this picture of Cheryl in her pink barrettes and her mascara and her pony. That's what my father did, as if she were some kind of joke. But she was real. A real girl had that life.

The month of June, I had gone every morning to that barn to help feed and brush the pony and to watch Cheryl ride. I even got up on him once myself, and Cheryl led me around the paddock. I remembered the sway as his haunches shifted side to side. The thud of his hooves in the dirt.

What was his name?

I stared out the leaded glass of my window. A breeze ruffled the dark green leaves.

What was his name?

I remembered the way he nudged me for more apples. How he lifted his foot as Cheryl showed me how to tend to his hooves.

And then I was sitting in that armchair by the window crying. God, why? Why should a grown woman be crying over a horse from almost thirty years ago? I asked myself again and again, but it only made it worse.

I gripped the blankets, and my body shook.

My father had no patience for the friend, or the mascara, or the pony. A girl like Margaret Brightwood didn't have time for that. Summer wasn't for friends and ponies. Summer was when I didn't have to waste my time with insignificant subjects like social studies and Spanish. Summer was the time when I could devote the full power of my mind to math.

He put up with it for a month—not even quite a month— before he declared that these barn visits were interfering with my studies. I was to go with him to the university in the mornings—not with Cheryl to the barn. And he kept me there all day, every day. When I persisted in seeing Cheryl in the evenings, he took me to Cambridge, Massachusetts, and we spent a month—an entire goddamn month—in some faculty apartment where I studied with Dr. Olbermeyer, one of the great number theorists. Olbermeyer died a year later, and what he taught me changed my life. But when I finally came home, Cheryl had moved on to another friend, another girl who wasn't so strange and skittish, who had a normal father and mother and a normal life.

I loved math. I could lose hours and days in books and blackboards. But I loved that pony too. God, what was his name?

Wiping my eyes on my sleeve, I walked down the hall to the bathroom to pee. My legs felt shaky.

That month of June had been the closest I ever got to a normal childhood. For years after, I had looked back on that memory as if it were something of a joke. The girl with the pink barrettes. The pony named Sassy—*Sassy*, that was it. As I got older, I learned to smirk at Cheryl and Sassy the way my father did. *Can you believe? It's like someone made them up for a picture book. A girl and her pony.* As if they weren't real. Research was real. Figures on a board. The language of eternity. That was real.

Walking back to my study, I nestled into the chair again, looking across the room at my notebook, inert on the desk. My life's work. My crowning achievement. The proof that would change the world. Exhausted in heart and mind from my breakdown, everything seemed wrong. I was thirty-eight years old, and though I raked through my memories, that was it. I had one goddamn memory of being a child. Of getting to love what I loved just because.

I hadn't seen it when I was ten, but I saw it now—my father's contempt. For people who were beneath me. Beneath *us*—because my father and I were two members of an exclusive club. All those normal people—they may have been charming in their way, but they weren't like *us*.

You're special, Meggie. You're different from those other girls. So your life is going to be different too.

And what ten-year-old girl whose mother has just up and left the family for an investment banker in London doesn't want to hear *You're special*?

My mind writhed and snapped as I sat curled in that chair, playing back every bit of my father's language, all his derision, all his praise. It was like he made me walk a path that went ever upward, but not into open sky. I always knew I was climbing toward a ceiling—the point where I would fail. Over the years the path brought me closer and closer to that ceiling, and yet he drove me on until I was crouched down, wedged into that narrow space. Unable to stand.

And there were never people alongside me on that path. Only below and above. Always either below or above. At some point my father himself had stepped aside, and there I was. Alone.

Sitting by the window at the very top of that grand gray empty house, with my mind worn down to a dry husk, my heart at last asserted itself. Through sheer, unrelenting stamina, it asserted command, and it mourned the loss of that friend, and the pony, and everything else it had yearned for and been denied.

Everyone wanted to see what was in that notebook on my desk. My father wanted to see it. All those professors in the auditorium wanted to see it. The engineers and executives and deans and who knows who else were filling up my voice mail and my inbox.

I, on the other hand, did not want to touch it. I stared at it from across the room. The sum total of my life's effort. I didn't have kids or a job or a husband. My only real friend was my own cousin. I had no hobbies. I didn't bake or quilt or garden or any of that bullshit. I had read a lot of books, but other than that... And I had one goddamn memory of doing normal kid things. And for what? That notebook. That was all. And here I was, recovering from an emergency-room-worthy panic attack alone in a splintery mansion. No one knew. No one cared. Not even me. And for what?

I had to do something. I wanted it out of my sight, yet I would be damned if anyone else got their hands on it, and I couldn't go around my whole life clutching that leather bag.

I thought about the file drawer, the bookshelf, a box stashed in a closet. But I would worry every time I left the house. I am not exaggerating when I say that I had thirty emails in the two hours it took me to drive home. I had gotten far enough in the proof that people knew it was real, and it wouldn't be long before they figured out where I lived.

It may have been unreasonable, but I did not find it beyond belief that someone could gain access to the house and go rifling through my office. Half the family had keys. Dad and Sharon loved to show people around and were not very concerned about my privacy.

A safety-deposit box. But the banks would be closed, and I wanted this done now. Out of my sight *now*.

Suddenly I knew what to do.

The safe. My grandfather's safe.

I snatched the notebook off the table. From the file drawer I collected my loose pages. The papers scattered around my desk and on the floor all went into a pile, and I carried the stack in my arms out of the room.

I marched down from the third floor to the second, down

to the grand entry foyer and through the center hall. I turned right at the kitchen, but just before reaching the side door and marching straight outside, I turned right again and wrenched open the door to the basement.

Bare bulbs illuminated the stone foundation walls, the huge iron furnace. With so much cleaner, drier space around, there was never much need to store anything in this damp basement. The floor was cement, painted gray-blue. A few spidery piles of boxes and boards leaned against the wall. A metal shelf with some ancient kitchenware. And in the corner, my grandfather's safe.

My grandfather had encoded the combination and kept it in a secret drawer in his desk in the library. No one knew where it was—except for me. Lila had forbidden me and Lizzie from playing in the basement when we were children because the safe was large enough for us to climb into, and she had what I later saw was an irrational fear that one of us would get locked inside. As she grew old and her mind released its hold on time, she retained that one fear, so she gave me the combination, just in case I should have to free a small child.

My grandfather had mistrusted banks and kept much of his wealth in gold, and he was serious about his safe. It was a beast. Probably built in 1950. Steel walls four inches thick, bolted and welded to a base that was too big to go up the stairs. No one was busting this thing open or hulking it off in a truck. It had been empty since he died.

The combination worked, and the door swung open wide with barely a hint of complaint. I knelt on the floor, piled the notebook and all my papers inside, and without a single doubt, I closed that door and turned the locks. If anyone had the chutzpah to get in the house, they might go through my files, they might violate my study, but no one was going to come down here with power tools and try to drill open the safe. Frieholdt's was of great value to a few people, but it was obscure. Not like a bag full of diamonds or anything.

Starting now, the Impossible would be banished from my consciousness until I was good and ready to bring it back. For a lifetime, I had let other people tell me what was important— why *I* was important. I was finally going to give myself a say.

On the way through the kitchen I collected a bottle of wine and a glass and continued back up to my study. The waning, rainy daylight showed every scratch and stain on my empty desktop. I nestled back into the armchair by the window, tucked up my knees, and after two sips of wine, the cogs finally stopped turning.

6

I woke, stiff and thickheaded, to raised voices on the street. It was evening. The streetlights were on, but it was not quite dark yet, and the same heavy drizzle was falling. I shifted my body in the chair to look outside. The driveway at the General's was empty of its usual half-dozen trucks, but out in the street, the carpenter—the one with the saw on the porch—stood arguing with a man in a black T-shirt next to a brown Land Rover. The carpenter stepped back, holding up his hands. The black T-shirt guy was bigger, but the carpenter appeared to be the tougher of the two. He was balanced, while Black Shirt looked angry and top-heavy.

Their voices grew louder. The carpenter stopped backing up and took a defensive posture. I gripped the windowsill. I wanted to open the window, but it would make a noise. I might be heard and looked at. I couldn't understand their words. Black Shirt advanced again. The carpenter retreated. Then Black Shirt swung.

The carpenter dodged and struck back, hitting Black Shirt hard under the ribs. Black Shirt lunged.

I jumped to my feet. He had the carpenter by the arm, trying to shove him to the ground. The carpenter twisted around and pushed Black Shirt into the Land Rover but Black Shirt swung again. The carpenter raised an arm. Not fast enough to protect his head.

Do something. Something. You can't just stand here and watch.

I ran to the bedroom and tore through my bag until I found my phone. Calling 9-1-1, I took the stairs in twos and threes. When I finished with the dispatcher, I flung open the front door.

"Stop. I've called the police. Stop!" I held up my phone, video on. In my haste, I ran all the way to the sidewalk, less than twenty feet from them, before I realized and stopped.

"Fuck." Black Shirt twisted his face away from the camera and let go of the carpenter.

The carpenter stumbled backward, and Black Shirt jumped in the Land Rover, slammed the door, and gunned the engine. The carpenter lunged out of his path, but not fast enough. The corner of the vehicle clipped him as it roared past.

He spun and fell.

Breathing hard, he tried to get up but fell again. His right leg twisted at an unnatural angle from the knee. The third time he made it to one foot. Hopping forward, he tried the right leg and, with a grunt, fell again.

I stepped forward, heart racing. Then back again. The drizzle turned to rain. He crab-walked on his arms and his left leg, dragging his right across the pavement. The rain began to fall harder. I backed away as he approached. When he reached the curb in front of my house, he hauled himself up to standing, holding on to the telephone pole and looking at me.

As if he were waiting for something.

Our eyes met, and before I had a chance to name it or know it, joy raced through my every nerve, and I gasped.

"Oh my god." He didn't just remind me of Isaac. He *was* Isaac.

His brow furrowed, the stoicism breaking down. At last I could see. His nose was crooked in a way it hadn't been before, but the eyes—unchanged. I don't know how I missed it, even with the hat and sunglasses he always wore, even from my third-floor window. Isaac Wells.

I ran to him. Not knowing what else to do, I reached out my hand. His was cold and wet, gritty from the asphalt.

"I'm sorry." He panted and squeezed his eyes shut, his face twisted in agony. "I'm so sorry. Holy fuck."

"Let me call 9-1-1 again. We need to get you an ambulance."

"I can't. I have to get away."

"From what? No. Why?"

He looked away from me and around the street, like a hunted animal. "I can't be here when the cops come. Do you have a crutch, or a cane? Or a fucking—stick? Anything." He looked pale, and his arms trembled.

"Please let me get you an ambulance. Your leg."

"Fuck's sake," he muttered and tried to hop away from the street on his left leg.

"Okay, okay. Yes. I have something. Just a second." I started for the door.

But before I reached the front walk, sirens wailed only a few blocks away.

"Meg?" His voice had an edge of desperation. "I really can't... Can you please help me?"

"You mean—?" I pointed in the direction of the sirens.

He looked down and held out an arm. "Yes. I'm sorry. Just to somewhere they won't see me."

The rain fell harder and dripped in my eyes. He needed an ambulance. A hospital. He needed someone to fix that leg. Not to be hobbling around in the rain hiding from the police. But all my life, people had told me what I needed when they should have asked *What do you need? What do you really need?* And they should have actually listened to the answer. It might have changed my life.

What difference did it make to me whether he went to the hospital? But it might make all the difference for him.

His shoulders slumped with relief when I stepped forward.

First he only gripped my forearm for balance as he tried to hop toward the house. He breathed hard through his nose, jaw clenched tight.

He stopped. "I'm sorry. Just one second."

"If I do like this, maybe." I stood awkwardly at his side and motioned for him to put an arm over my shoulder. Lucky for him, he wasn't much taller than I, and though he tried not to, he leaned on me heavily. His clothes smelled like woodsmoke. His waist was lean and firm. He wore a cap pulled low on his forehead.

"No, not that way," I said. "We'd have to go the whole block before we could get you out of sight. Come around the driveway."

Getting up the steep part of the driveway was no easy task. With his arm over my shoulder, I stepped forward. He leaned on me and hopped, wincing every time he landed.

"Why were you hiding from me?" I said. "You've been working across the street all this time."

"I'm sorry."

"But why?" I felt myself smiling and wondered if I should stop.

"I can't—oh fuck. I'm sorry. I needed some quick work, and I was hoping Lila—" He winced again.

"You were hoping Lila could give you some work?"

"Yes, but…" He hopped again. It was slow progress up the driveway.

"But she's—" The words caught tight in my throat. "But she couldn't."

"And there's half a dozen houses in this neighborhood that need work. I only had to look across the street."

The stew of joy, grief, and confusion were making full sentences, even full thoughts, difficult.

"But why didn't you let me know?"

"I can't explain right now. I didn't want to make trouble for you." He scowled and moaned as his toe caught on the asphalt and wrenched his leg.

"Isaac—trouble? Jesus, let's get you inside."

"No. Don't take me in your house."

"I don't understand. What's going on?"

"It's really better if you don't know."

The sirens approached, winding down the road that crossed the park. Their tone shifted as they made the turn into the neighborhood and under the heavy tree cover.

He gripped my shoulder harder and doubled our pace until we stood in the dark space between the side door to the house and the big, freestanding garage.

"This is fine," he said, leaning against the wall. "I'll get to the back alley."

"You mean… No. You can't. Please." I scrambled for a solution between the sirens and his pained eyes, so withdrawn, as if he were already trying to escape. I opened the door to the garage. "Here, this isn't technically the house."

The air inside was cool and smelled of motor oil and concrete. Along the wall near the door, an ancient sofa stood next to a side table with an ashtray piled high from when my grandfather used to sneak out here twenty years back to smoke.

He hopped inside, gripping the door frame.

"Stay in here," I said. "I'll let you know when they're gone."

He dropped onto the sofa and looked up at the ceiling, his eyes little more than a gleam in the darkness.

"I'll go talk to the cops," I said.

"Please don't tell them anything."

"I won't. I promise. I won't let them near you." I felt like I was desperately grasping for a hold on something that kept slipping away. "Please promise you'll stay."

He gripped his temples with his hand and muttered, "Fuck."

The sirens stopped and a big engine pulled up and idled in front of the house.

"Isaac."

"I'm sorry. Okay. I promise."

I lied to the police. I told them that both parties to the fight had run off. The officer who came to the door did not seem particularly impressed with the situation, but he and his partner walked up and down the block, then sat out front in their squad car. I was horribly impatient for them to leave. Isaac might have changed his mind and managed to limp off.

He was hurt. He needed an ice pack at the very least. The cops in their car weren't watching. I could probably go out to the garage without them noticing, but I couldn't take the chance. I promised. He promised.

The rain slowed and stopped. It was fully dark when at last the big engine in the police car rumbled, and they pulled slowly into the street and drove off.

Long accustomed to caregiving, I had ice ready and went immediately to the garage.

"They're gone. Put this on your leg. Is it your knee? Who was that guy?"

"Thank you," he said. "He was nobody."

"And here's some ibuprofen." I turned on the light and handed it to him with a cup of water. "We need to get you to a doctor. And we—or I—need to report him to the police. He hit you with his car. He can't just do that and drive away."

"No. Just…no. Please don't call the police again." He swallowed the pills. "I'll just rest for a little bit in here. If that's okay."

A heavy beard made him look older, and his brow was tight with pain.

"Of course it's okay. Here." I crossed the room and turned on my grandfather's old space heater. "You should just stay the night. But I don't understand. Why don't you come inside?"

At last he looked me straight in the eyes. It was a look that admitted no argument.

"I can't."

I felt powerless in every limb, but I returned his gaze. "I'm so happy to see you."

His was a face I had known so well, but at that moment it was unreadable. He was silent, yet looked so much as if he wanted to speak.

I shook my head. "Okay. So…good night?"

He nodded. "Good night."

Climbing the stairs to my room, joy, confusion, fear, even a kind of regretful sadness all wrapped around me like a web. He was back. He was sleeping in my garage. He needed a blanket. Mid-September the weather could go either way, and it was cool with the rain. His clothes were probably wet. I pulled a mothball-smelling quilt from a chest in a second-floor bedroom and took it outside. This time I tapped on the door to the garage. He gave no response, so I let myself in. He had turned off the light again.

"I brought a blanket."

But he was fast asleep, head on the armrest. Leg and ice pack raised on the back cushions of the couch.

The concrete floor cooled the soles of my feet. I folded the big blanket in half and laid it over him, careful to avoid the knee.

I switched off the house lights before heading to bed, and before I went up, as always, I turned on the light on the porch. The entrance to the library was to the right of the main stairs. It wasn't a room we had used much when Lila was alive. Since the bathroom above had flooded a year before I came home, the plaster ceiling had fallen in and the room was a mess. But worse, the bookcases that had been custom-built for the curved room had warped and pulled away from the walls. Dust and boards still littered the space.

I stood at the door, arms crossed, looking at the big empty room, lit only by the light from the porch through the windows.

I was twenty-three, he was nineteen, and Lila had set us to work on the library. It was a big job. The books had to be taken off the shelves and cleaned before Isaac could even get to the woodwork. It was precisely the kind of job where I could be useful.

On a little card table near the big double doors from the foyer, I gathered my collection of instruments. Small paintbrushes for brushing the plaster dust from the pages, leather conditioner, and soft rags. Even a tiny vacuum. The kind they use to clean the dust out of computers. And on the floor, a pile of clean cardboard boxes to put the books in until the shelves were ready to welcome them back.

Isaac did the heavier cleaning, bagging up the big chunks of fallen plaster. He gave me a mask to wear in the beginning when the dust hung in the air like a white haze. Winter sun shone through the windows, and the leafless boughs of a giant oak cast a thousand tiny shadows on the floor.

We fell into a routine. He arrived at nine, had coffee with Lila, and attended to any odd jobs that needed doing. Then around ten I would join him in the library. He took the books down from the shelves and piled them near my table, and I sat paging through the old volumes. I was a slow worker because I did as much reading as I did cleaning.

"Look. 1856," I said one day when the sky was so dark with rain that we had all the lights on.

"What about 1856?" Isaac said.

"This book. Published in 1856. It's the oldest one I've found yet."

He took a pencil from his pocket and wrote on a patch of intact wall. *1856.*

"Where do you find the date?"

I got up and showed him how to look for the copyright page. Sometimes the date was easy to find. Sometimes it was a scavenger hunt—especially on the older books.

Half an hour later, he wrote *1849* on the wall.

"Let me see." I reached out for the small, thick book in his hand.

As he gave it to me, our fingers touched. His were rough and warm, and they sent a charge across my skin. He retreated quickly, and we worked in silence, avoiding each other's eyes for a solid hour.

Finally I held up a book with gold letters embossed on its brown spine. "This one's 1829."

"No way. Show me."

Somehow, given a little time and space, we always started talking. Maybe the silence took the place of small talk, and when we finally got to a conversation, we skipped straight to the real stuff.

Over that winter, I told him all about coming to Lila's house as a child. How it was never as often or for as long as I wanted. I told him what a misfit I was at school, and how lonely. How hard my father drove me, and how hard I drove myself.

He was a misfit too, he said. His father had left when he was two, and his mother was bipolar, so his older sister had all but raised him. She was working her way through community college, and they shared an apartment. Things were in a rare state of stability, but he was afraid it wouldn't hold.

"Nothing ever lasts long in my life, good or bad." He held up a book. "This is 1822."

The list on the wall got longer and longer.

I dreamed of solving Frieholdt's. He dreamed of becoming a blacksmith, like his great-uncle who had made beautiful knives that never seemed to lose their edge.

He visited us on Christmas. Lila gave him a card in which she had tucked a substantial amount of cash. He gave us a birdhouse he had made, and he mounted it to the trunk of the closest maple in the back, where we could see it. In the spring, he said, wrens would nest there, but we had to watch closely because they were shy.

He seemed so able. So normal. He may have felt like a misfit. He was poor, and his family was broken, but he was warm and kind and handsome in a way he didn't seem aware of. And everything he touched worked.

However long he stayed, I wanted it to be longer. Wherever he was, I wanted him closer. But I was so afraid of everything then. Coping with anxiety and panic almost daily. My research felt more and more like a castle made of smoke. I had no job. No future. The best I could do was get through a day. I had no business thinking about a relationship with Isaac Wells, who was so capable and young and had everything going for him.

By February all the books were clean and our list went to 1799. A cookbook, of all things. We read through it, laughing at the recipes for rabbit stew and something called piccalilli.

On a dry, bright day, when the cold seeped in through all the loose places in that big wooden house, Isaac arrived on his motorcycle at his usual time, but instead of getting to work, he and Lila sat and talked. I liked to let them have their hour in the morning, and it gave me a chance to adjust myself to his presence, but this time I waited impatiently on the back stairs. There was something different in the tone of their voices. Lila sounded animated, and Isaac talked more than usual.

At last, I heard their chairs scraping the floor. I thought Lila said, *She's upstairs.*

I stood up, nervous. Why? I took a deep breath, closed my eyes, and blew out slowly. Slow the heart. Slow the mind. Then I gripped the rail and started down the stairs. Whatever it was, I was about to find out. I went down. Isaac turned the corner from the back hall and started up. We found ourselves one step apart. So close, I could smell his hair.

"Hi… I was…" He looked pale.

I froze, and for a moment neither of us moved.

Then he turned around and went back down, waiting for

me at the bottom. It took a second to get my joints mobile again, but I managed. The back hall wasn't much better than the staircase as far as room to maneuver, but at least we could stand a few feet apart.

He wore jeans and a black cotton sweater. He put his hands in his pockets.

"I was coming up to find you," he said.

"Why?"

"I'm leaving…"

My face burned, and I fought the urge to cry. An apprenticeship three states away. With a blacksmith. I could feel the pain in his voice. The only time he seemed happy was when he told me, "He knew my great-uncle Kimmo."

As horrible as I felt, I managed a smile. For him. It was his dream.

"How long?"

"Three years, if I don't fuck it up."

I couldn't do any more. I couldn't talk. I could barely breathe. But we were used to long silences.

I managed to whisper, "I'll miss you."

He held out his hand and waited while I willed my body to move, to reach out. His skin was dry and warm, calloused. His knuckles bony. My own hand felt inert. The signals from brain to muscles moving erratically. Too slowly.

"I'll miss you too," he said and held my hand a little tighter. He was shaking.

I have never wished harder to be someone other than I was. Someone who could take him by the shoulders and tell him everything that was in my heart. But wishing had never changed anything and never would. He came to Lila's to work for three more days, but I didn't come down. I couldn't. Then he left.

I wept. I sank into a month-long depression. It sounds so old-fashioned to say that I loved him, when I had never done more than hold his hand. But so it was. Spring advanced through the garden with its insistent will to grow, and wrens nested in his birdhouse.

7

It took some doing, but I persuaded him to let me take him to a doctor. At the clinic, he gave a false name. Ignoring his protest, I paid the bill.

It was a bad sprain with a fracture of the tibia near the knee. Not bad enough for surgery, but bad enough that he walked out with a hinged brace from his thigh to his ankle, and strict instructions to stay on crutches for three weeks.

All the sitting around in waiting rooms that morning allowed us some time to recover from the shock of the day before. We could ease back into acquaintance. As much as I felt like he was part of my soul, I had not spoken to him in fourteen years. A lot had happened.

He finished the apprenticeship, he told me. Loved it. He was saving money to set up shop when his mother had a manic episode. She ran up thousands in credit-card debt and couldn't pay rent. He went back to bail her out, and he met a girl.

My gut cramped at this part. I knew he had to have, but at the same time I couldn't bear the thought. I stared out the window of the X-ray waiting room. The air-conditioning vent blew cold air at my shoulder.

They married. He tried. He worked. He supported her for three years. And she cheated on him.

"It's maybe the one smart decision I made in my life," he said, "to get out of that relationship before we had any kids."

The divorce was draining and expensive. Between his mother, his ex, and being a high-school dropout, he never could get ahead, and he had lived paycheck to paycheck ever since.

And me? Work, work, and more work. A few dates. I didn't tell Isaac, but there had been a brief reunion with the physics professor I almost married in graduate school. That was it. Research. Caring for Lila.

I almost laughed at how we gathered this vital information about each other in and among more benign subjects. Not married. Not—that I could tell—partnered.

On the way home, I took us for drive-through burgers and fries. The young woman at the window smiled as she handed us the bags. From her vantage point, we were a couple in a car, getting lunch. Regular people doing regular things. But what was stranger was that for a minute I felt like we were regular people too.

We ate in the parking lot, windows rolled up against an unseasonably hot afternoon.

Isaac wiped his hands on a napkin, staring hard at the parking lot. "Thank you. I don't know what I would have done without you. You can drop me on Piney Branch and Sixteenth Street. I'm staying with one of the guys from the job."

It was as if someone punched me in the face. My neck grew stiff as I pulled out onto the road. Then the creaking feeling in my ribs. He wasn't staying. He was trying to get away from me. Something was wrong. Bad wrong. Was it me? I couldn't tell.

"Take a left up here." He brushed the crumbs from his beard and balled his trash up into the bag.

I gripped the steering wheel. He gave directions, and the distance grew shorter and shorter between our point on the road and the point at which he would get out and hobble up to a door that was not my door and a house that was not my house.

I pulled over to the side of the street.

"What are you doing?" Isaac said.

"Please come back and stay with me." My voice felt thin and reedy, like it was escaping through a tiny aperture in my spirit. It frightened me how much I wanted this.

"Meg—"

"I know you're going to say how you don't want to bring your trouble into my house. You've been apologizing for that all morning, so let's skip that part, okay?"

"No. Not okay. That's the important part."

I lifted my hands from the steering wheel and dropped them again. It wasn't going to work. I looked away, out my window, through the traffic passing, at the gray trunk of a beech across the street.

"We're adults now," I said. "We don't—or at least, I don't want to play games. We had something together. I don't even know what it was, but it was something."

He looked at me a moment, brown eyes wide and bright. Then he sighed and dropped his head. "It's really better if you don't have me in your house."

He wasn't even saying he didn't want to, just that he thought he knew what was *better*. I hit the steering wheel with the heel of my hand.

"How do you know what's better for me? My whole fucking life, people always think they know what's better for me. How about you let me decide that?"

"Listen." The edge in his voice cut through my petulance. "I don't know what's good for you or not. It's not about that. But with my situation… If you knew, you could be in legal trouble already."

Something like electricity prickled down my spine as I turned. Being this close to a panic attack involved unusual physical sensations. Unpredictable, like a neon sign popping and flickering, trying to turn on.

"I'll be fine," he said. It sounded awfully close to goodbye.

I took a deep breath, not sure I would be breathing much after what I was about to say.

"But do you want to? Do you want to come home with me?"

He stared ahead and did not speak.

The loss of something you thought you already lost is the worst loss of all—when you've learned to live without it, and then face having to learn how all over again.

I sank in my seat. "I still don't understand. Why didn't you tell us—me you were working right across the street?"

"I wanted to. She was alive when I first came." He shook his head and looked at me. There was shame in his eyes. "But when I saw how things were—"

"How frail she was?"

"I saw you out walking with her in the wheelchair. I couldn't. I would've only made your lives harder. She might not have even remembered me."

"She would have remembered you."

He rubbed his eyes with thumb and forefinger.

"So you just walked across the street?" I said.

"It's a huge job. And they could pay cash. And then I saw the ambulance come to your house."

"When she died."

He covered his face with his hand. "I wish I had come over. Just to see her."

A bus rattled by, and I waited for quiet.

Then I turned to face him. "If it weren't for everything else, all the stuff you're not telling me, if it weren't for all that, would you come back with me? Please tell me the truth."

His eyes softened, and the deep lines disappeared from his forehead. Like he looked when he was nineteen, before any of the things that had creased his face and put that bend in his nose and the scars on his hands. He pressed his lips together, chest rising and falling.

"Of course I would."

And that was enough. I turned the car on, checked my rear-view mirror, and pulled a U-turn back home.

Did he argue with me about it? Yes. Did he try and persuade me to turn around and drop him at the apartment of some near stranger from the worksite where he slept on the couch and didn't leave a trace of his presence from when he left in the morning to when he returned at night? Yes. But did I? No. I wasn't a scared little girl anymore. I was a scared grown woman—which is different. I drove back to Lila's and up the driveway, and I helped him inside, all with a lightness in my body that I couldn't remember feeling possibly ever.

He was back. I thought it would never happen. He was awkward and in pain, working his way up the steps on his new crutches. I waited holding open the door.

"Back here." I waved him through the center hall to the narrow passage between the kitchen and the side door. "They're the old servants' quarters. It's the only bedroom on the first floor."

They were designed for a single housemaid. One room held a bed on a carved bedstead with just enough room to stand up, if you weren't too large a person. The other room held a small chest of drawers, a chair, and a delicate round side table. Each had a small rug, with a faded pattern of roses.

Isaac peered in. The rooms were connected at either end by short passages. Between the two rooms were a closet and a bathroom not much bigger than the closet. At the closet end, a tall narrow window looked out over a weedy part of the garden. It was an efficient use of space, unlike the rest of the house.

"Servants here lived better than I ever did." Isaac rummaged in his pockets. "Could I have a glass of water please?"

I brought him one and found him sitting on the bed.

He took it and downed two pain pills. "I imagine you'll google me. If you haven't already."

"I haven't."

He seemed relieved. "If you do…don't let it be trackable."

"Let me get you something to elevate your knee."

"It's important. You don't want to have me in your search history."

"I've got a good VPN on my whole system," I said. "I thought someone was hacking my research once."

From the big parlor with the fireplace, I gathered scratchy old sofa cushions in my arms.

Isaac eyed me when I returned, then groaned a little as he lay down and propped his knee up on the pillows. I opened the window.

"Just for a couple of days. Then I'll be out of your way," he said, his voice already growing thick with fatigue and pain.

Since I could remember, knowledge was the currency by which I transacted my life. Knowledge bought me my parents' love, but it was not a stable currency. There was an unpredictable inflationary cycle. Sometimes I would find that the fortune of knowledge I had worked so hard to amass suddenly failed to impress. But I could stand on my hoard and see the next shiny jewel, and when I got to it, approval and love would flow in again.

With Isaac asleep in the servant's bedroom, sedated by pain medicine and his knee elevated, I contemplated the value of knowledge. I could open up a browser and within seconds know what the internet had to say about him. But I didn't. It couldn't possibly make anything better than it already was.

8

He slept through the afternoon, and I spent the day in the living room, listening for him to wake. I hadn't spent a day away from my tower study in years, and my neck felt softer. My shoulders lower. In the kitchen, warming up soup, I finally heard thumping from Isaac's room.

The look he gave me when he limped into the kitchen on his crutches asked the question, and the look I gave him must have answered it. No. I had not searched his name.

He frowned and sat at the table in the breakfast nook. I set a bowl of tomato soup in front of him.

"I was going to make grilled cheese. Do you want one?"

"I'm wanted for murder."

I sat down, a prickling feeling all over my skin. It couldn't be true. But no. If he said it, it must be true. But there had to be more.

"What happened?"

He was silent a minute, and when he spoke it was in a soft voice, like a confession.

"We never really talked much about, you know, anything

before we met. You don't really know how fucked up my family is."

I nodded, eyes stinging from failing to blink, waiting.

He sighed. "My mom has bipolar and no insurance, so things get kind of...out of hand. My grandmother put a roof over our heads, but..."

There was so much he was leaving out in those long pauses, but I committed them to memory. I would learn later. I nodded again.

"My big sister, Kate, pretty much raised me, but a couple of years ago she started doing meth and got involved with this dealer, Danny DeVries. Scrawny little jacked-up asshole."

Deep creases showed in his forehead.

"Is he the one you—?"

His shoulders were rigid as he leaned back in his chair, but his face softened. "It was fucking stupid of her. But she's my sister, you know? And she tried. She tried to get out and get clean. She wanted to go to college."

"But..."

His eyes go flat. "Then he started hitting her."

So they made a plan.

Five months before he staggered up my driveway, Isaac went to her house when the boyfriend was away. Kate had her bags packed. All her papers in order. She threw everything in Isaac's truck. But there was a dog. She had to take the dog—the only living thing besides Isaac that she really loved.

She called and called for him, and finally he came running around from the back of the house and bounded happily into the back of the truck. But just as they closed their doors and started to back out, DeVries came tearing down the road and skidded into the driveway, blocking the way.

He jumped from his car, but Isaac hit the gas, cut across the

yard and over the ditch into the road. The boyfriend took out
a gun and fired. It hit the back panel. Kate screamed. He fired
again and hit the tailgate. Then he got in his truck to follow.

There was no way Isaac would win a chase. DeVries had
more money and more engine, so Isaac grabbed his own hand-
gun from the center console and fired at the front tire. Missed.
Fired again. Weaving down the two-lane road a hundred feet
ahead and losing ground, he got off one more shot and floored
the gas. In the rearview mirror he saw the boyfriend's truck
veer off the road, flip, and roll.

Kate begged him to turn back. To help. But Isaac knew
this guy. If he was still alive, he'd still be shooting. So he told
Kate to call 9-1-1 and kept driving.

"Kate's four states away now. I gave her money for an apartment and to get settled. It was nearly everything I had." Isaac
leans forward, arms wrapped tight across his stomach. "I was
fueling up on the way back, and my friend Darrell called. He
was like, 'What the fuck, Isaac? They say you killed Danny
DeVries. They say you shot him in the neck, man.'"

Isaac stared hard at the water-stained top of the breakfast
table. The groove between his expressive brows had deep-
ened. Every few seconds he shifted in the hard seat. He had
to be in pain.

"I couldn't go back. I can't. I have a juvenile record. Plus
some other…like fucking pot possession. Disorderly conduct.
And I'm fucking poor. Danny has a brother, and they have
practically everyone in their pocket, including half the police
department. Blind Fork would like nothing more than to see
Isaac Wells finally go to jail. There's no way I'm getting away
without time." He lifted his hands, then dropped them in his
lap. "My mom is on disability. She can't get by without help,
and if I'm in jail, there's no one to help her. So here I am."

Since he got hired on across the street, he had been sleeping on a coworker's couch for a fee. He couldn't register a car, so he couldn't drive. He kept a burner phone, and no one knew his number. He conducted his entire life in cash.

"If I so much as get caught jaywalking, the cops will do a search and find the warrant and send me back to Blind Fork. And then I'm fucked." He looked up and waved at me impatiently. "Just look it up. Get it over with."

I reached over to the counter for my phone.

Wanted. Isaac Wells of Blind Fork, North Carolina. Thirty-four-year-old Caucasian male. Five feet eleven inches. Hair, brown. Eyes, brown. Wanted in the death of Daniel DeVries of Bent Tree, Tennessee.

Information on his whereabouts could be relayed to a toll-free number.

His voice was weary but less strained. "Now you can decide what to do."

I stood and picked up his bowl. "Let's go outside. It's easier to think out there."

He followed me on his crutches to the back porch, where we settled at an angle to one another. Him with his leg extended on the wicker couch. Me in the rocking chair. He sipped the soup straight from the bowl. The magnolia leaves made a sound like rustling paper in the light breeze. It was remarkable how little it looked like a city from Lila's back porch.

"I remember Kate," I said. "She came to the door a couple of times to pick you up."

I wasn't ready to tell him that the first time she came, I had been jealous, and jealousy had made me brave so that the second time, I actually answered the door, hands sweating, back stiff as a plank. And when she said, "I'm here to pick up Isaac," I said, "And you are…?"

I probably sounded like the worst kind of upper-class bitch. But she smiled like she could see right through me and said, "I'm Kate Wells. His sister."

Isaac looked sideways at me. "Yeah, Kate's memorable, all right."

"So she was a witness. She can help you."

His face hardened. "After everything I did to get her away from that motherfucker? She's safe now. She's finally in school."

"Wouldn't your car have bullet holes in it? It would show you'd been shot at."

"My truck is locked up in some dude's warehouse across town from Kate. I paid him up front for a year and took off the tags."

"But you didn't abandon it?"

"Abandon my truck?" He laughed, it seemed at himself. "It's a good truck. When this all shakes out, one way or another, at least Kate can use it."

I rested my elbows on my knees. "Wouldn't she want to help you?"

He shook his head. "Of course she would. That's the problem. She'd ride hell-for-leather here and testify, and then DeVries's brother would know exactly where she was, and I wouldn't be able to protect her."

"So you're deciding what's best for her, without giving her any input."

Isaac glared at me, brow furrowed, then dragged a hand down his face.

"She was an addict, Meg. It's different."

My thoughts resisted arrangement. They swam around in my head and bumped against each other like atoms in entropy. I readied myself to speak, and the doorbell rang.

Isaac jumped up and scrambled for his crutches. "Fuck."

He hurried to his room, turned off the light, and closed the door. I collected myself, took two deep breaths, and headed for the front of the house. It would be easy to explain why I was so nervous answering the door. I am always nervous answering the door.

Dusk had fallen, and I switched on the porch light.

That was an oddly dressed cop. Baseball cap in hand. T-shirt. Work pants. A pair of earplugs attached by a cord dangling around his neck. Old too. Gray stubble of a beard. It took longer than you would think for me to realize this was probably not a cop at all.

I opened the door.

He nodded. "Ma'am, I'm sorry to bother you. I'm a foreman across the street."

"What can I do for you?" I wasn't trying to be cold, but if I didn't act it he would see how scared I was.

"Well—" he switched his cap from one hand to the other "—I had a guy who didn't show up for work today. A lady came looking for him."

"It wasn't me."

"No, ma'am, but I heard there was a fight, or something that happened last night. I wanted to ask if you...if you saw anything. We just want to make sure he's okay."

I couldn't have turned my head at that moment if you had paid me a million dollars, my neck was so rigid.

"There was a fight. Right out there." I pointed to the street. "I called the police, but by the time they got here, they had both disappeared."

"All right. Okay." He nodded several times and stepped back. "Thank you, ma'am. Sorry to bother you. I just hope he's okay. Good carpenter. Could use him back." He smiled and put on his cap.

I tried to smile back. "I wish I could be of more help."

When he got in his truck and drove away, I locked the door and nearly ran for the back of the house.

"It's okay." I knocked on Isaac's door. "Isaac, it's okay. It wasn't the cops. Just a guy from your work."

He opened the door, then dropped back to sit on the bed.

"I can't do this to you. I can't stay here." He stood up and put on his jacket, gathering a set of keys, his phone and wallet and crutches. I stepped back as he excused himself around me in the hall.

"Isaac, no. It wasn't the cops. It was just a guy from across the street, wondering if you were okay. He said a *lady* came looking for you."

"God. Fuck." His face darkened. "Listen, eventually it's going to be the cops. Do you know you can go to jail for harboring a fugitive?"

"Yes, I do know."

I stood between him and the side door.

"Excuse me," he said.

"No."

He waited, then rolled his eyes and started down the center hall for the front door. But I went through the dining room and the parlor and intercepted him before he got to the foyer.

He scowled at me. "I'm leaving."

"No."

"I can leave if I want."

"But you don't want to."

"Yes, I do."

"No, you don't. You just think you should."

"If the cops—"

"If the cops know anything now that they didn't know yesterday, then they'll be knocking on the door of whoever's house you were staying at. Or they'll be talking to the lady who's looking for you—which we are going to get to in a minute. They won't be coming here. At least not yet. And if they do, they have no justification to search."

He tried to sidestep around me, but I stopped him. I could act as brash and smart-ass as I wanted, but he was really trying to leave. Desperation dug a yawning chasm I would fall into if I didn't act.

With the grown-up Isaac Wells in front of me, I did what I had wished a million times I had done fifteen years ago. I stepped forward, close to his body, and placed my palm on his chest. My heart glowed hot. I could smell the sawdust on his shirt and the worn leather of his jacket.

"Please stay."

His shoulders softened. He leaned his head down next to mine, rough beard grazing my cheek. "I'm afraid."

"So am I."

"Not even about the cops. But that you won't—that I'm too much of a fuckup."

"Me too. That I'm a head case."

"No, you're not."

"Yes, I am. How do you know I'm not?"

"How do you know I'm not a fuckup?"

"I didn't say you weren't."

He laughed, deep and low in his chest. "True."

"Postulates one and two: you're a fuckup, and I'm a head case," I said. "Please don't go. Not yet."

"I remember it was just like this," he said. "You were so brilliant, but when you talked to me it was like we weren't different at all."

"We're not."

"Of course you would say that, but yes, we are very different."

"Don't patronize me." I leaned back so we could look at one another. His eyes. I remembered them so well. That brown where if you looked long enough you saw the glint of red-gold. "Your whole life, people groomed you for failure. My whole life people groomed me for greatness. Have you ever thought that those two things aren't all that different? Neither of us got to just be ourselves."

"I've never thought that, but I do now," he said. "And I'm sorry for patronizing you."

"Postulate three—" I laid my other hand on his chest, feeling his heart beat underneath "—I am responsible for what is good for me. And I am the only person who has the right to act on what's good for me. And you too. You do what's right for you. I do what's right for me. Not what we think is safe. Not what other people want. Not what we *think* other people want—including each other. What we truly want. Okay?"

"What's a postulate? Like a precondition?"

"Yes. A premise that serves as the basis for a line of reasoning."

He nodded. "I can agree to those postulates."

The light from the porch shone through the front windows. Otherwise, the house was dark throughout. We were invisible to the world, concealed in the narrow hall. He hopped to the right and leaned against the wall for balance.

"Do you remember," he said, "the time we nearly ran into each other in the back stairs? You were coming down—"

"And you were coming up. I wasn't paying attention. It was the day you told me you were leaving."

"We were so young."

And suddenly it hit me. We weren't young anymore. Fifteen years had come and gone since we met.

I fought the grief that constricted my throat. "Under postulate three, I want you to kiss me."

He reached up and stroked my hair. "Under postulate three, I want to be able to see your face."

I ran down the hall. The nearest lamp I could reach stood on a table in the foyer. I flipped it on, and it cast enough light in the center hall to see by.

When I turned back, Isaac was already coming to me, swinging his bad leg between the crutches. He stopped at the end of the hall, dropped his right crutch, and leaned his left shoulder on the door frame. He got one good look, then he kissed me.

I started into that kiss from far away. It had been so long. He cradled the back of my head, his thumb behind my ear. The gentlest suggestion that I should open my lips, and oh I had forgotten…my personal brand of anxiety was obliterated by pleasure. His beard scratched my chin. Warmth spread through my limbs, rushing toward my fingers. I felt the cool wall under one hand, his arm under the other, and I swear something realigned inside of me. Angles became curves. Particles became waves. For years, a set of brackets had defined the boundaries of what I was able to experience. Isaac Wells erased them.

Suddenly every feeling I could name—and more that I couldn't—flooded my mind and heart. Isaac leaned his head beside mine and held my shaking body firm and strong.

"It's okay. It's okay."

"Where have you been?" My voice struggled out, wanting to break apart.

"I'm sorry." He leaned his head down to my shoulder. "I'm sorry it took so long."

I held on, one hand around his waist, one hand on the wall.

"Postulate three is a bitch," he said, his breath warm on my neck.

"What do you mean?"

"If it's all about what I want, then what I want is to take you back to that ridiculously small bedroom you've got me in and make love to you. Am I not supposed to think about what's good for you? That doesn't seem right."

I smiled through the chaos of emotion in my body. "You're right. I think I was inexact in my language."

"And math is all about being exact."

"Not really. It's more about clarity. Postulate three should really be that only I can really *know* what's right for me. And same for you. Everything else—what's safe, what the other person wants—is speculation. But it doesn't mean we shouldn't talk about it."

He kissed me again. "I could listen to you talk forever."

9

We did not go back to that ridiculously small bedroom. We went to the kitchen, kissed, shared a beer, kissed some more. I liked this new state of things—not having to do a damn thing about Frieholdt's. Isaac Wells in my arms at last. Was this what it was like for people without an all-consuming obsession? To be able to pay attention, to enjoy what is right in front of you?

Neither of us felt like eating, so we talked and laughed and kissed some more. As it got late and he grew tired from the meds, I took him to the ridiculously small bedroom and sat down next to him as he took the brace off. Free of that limiting contraption, he pulled me onto his lap. He winced and adjusted me to the side.

"I'm going to hurt you," I said.

He wrapped his arms around me and buried his head against my neck. "No, you're not."

He kissed my shoulder, my collarbone. His hair smelled of wood dust and a little bit of car exhaust. His beard brushed my breast through the fabric of my shirt, and when he touched my bare skin, I gasped.

Then he paused and heaved a noisy breath. "We better stop. I've thought of this for so long, I don't want to rush it."

"You did?"

"Did what?"

"Thought about it?"

He laughed. "Of course I did."

"Since…"

He tilted his head and looked at me as if I were a little dim. "Since *forever*, Meg."

Even after all the kissing, I blushed.

The first thing I did when I reached my own bedroom was open the window. I wanted to shout into the night, but I did have neighbors, and I didn't want the attention. The second thing I did was to open the small top drawer of my bureau. I had two condoms in there from who knows how long ago. Expired. I swore out loud and paced the room. There was no way I was going to sleep so I went down the hall to my study. The shorthand version of Frieholdt's was still on my board. Looking at it at that moment, being so completely in my body, it looked as if it belonged to some other world. Some other Margaret Brightwood. It didn't matter. It could wait.

Technically, acquiring birth control could wait too, but it didn't wait.

I tiptoed back into the house with my little bag from the twenty-four-hour convenience store a half mile up the hill. I had thought about driving, but I worried it would wake Isaac, so I walked. And it's a good thing. It cooled my engines a little. Let me get a little think in. Maybe he was right. Maybe we shouldn't rush it. I should cool down and go to bed.

But the moment I walked back in the house, it was no use. There was going to be no sleeping for me that night.

Trying to be as quiet as possible, I got a glass of wine in the kitchen. The room where Isaac slept was only a single wall away. I didn't know how heavy a sleeper he was. Maybe he wasn't sleeping either.

Swirling the wine in my glass, I leaned my forehead against the window in the breakfast nook.

Wanted for murder.

But he didn't mean to kill the guy. It was self-defense. The guy was shooting at him.

But who would know that? Only Kate. I could hire him a lawyer, but without a witness...

I rolled my forehead against the cool glass. Something rustled in the garden. Probably deer. This close to the park, they were our daily companions.

"Meg?"

I startled, splashed wine on my arm, and spun around.

"I'm sorry," Isaac said.

His hair was pushed back from his forehead. Rumpled T-shirt, and some soft pants which dragged on the floor around his bare feet. My mouth hung open.

He leaned on his crutches. "Um...say something."

"Sorry. Hi."

He smiled. "Hi. Did you go some—"

"I don't care about rushing it. I don't want to wait." I set down the glass with a trembling hand. I was one ionic bond away from lighting up like a solar flare.

He hobbled over, pausing to look at the bag from the convenience store.

"Did you—?"

"Yes. I went and got condoms."

"You walked all the way?"

"Yes. Yes, I walked to the store. Isaac, please."

The floor creaked under his crutch as he shifted and leaned against the counter. I felt frozen, as if even lifting my feet would tear up the floorboards.

"It's been fourteen years," I said. "And if we wait, you might figure out what a mess I really am, and you might think you don't want to deal with all that. I don't want that to happen. I don't want to miss my chance."

"I think I'm the one *you* won't want to deal with. I want you to have time to think it over before—"

"Think it over? We already established I'm a head case, you're a fuckup. Those are—"

"Postulates one and two."

"Yes. Preconditions. They're built-in. If you killed that guy—*if* it was actually your fault—you did it in self-defense. You may be a fuckup, but you aren't a bad person."

"How do you know?" He rolled his eyes. "How do you know I'm not a fucking horrible person who you should run away from as fast as you can?"

"Quit rolling your eyes at me. I just know."

He held out his hand for my glass, and I gave it to him.

His face softened as he took a slow drink. "Are you really sure?"

I nodded, practically vibrating with impatience.

He reached down the counter and looked in the bag. "What kind did you get? I hope not the cheap ones."

I laughed and snatched at the bag. When I came within reach, he grasped me by the waist and pulled me in, dropping his other crutch, both hands up my shirt and his tongue in my mouth.

I dug my fingers into his hair with one hand and untucked

his shirt with the other. The muscles along his spine flexed under my fingers. Then he sighed, and his back relaxed. His hands softened. Pleasure washed through me. Cleansed me. Brought movement and life into places that had been rigid for so many years.

Looking in my eyes, he said, "There's no going back after this."

"Yes. Yes."

Yes was the only word I had. The only thought I had. *Yes* was the answer to everything in that moment.

We stumbled comically back to his bedroom, crutches and elbows bumping the walls, and dropped into the narrow bed.

He gritted his teeth. "Shit."

"What happened?"

"My knee."

I stood up. "Do you want the brace?"

"Fuck, no. Come here." He sat on the edge of the bed.

I peeled off his T-shirt as he undid my jeans. Moonlight through the window shone off his shoulder.

"Is your knee okay?"

"If I don't move it."

He pulled up my shirt, rough beard, warm lips. I was about to explode. He took a long, stuttering breath, then reached between my legs.

"I think if you're on top—"

I climbed gingerly over him as he leaned back.

"Like this? Are you okay?"

"I have never been better in my entire life."

"Oh shit." I clambered off again.

"What?"

"I forgot the bag."

He groaned. "Hurry up."

I dashed out of the room, ran on tiptoes to the kitchen, and grabbed the box of condoms. That half-minute, ten-yard dash down the hall was just enough time to notice what was happening. Laughter filled my chest like big bubbles which broke as I ran back to the room.

This was fun. *Fun*. When was the last time I had fun?

I straddled his legs and fumbled with the box. "I'm sorry. I haven't had a lot of practice."

He smiled. "Here. Let me."

A breeze rattled the magnolia leaves, carrying the scent of late-summer decay from the garden. He grasped my hips, and I held on to his forearms to steady myself. The cool evening air washed over my bare skin as fourteen years' worth of hopeless dreams I had indulged—and then scolded myself for—were realized.

My body shivered and shuddered, and as we both neared the climax, Isaac sat up, propping himself with one arm and holding me with the other, our bodies bonded together, breathing together. And when it was done, the joy tipped over into tears.

"Are you okay?" he said. But as soon as he spoke, he wept too, holding on to me for dear life.

"Yes. Are you?"

"Yes."

And then we laughed. Nothing was okay, but everything was perfect.

I can't believe I actually slept, with my back pressed against the cool plaster wall and my leg hiked up over Isaac's hip bone. But sleep I did, and so did he. Until nearly ten the next morning. I woke to the tickle of his chest hair on my cheek.

Isaac wasn't one of those guys with bushy fur like a bear. I stroked his arm, and he shifted in his sleep. His hair was smooth.

If there had been a lot more of it, he might have been sleek like a seal. Extracting myself from the bed was no easy task. Being much closer to forty than to thirty, the cramped arrangement—as wonderful as it was for my heart—had been no good for my back, and my right shoulder ached. I hoisted myself up.

Isaac woke, sucked air through his teeth, and muttered, "Fuck."

"Your leg? I'm sorry."

"It's okay. Don't go."

He reached up to pull me back.

"Wait. Scoot over." I climbed awkwardly off the end of the bed, and lay down on his other side. "I've been lying on my right shoulder all night. It's killing me."

I nestled close in the crook of his arm. His ribs expanded for a deep breath.

Isaac ran his hand down my back. "Okay. So now what?"

My face nearly hurt from smiling. "I don't know. Coffee?"

"That sounds like heaven." He plucked his pants from the floor and began to work them up his bad leg. "Why don't you start it? This could take a while."

As the pot hissed and sputtered, I checked my phone. The voice mails and emails were tapering off, since I was wholesale ignoring all of them and assigning most of the repeat offenders to spam. But there was a message from my father.

I've arranged movers. We're coming over tomorrow morning to divide up the furnishings.

I muttered *fuck* through clenched teeth. Already? He could have given me more than a day's notice. But it was in character for him, acting like I was just another object in a house he now owned.

★ ★ ★

We decided it was best if Isaac spent the night on the third floor. Sharon said Dad and my uncle Stuart would arrive at eight, but seeing as Henry thought he owned the place already, he might well come early.

It was no easy task getting Isaac to the third floor on his one leg. Of course, easy enough for me. I basically stood behind him in case he started to tip backward. He had to do the work of hopping on one foot up the back staircase without the crutches, one hand on the handrail and the other on the wall, and I would be lying if I said I did not get a bit of a thrill watching the muscles in his back work. The stairs from the second to the third floor were too wide for this method, and it was considerably more awkward with the crutch.

"When they get here, you should stay in my study," I said when we reached the top. "It's the only door that locks."

He stopped at the tiny bathroom. I waited in the hall.

There was a man in my house. Lila and I had been two soft, pale women who spent a lot of time indoors. There had not been a man in the house overnight in years. Not since my brief reunion with the physics professor. And even then, it hadn't been like this. All the grunting and breathing. The calloused hands. The beard. Those shoulder muscles.

The tap ran, then Isaac came out.

"This house needs so much work. You've got rot under the sink in there."

"It would look amazing all fixed up."

He followed me down the hall. "Like a palace."

As we entered the top room of the tower, he looked over at the board.

I pointed to it. "Remember?"

He stood behind me and kissed my temple. "Of course I remember."

"You designed it, didn't you? Because the other one was too small."

He nodded. "Lila didn't tell you that?"

"No. Just that it was a surprise." Somehow I had not, until that moment, thought it was odd that she never told me Isaac was the brains behind my board. Lila was the money and goodwill, but Isaac was the one that created a twelve-foot-wide chalkboard on a concave wall. Lila and I had barely talked about Isaac over the years. Attributable, I supposed, to the depression that crushed me for months after he left. And to her generation, who thought that if you didn't talk about things they got better, not worse.

"I had to carve that ledge by hand," he said, putting his arms around me. "Is that the same problem you were working on before?"

I nodded. "Since I was—"

"Fifteen. Where are you with it?"

I tilted my head so it touched his. He was only maybe four inches taller than me.

"I solved it."

He pulled away to look at me, eyes alight. "You solved it?"

"Yes."

"Meg—you solved it? You solved it. When?"

"Last month."

"Is that it?" He pointed at the board.

"It's kind of a shorthand of the central function."

He hobbled over to the board. "Holy shit. Your whole life's work. So last month—then what?"

I told him about the night I solved it and about missing Lila's funeral, then all the time I spent writing it out. Isaac had dropped out of high school and gotten a GED. He didn't comprehend the smallest fraction of what Frieholdt's actually was, but—and this was a revelation—he understood what it meant to me. That's what really mattered. I told him about the presentation and the panic attack, and he understood well enough not to burden me with too much eye contact. And I told him about throwing it all in the safe and locking the door.

He ran his fingers along the chalk ledge, tested it to see that it was firm, but I knew I had his full attention. I could feel it.

"That's some safe down there." He rubbed his beard. "I remember it. So how long is it going to stay there?"

"Until I'm ready to get it out."

He hobbled over to the windows, pausing in the center of the room and pressing his crutch into the soft spot in the floor. "Better fix that. You'll put your foot through, if you're not careful. And this window's cracked. Jesus. If I lived here, it would drive me crazy. I would just want to fix everything."

I laughed. "Clearly."

He lifted the curtain and looked out at the street.

"Who was it?" I said. "The guy. Why did he attack you?"

Isaac turned to face me, looking pale. "I was sleeping with his wife."

My gut flushed hot. "And that's who came looking for you."

"It's over. Please believe me. It was already over."

"Of course I believe you, but—"

He crossed the room to me, avoiding the soft spot this time. "But what?"

"You were here all that time. Why didn't you... Why did you...pick someone else? If you weren't going to come over... to me, why didn't you just leave?"

He pulled me in close. My spine felt like a spring that had

rusted and fused. Bones grinding grittily against each other. His heart pounded, but my chest felt hollow.

"Postulate one." He stroked my hair. "I'm a fuckup. But after I got all the way here and realized I couldn't work for Lila… I needed money, and they were willing to pay cash across the street. It's harder than you'd think to find work for cash."

"You're changing the subject."

My body began to soften, the way he kept lifting my hair, wrapping it loosely around his hand, then letting it go.

"Yes and no. I'm essentially homeless. I'm using a fake name. Makes decent work difficult to find." His brows lowered. "There was no way I was going to get you involved in my problems. I figured maybe if I got laid, I could let go. I could stop looking over at your house all the time. But as usual I just fucked things up more."

I held on to him and in his body he seemed so firm and sure. So different from his words.

"I'm glad you fucked things up. That's what got you here. I'm going to send that guy a thank-you note."

Isaac frowned, then kissed my forehead. "Maybe don't."

Far below, the doorbell chimed, and we both stepped back, listening. On high alert.

"Sharon?" Isaac whispered.

I shook my head. "They're not supposed to be here until tomorrow. Besides, she doesn't ring the bell. She has a key."

There was no reason to be whispering. We could have shouted and not be heard from the front door.

"I better go see," I said. "Stay up here. Lock the door."

10

It was not Sharon. Instead, a stranger waited on my porch, looking to her left at something. She noticed me through the glass and turned her head, but her body remained remarkably at ease. Her hair was more gray than black, tied back in a utilitarian ponytail, no makeup, wire-rimmed glasses. She stood back several paces, as if she had no intention of coming in.

I opened the door, only as wide as my shoulders.

She did not move. Only looked at me straight on.

"Dr. Brightwood, I'm Anne MacFaull."

She wore a T-shirt from some running event, jeans, and well-worn sandals.

She had been at the presentation. In the center, by the aisle, very near my father, in the periphery of my vision. Now I could put the face with the name.

The luminaries of academia and business knew very well that I was presenting on Frieholdt's, and those in the know understood my career well enough to know I might very well have done it. The more money they stood to make from my breakthrough, the more persistent the interested parties had been in the days following. The university deans and math department heads had given up after I ghosted them. The R & D people at oil and car companies had kept trying to reach me by phone and email, but even they were tapering off. But Anne MacFaull had stamina. At first she asked to meet, then she talked about how interested she was in my research, but after I failed to respond, she began to send articles. Obscure historical pieces on Bonnie Fenty, Emmy Noether, and Frieholdt himself.

It was not ineffective. Someone had to do some digging to find those pieces. And yes, I was interested in them. I doubted, however, that the someone who did the research was Anne herself. She was the vice president of research and development at Nautilus, which was kind of like Tesla, only for ships. Chances were very good she directed an underling to do the labor.

"You're not what I expected," I said.

She smiled. Deep creases around her eyes. I guessed she was around sixty.

"What did you expect?"

"Someone more corporate-looking. But mostly, I didn't expect you would come to my house."

"I realize it's unconventional."

"Invasive, even."

She frowned but nodded. "Yes. I suppose so."

Notably, she did not apologize.

"What do you want?"

She eyed me discerningly. I knew that look. I had felt it on my own face. When you are taking in information and your mind is at work. When you are asking yourself, *What am I seeing here? How do I work out this puzzle?*

"I'd be very grateful if you'd come out and talk with me

for a bit." She nodded toward a black car on the street. "I can have my driver go get coffee. How's that for corporate?"

I stepped out and shut the door behind me.

The driver brought coffee from the store on the avenue, and we rocked like two old housewives in the rockers at the corner end of the porch. A cool front was coming through after all the rainstorms.

"I know a good deal about you," she said, reaching out to pluck a leaf off the trumpet vine that trailed over the rail. "What would you like to know about me?"

"Why you're here," I said.

She eyed me as if she knew me well. "Dr. Brightwood, we are women of above-average intelligence. You know why I'm here. And I do have an offer for you, which I'll give you in writing when I leave. I don't think you'd be out here talking to me if that was all you wanted to know."

I nodded and crossed my legs on the rocker. She was right, of course. I knew that Frieholdt's had value to her, and she wanted some kind of privileged access to it. That's what all the corporate types wanted. I also already knew about Nautilus. Their CEO had been all over the news. So why was I out there talking to her? I asked myself that very question.

She was disarming. No immaculate suit. No heels. She looked like she was going to take a walk in the park when she was done with me, which I figured she very well might. It was warm for September, and a light rain the night before had washed the dust from the leaves. The park would be a riot of color around the sparkling creek.

What did I want to know? I looked at her profile. A strong nose. Receding chin. Those minimalist glasses nearly floating above her cheeks.

"I do want to know why you're here," I said. "I've gotten a lot of correspondence, but you're the only one who has actually knocked on my door."

"Well, for one, I'm not afraid of having a door closed in my face." She looked over her glasses at me. "You'd be surprised—the fragile egos of powerful people. But that only explains why they are *not* here. Not why I am."

The coffee was delicious, and I sipped in silence.

"I've followed your career a long time," she said, eyes focused through the trees. "I've met a number of your colleagues. Even your father. I think it's a shame you were guided down such a conventional path. I almost approached you when you left Halberstam, but I didn't have the power then to give you the position I thought you needed to do the work you were capable of."

"But you do now?"

"Yes. I do. It will all be in the letter I'm going to give you. That part is best explained in writing. It's the human understanding," she said and gestured back and forth, from me to her. "That's what requires a visit and a knock on your door. If you'd like me to give you the letter and leave, that's fine. But I'm offering you an opportunity to understand, and perhaps be understood."

I looked at her, then out at the street, and thought for several minutes. Finally the question became clear.

"I want to know if you understand that you can work on something for a lifetime and it might be everything you ever dreamed of, or it might come to nothing," I said. "I've been working on this one thing for twenty years. What about you? What's your Impossible Theorem?"

"That is an excellent question." She looked directly at me, eyes bright, her posture suddenly animated. "Individualized molecular proteins—for customized pharmaceuticals. The theory is there—absolute sci-fi-level potential to cure disease—but it's twenty years ahead of its time. I've got a bit of discretionary budget and the most amazing people working on it." She stood, as though she couldn't sit still while she talked. "The computing power required is immense. The biggest challenge right now is to streamline it to what we have available."

She went on, punctuating everything with a gesture, raised eyebrows. She dropped the f-bomb a few times. I didn't fully understand, but she talked to me as if I did. Not talking down. Not making assumptions. I noticed where she translated the overly technical and where she let complex concepts be complex. I asked questions. She listened and thought and gave me nuanced and coherent answers. I hadn't had a conversation this interesting in years.

After twenty minutes, she sat down again, looking slightly sheepish. "I tend to go on and on when people ask about that. I don't want to keep you too long. What else can I tell you? Or do you want to tell me?"

"Nothing." I set my empty cup on the floor. "Whatever you're offering, the answer is still going to be *no*. But I've actually enjoyed meeting you."

She smiled. "As have I. I'll ask Jason to bring the letter."

She pulled out her phone and sent a text. Her hands were unmanicured. Every powerful woman I had ever met under the age of seventy used the tools of personal appearance to augment their power. This woman did not.

"Dr. MacFaull—"

"Please, call me Anne."

"What is it you think I want?"

She put down her phone. Her body grew still, and a softness, something almost motherly, came into her eyes.

"I think you need an equal."

I closed the door with a quiet click and listened to the near-silent electric car pull away. In my hands was a box. Smooth, matte, black. Thin and about the dimensions of a magazine. I sat on the first step of the grand staircase and opened it. On top was a slim envelope. Creamy white, with the Nautilus logo in the corner. Underneath, I lifted a piece of tissue and found a brown archival sleeve set in a custom-cut piece of dense black foam. It fit snug, as if it were meant to be stored there.

With the box on my lap, I opened the flap. A thin volume slid into my hand.

Discourses on the Loading Hypothesis. By Claude Lemaire and Boris Fenty.

Boris Fenty, the pen name of Bonnie Fenty.

Eyes wide, I paged through it. Mathematicians I respected believed that the Loading Hypothesis, which was postulated before Lemaire and Fenty were born, played a role in Frieholdt's Conjecture, but it was poorly understood. There had been work published over the years, but I had no idea that this particular piece of research even existed before that night. I had researched Bonnie Fenty more than most historians, but these old journals were printed in such small numbers and were so obscure that they were lost to history. There were no publications on the Loading Hypothesis to be found—until now.

As I gathered myself and began to climb the stairs, I felt like a little girl on her birthday, cradling my treasure in my hands.

I knocked on my study door. "Isaac, it's okay. It's only me."

He clumped across the floor and let me in. We sat together

on the couch, legs touching, with Anne's letter in my lap. One page, with her signature at the bottom. Her offer was thus: Give her exclusive access to the proof of Frieholdt's Conjecture. Give no interviews, do no press, do not submit for the Beckett Prize. Keep it for all intents and purposes as if Frieholdt's remained unsolved, for a minimum of five years. Allow Nautilus consultation access on a regular business schedule. Meet with her team quarterly. In exchange, Nautilus would give me three hundred thousand dollars a year, a monthly stipend for living expenses, and a visa to live anywhere in the world. If I agreed, a contract would follow, and the arrangement could commence immediately upon approval of the proof by her team.

It was a way out. No presentation, no publicity, and the chance to disappear, if Isaac Wells weren't at my side, leaning his head toward mine... But what if we could disappear together? Anne was clearly a person with a lot of power. What if there were some way...?

"You could do this," Isaac said.

But the longer I sat there, the heavier the letter grew in my hands. Yes, I liked Anne MacFaull. Yes, it was a generous offer. Yes, she had softened the ground effectively with the copy of *Discourses*—acquired, as she mentioned in the letter, from an obscure historical society in a small English village. But Frieholdt's wasn't just a mathematical showpiece. Its real-world implications were important and had the potential to be incredibly valuable. Here was one place where the awesome engine of capitalism would work toward a global good, but only if people were competing to put it into practice. Not if it was secreted away in the research and development department of one company, even one as powerful as Nautilus.

"It doesn't feel right." I stood and crossed the room. Lifting the white curtain, I looked out the front windows. The crew was at work on the house across the street. The house where Isaac had worked until only the day before yesterday.

For all of Anne's good intentions, this was still all about Nautilus owning and profiting from my work.

I turned around, still holding the letter in my hand. Isaac was looking at me, shaking his head.

"Must be nice, to be able to turn down an offer like that."

"I don't know if I'm turning it down."

"But why not take it? It seems obvious."

"I'm a researcher, Isaac. It's not sales."

He raised a judging brow at me.

"Of course I want to make a living, but it belongs to everyone." I flared back at him. "You need to understand, this will change the design of every object meant to move through air or water. When physicists and engineers get their hands on it, the results could alter the course of climate change, and when it comes to climate change five years is a lot. I want the collective brainpower of the whole world to have at this thing. I'm not going to leave it in the safe for long. Just until I'm ready. But if taking Anne's offer should be the *obvious* choice, then I must be naive, or spoiled, or—some kind of sheltered rich girl, right? That's what you're thinking."

"No. I wasn't thinking... Not like that."

"But something like that, right? My dad sent some money when I was caring for Lila, and she left me a little cash in her will—a little, all right?" I spread out my arms. "Do you see a show house here? And she gave me two years to live in it before they're allowed to sell it. That's it."

"Okay. I just thought—"

"People think all kinds of stuff about me." I rattled off the familiar parody. "She's a trust-fund baby. She lives large off her daddy. She should suck it up and work for a living like everyone else. Like I have this great fucking life."

Isaac stood. "All right. All right. But I'm not *people*, okay? I grew up poor. I learned to shoot so we could eat. Give me a break. I hear money like that, and I can't help it."

I saw the worry on his face, and my indignation vanished.

My hands fell to my sides. "Of course you're not *people*. Of course. I'm sorry. I see those figures. I know they're real. And I don't have many options. I'm going to need money pretty soon. But I can't sell it. I just can't. Not yet."

I went to him, and he put his arms around me and spared me having to look in his face.

"Back in graduate school, there were times I felt suicidal." I leaned rigidly against his shoulder, my face turned away. "People don't understand I can't just *go get a job* like a normal person. But at least I have resources—"

My voice caught in my throat. I had come to accept who I was, but god, sometimes I just hated it. I just wished I had so-called normal options.

"I'm going to have to do something for money. I know that. Being *me* plus being really poor? There are people who have to do that, and it's not pretty."

He leaned his cheek against my hair and said sadly, "That's my mom. And no, it's not pretty."

"I'm sorry." I shifted my weight toward him. "It's on me to get my shit together and learn to live in the world so I *don't* have to take an offer like this. So I can make a real choice."

"Quit being sorry," he said. "You get to decide what's right for you. Postulate three, right?"

He slid his hand over my ass and kissed the taut muscle in my neck stretched from turning away. Ease crept into my body. Things flexed where they had only just now been frozen.

I turned my head toward him. "It's amazing how you can do that."

"I wish I had money too, but this'll have to do."

He reached under my shirt, caressing my ribs and back.

"I know so much about this one thing," I said, "and so little about myself."

Isaac murmured next to my ear. "What do you mean?"

"I've been killing myself to finish this proof, and the whole rest of my energy went into keeping Lila comfortable. Now both those jobs are done, and I don't have a clue who I am. What do I like? I don't even know." What a sorry thing for a grown woman to say. I found Anne's letter still clutched in my right hand.

Isaac leaned back a little and smiled. A gentle, thinking kind of smile. "Do you remember when I was clearing that big tree that fell in the backyard? You came out and gave me a beer—"

"And we walked around the garden, and you told me the names of all the plants. All the plain little green plants—"

"And you said you had never thought about how each one of them had a name." He brushed my breast, and a warm ache bloomed inside me.

"Of course I remember. Sassafras. And mayapple. I was so surprised. I think that was the longest conversation we had ever had. It was like a botany lesson."

He shrugged. "Childhood hobby."

"Come on. More like encyclopedic knowledge."

"You liked spicebush," he murmured in my ear. "The long, leggy one that smells good when you crush the leaves."

I broke free. Still holding his hand, I reached over and stuffed Anne's letter in my desk drawer. I had time. A little bit of time to understand my own soul before I had to sell it.

He gave me a wry smile, looking me over. "I'm pretty sure I know what else you like."

This man with his shaggy beard and his busted leg looked sexier on crutches than anyone I had ever seen on their own two feet.

We moved the nightstand in my bedroom and pushed the two twin beds together. We took up more space and more time. We talked, and kissed, and talked some more. Then finally made love. There was no air-conditioning, and we lay damp and sweaty, sheets tossed aside. The dormer which overlooked the front yard had a big circular window, hinged at the top. Isaac pulled himself up and hopped over to it, gently working it open and propping it with a crutch. The outside air moved around the room, raising the hairs on my arms.

"They could have just stuck a regular window up here. But instead, they did that." He sat on the end of the bed. "It must have been amazing to come here as a child."

I rolled onto my side as he stretched out again in the bed. "It was. But I never got much time off."

"Time off?" Isaac interlaced his fingers with mine. "Time off what?"

"Studying."

"When you were—"

"Nine. Ten. That's when it got serious."

"You must have had some time for fun. I mean, with all this money."

"Money didn't have anything to do with it."

He kissed my knuckles. "Growing up without it, I always thought money bought freedom."

"Money doesn't buy anything. People buy things. And it has to be *your* money. And your choice."

"But a ten-year-old has neither."

"I didn't, anyway."

He pulled me close, and I took a long, deep breath. Cicadas sang in the treetops.

11

At first we planned to lock up the study and let Isaac hide out there while my father and Uncle Stuart went through the house. Downstairs was not an option, and I was pretty sure they'd look through the garage too. My study was the only room I could plausibly lock. But Isaac couldn't get around the idea of having no exit route, so at six in the morning, I drove him up to the avenue. There was a decent coffee shop and a public library, and he seemed notably more comfortable with this arrangement.

I, however, was fidgety and irritable, and I held his hand tight.

"You're not going to leave are you? Don't disappear. Please, don't disappear."

An electric bus hummed by. Isaac kissed my lips. "Not going to leave. I promise."

It was a pain in the ass not to be able to text him, but he insisted that even though he was using a burner phone, I was not to have the number in my history. Nothing that could tie me to him. It seemed like an overabundance of caution, but then again, I wasn't the one with an arrest warrant. So we had arranged a time for me to pick him up.

"If I'm late, don't go anywhere. It'll just be that they're taking forever."

He pried his fingers free from mine and nudged me toward my car. "Don't worry. This isn't goodbye."

Driving down the hill back to the house, I still couldn't shake the feeling that it might have been.

Once home, I scoured the maid's quarters for the twentieth time—no trace of Isaac—then my bedroom and study. Again, no trace. My heart rate dropped slightly from its anxious high.

Then the front door swung open.

"Meg?" My father's voice moved through the foyer. "You up there?"

"Be down in a second."

A second set of footsteps crossed the porch and the foyer. My uncle Stuart. Their deep voices and hard-soled shoes drifted through the first-floor rooms. I padded down the back stairs in my socks and met them in the dining room.

My father patted my arm. "You're looking much better."

"I feel fine."

Uncle Stuart muttered, "Ridiculous. One person living in this huge place."

"Nice to see you too, Uncle Stuart."

I nodded when he turned to look at me. He was a taller, leaner, balder specimen than my father and apparently had been especially put out that I had missed the funeral. What charm there was, my father had gotten almost all of it.

"Listen," Henry said, "I told Sharon to come over after we're done. At about ten. We don't need all this." He waved his hand around the room. "You two can divide up the remaining things when we're done."

"Fine. I'll be upstairs."

Shit. This was going to take longer than I thought.

And did it ever. They spent two hours going through the house. By the time Sharon arrived, I was exhausted from vigilance.

I didn't want much. Some photo albums. The handmade quilt from Lila's bed. For some reason, I was attached to the fireplace irons and a slouchy old chair badly in need of reupholstering. All of which Sharon was happy to part with. And then there were the books. When we went through the library, I saw that my father had already picked over the science section. Sharon wanted the Thoreau and the matching set of Dickens. I wanted that cookbook from 1799. I didn't tell her it was the oldest and probably most valuable of all. Just that it had sentimental value.

It wasn't until the moving truck rumbled up the driveway and six young men arrived to move things out that the grief hit me. They rolled up rugs, took down paintings, and lifted furniture that had not been moved in fifty years, revealing pale patches of floor and wall, scuffed, dusty corners, chipped baseboards, mouse holes.

I stood watching from the lower landing of the big staircase. People say the grieving heart is heavy, but I didn't feel heavy. I felt much too light. Unmoored. Lila had loved the portrait of her aunt that had hung on the dining room wall. As a joke, she used to talk to it about me. *Meg's in quite a mood this morning, don't you think, Agnes?*

Her bare feet had traversed these rugs for decades. Not only was she gone—the one person I had in my corner—but the space that had held her memory was being erased before my very eyes. It wasn't her home anymore. It was just a house, with one lonely person rattling around inside. Stuart was right. It was ridiculous. But Lila had understood me. I needed time.

Sharon came down the stairs from the second floor and stood beside me.

"It's the end of an era." She put her arm around my shoulders, and even though we were never close, I accepted the simple kindness.

The side door opened.

"Meg?" My father's voice. "Will you come here a second?"

I flushed hot and followed him outside. And into the garage.

He turned on the light. "It looks like someone slept in here."

Fuck. Fuck fuck fuck. The couch. The blanket. That first night Isaac was here. I had forgotten to put it away. Dad knew I never had anyone over.

"Meg?"

"Oh." I shook my head as if I had forgotten something. "I was… There was one time when I was working, and I just needed a change of scenery, you know? So I came out here and sat on the couch, but it was kind of cold. Last winter."

But the blanket didn't look like it had been there since last winter. I picked it up and started to fold it, and a handful of change rolled onto the floor. I should have played dumb.

"I still come out here from time to time when I need to, you know, refresh my head." I leaned over to collect the change.

Shut up. Shut up. Don't talk so much. It sounds fake.

My dad frowned. "You did always have strange work habits."

Oh thank god.

He picked up a stray quarter from near his feet. "I've been meaning to ask about your paper."

I waited.

He sighed. "Have you figured out what you're going to do with it?"

"No."

"So you're just sitting on it."

"Yes."

"Until?"

"Until I'm good and ready."

This was a topic on which I had no need to waste words.

"What's going to change before you're *ready*?" He didn't wait for me to answer. "You really ought to get some help. But you never did like to share."

It stung. *Share.* In his world, sharing went one way. He only resented my unwillingness to *share* with *him*.

It was midafternoon by the time the last moving truck rolled out of the driveway and I had the house to myself at last. Then I snatched my keys, looked up and down the block to make sure no one was coming back, and jumped in my car. My heart pounded, and my hands slipped, sweaty on the steering wheel. I ran a yellow light, turning onto the avenue, then right on the side street by the library.

And there he was, sitting on the park bench, just as we had arranged. A book lay in his lap, and he didn't look up until I stopped the car in front of him. Then he smiled and got to his feet.

"No, I can do it," he said, when I started to get out to help him. He clambered in, tossing his crutches in the back seat. "You know you can get a library card without an ID? You can say you're anyone. Look what I found."

He held up a black hardback book with old-fashioned print. *The Blacksmith's Companion.*

I threw my arms around his neck and took a deep breath. "You're still here."

"I promised."

The rug in the foyer was gone. The rug I had sat on as a child, waiting for my father. The rug with the woolly tassels that I had rubbed between my fingers to bring myself down from an attack. Now there was only a bare floor, paler than the rest.

Isaac and I drifted through the first floor, not speaking.

Half the contents of the house were gone. The big rug in the parlor by the fireplace remained, its pattern faded beyond recognition. And the couch that felt like it was upholstered with sandpaper. No one wanted that. The sideboard in the dining room was gone, but not the big dining table and those grand, heavy chairs.

The air felt different. There was more space where there had already been too much to begin with. The shelves in the library were half-empty, and a scuffed floor remained where my grandfather's leather chair had been, but his tall writing desk with the matted felt still stood by the wall.

The moment Isaac left my sight, the tears came. Only the kitchen resembled the house I had woken up in that morning, and that's where he found me sitting on the floor.

It wasn't easy for him, but he got down next to me and held me in his arms.

I pressed my forehead against his shoulder. "It's so empty."

"I'm sorry."

"I feel like a squatter in my own house."

He adjusted his bad leg. "I wish we could just take that third floor and transport it somewhere."

He went with me as I surveyed the second floor. No one had wanted the beds and mattresses, but odd pieces of Lila's world had vanished. A mirror. A nightstand. An armchair and footstool. Almost all the rugs. Dad and Uncle Stuart had a keen understanding of antiques, and now only the shabbiness remained. The things that didn't age well.

Someone had dropped a bit of lace in the second-floor hall. I picked it up. A small, finely made shawl that Lila used to drape over the back of a chair in her bedroom. I shook the dust off, and a strand of her white hair fell to the floor. It seemed all that was left of her, where once her being had suffused this whole place.

It was an effort for Isaac to get all the way to the third floor on the crutches, but he did it. I fell into my old couch while he stood at the window, looking down on the street.

It didn't feel like home. Only a bunch of half-empty rooms and Frieholdt's Conjecture locked up in the safe.

"I don't know what to do." My voice sounded small and far away. "There's nothing here but my proof. I have no other... anything. It feels so all-or-nothing. I make history or I—what? I don't even know."

Isaac leaned against the wall and looked at me with a kind but skeptical arrangement of his eyebrows.

"You can't do anything?"

"No. I can't do anything. I'm not good for anything. I can do math that no one understands except me. That's it."

"Stand up," Isaac said.

"Why?"

"Just stand up."

So I did.

"There," he said. "You can stand. That's something."

I rolled my eyes at him. "You know that's not what I mean."

"Maybe not, but it's what I mean. Can you lift fifty pounds?"

"I think so."

"Can you deal with leaving the house for a few days?"

"I think so. What are we talking about here?"

He went and opened the door to the balcony and looked out at the trees.

"My great-uncle has a place. It's way up in the Smokies. He's in a nursing home in Florida, and I'm supposed to go check on things every so often."

I hadn't necessarily wanted to be in this house as much as I had been the last fifteen years, but there had never been anywhere else I wanted to go. Now there was, but the prospect still made me anxious.

"What kind of place?"

"It's a log cabin he built himself. One room. Wood heat. It's on top of a mountain. Really remote."

Isaac had started out with some bravado, but now he looked worried, as if he thought I wouldn't like it. But the more I heard, the easier I felt. A place away from everything. I couldn't think in this big house. The rooms weren't even familiar anymore, and the whole place radiated grief and restlessness.

Locking Frieholdt's in the safe had been only the first step, I realized as I looked at Isaac. If I could actually move farther from this lifelong obsession, maybe I would find some space to stand.

"How far?"

"About six hours. I mean, we've got to make it up this kind of steep path and carry water from a well. I'll actually need your help. I don't know. Never mind. It's okay if—"

"No neighbors?"

"Not unless you count a bunch of wild turkeys and deer."

"When can we leave?"

"As soon as you turn off all your location tracking."

12

Before we left, I visited Frieholdt's in the basement. The lock on the safe complained a bit, but it opened, and there was everything, just as I had left it. Part of me wanted to take it along, as if it were a pet or a child that would need care and feeding. But the part of me that made the decisions resisted. If I wanted to get away, I had to learn to get away. Frieholdt's would be safe. The idea that someone would break in and try to steal it was paranoid. Even I could see that. And even if the house burned to the ground, Frieholdt's would come out unscathed.

So I shut the door and turned the dials.

Once we got on the road, my courage failed, but we were already an hour from home, and I was at the wheel. If Isaac had been driving, I might have asked him to turn around, and he would have. But I was in charge, and pride defeated fear. I was not going back. We drove for hours along the big highways that ran south-by-southwest down the state into the mountains. Isaac talked me through my edginess nearly the whole way in his low, easy voice, tinged with a mountain drawl. He told me about his great-uncle, the only sane member of his family. An immigrant. A great giant of a Finn who had built the cabin with his own hands from the trees that grew on the mountainside. Isaac would inherit the cabin when the old man passed away, and it was as good as his already.

Isaac pointed me to a turnoff which took us onto smaller roads, through small towns. We stopped at the last Walmart and bought some food, matches, a propane cylinder, and a couple of bags of ice. I stayed close at his side. The bright lights seemed to blaze right through my skin.

As we began the climb into the mountains, houses became sparse. Only a dirt driveway every mile or so. The road switched back and forth up the slope until we came to the parkway along the crest of the mountains. We climbed higher and higher, and the views got wider and wider, until we couldn't see another road for miles.

Finally we turned onto a narrow gravel lane that cut down a steep mountainside. It was rutted and potholed and lacked any barrier between the road's edge and the precipitous drop into the hollow below. After three miles we came to a pull-out and stopped.

After the cacophony of tires on gravel, my ears rang with the forest silence. It was ten degrees cooler up on that mountain, and sunlight filtered through leaves already beginning to turn. I saw no house, only three log steps set into the road's edge leading to a path that angled steeply up the hill.

I looked at Isaac, who was already unloading bags.

"There's no way you're getting up there on one leg."

He rolled his eyes, shouldered his backpack, into which he had shoved as much of our stuff as he could, and using only one of the two crutches, he started up.

"Stop it," I said, following. "You're not supposed to put weight on it."

"It'll be fine." He muscled his way up the steps and onto the rocky path without looking back. "Get some bags if you're coming up."

"Isaac, this is crazy. You didn't tell me we'd be mountain climbing. You're going to hurt yourself."

"Who's responsible for what's good for me?" he called down. "Postulate three, Dr. Brightwood."

He was covering ground faster than I thought he would. I groaned out loud.

"You're a fuckup," I yelled after him.

"Head case," he yelled back.

I picked up as much as I could carry from the trunk and began the climb. I would do any extra trips to the car. Once he got up there, he was staying. There, at least, I would draw the line.

I caught up to him without much trouble. By the time the path leveled out he was breathing hard, and he had started using the second crutch. He winced when his foot hit a rock, jarring the bad knee.

The trail took a bend and opened to a small clearing of tall grass. There under a high outcropping of rock was a single-story log cabin with a shingle roof. I had imagined something stout and square, like a child's drawing of a house, but this little dwelling looked more like it had grown from the mountainside than been built. The logs rested against one another, round and irregular, but fitted tight without mortar. Along the front ran a covered porch, and a dull gray flue rose from the back. An outhouse stood near the tree line on the far side of the meadow.

The low angle of the afternoon sun showed every blade of grass, every fly and moth, every spore and molecule of pollen that floated in the air. The cabin's two small windows reflected gold from the sky to the west.

I stopped and inhaled the scent of pine duff.

"It's beautiful."

A few paces ahead, Isaac leaned on his crutches and smiled. Something had shifted in his shoulders, his back. Something defended had let go. This, I thought, was what a person looks like when he is finally home.

"Come on." He started across the meadow. "It gets dark fast once the sun goes below that ridge."

Our feet knocked along the front porch to the door, and Isaac lifted the iron latch. It was not locked. I set my bags on a small table to the right of the door. Handmade. And the two chairs as well. The interior was cold and smelled woody and a bit like old leather.

Isaac circled the room as my eyes adjusted to the low light. He ran his hand lovingly over the log walls, brushed a cobweb from a window over a narrow wooden counter, and ducked his head into what looked like a sleeping nook. He finished his circuit at the fireplace. Although it could hardly be called a fireplace, which makes one think of a square recess with a mantelpiece.

This was a structure that extended from the back wall almost a third of the way into the room, smooth and white but solid. Isaac had told me about it on the drive. It was the size of three refrigerators pushed together, made of brick, but covered in plaster. Instead of a straight flue going up the inside, he said, it had a channel that made several turns before exiting through the roof so the bricks could absorb the heat from the smoke. His great-uncle had built special piers beneath the floor to support its weight. It rose almost to the ceiling with a broad ledge running along one side at about the height of my knee. This formed a hearth for the opening where one would make a fire. An iron poker hung on a hook.

The old man would make a fire in the winter, Isaac had said, and over several days the entire bulk would warm up. When it was really cold, a person could unroll a sleeping bag and sleep on top.

Isaac leaned his crutches against the wall and dropped into a leather armchair with a sigh.

"Welcome to heaven."

I walked over and tilted his chin up to look at me. "You stay in heaven. I'll go get the rest of the stuff."

He pulled me down by the arm and kissed me. "Thank you."

As I walked across the meadow to the path through the trees, the restless fretting left my body, and I felt an unfamiliar lightness. Pleasant, if not entirely comfortable.

13

Isaac had wisely opted for a trip to the liquor store and a bottle of bourbon rather than buying beer at the Walmart. I appreciated his foresight over the three trips I made to the car and back, glad that, along with the ice, I wasn't hauling glass bottles up the hill. He busied himself putting things away, but it seemed to drive him crazy that he couldn't help carrying stuff, and if I didn't drop the bags and turn directly around, he would get up and try to follow me. Ridiculous man, on that bad leg.

When I had brought up everything we needed, I stretched my back and went out on the porch. Below the meadow where the cabin stood, the mountainside dropped off so steeply that one could easily see over the treetops from the porch to the next ridge. The setting sun looked like it was burning a notch out of the crest.

Isaac came out and put his arm around my waist. Such a remarkable thing. Since he had crashed back into my world, I had had more physical contact, physical labor, conversation, everything in one week than I'd had in the previous year.

Or more. It wasn't even quantifiable it was so fundamentally different.

"What do you think?" Isaac said.

"He built this all himself?"

"You see how the logs are pretty small?" He directed my gaze over to the wall. "He could manage them himself. He got a neighbor to help with the big foundation logs, but he hauled all the other stuff up here himself. I mean, except for the logs, which were already here. The reason this is a meadow is because he logged it to make the house."

I leaned into him. Enough to get more contact without making him bear my weight. Part of me felt liberated. Free of that giant edifice that was Lila's house. It should have housed a family of ten plus servants, and it was a burden for one woman. But part of me also felt the vacancy of a lifetime of working with my mind and not my hands.

The work of the mind is real work. We would all likely be dead without it. What I was feeling wasn't judgment. It was imbalance. A normal girl would have played sports or an instrument. She would have been in the school play, and in art class, and maybe learned to make clunky, thick bowls on a pottery wheel, alongside being good at math. But not this girl.

And now that the Impossible was done and locked up tight in my grandfather's safe, that feeling of lightness was the absence of anything to take its place.

He was right. The cabin got dark fast once the sun fell below the ridge. On his one crutch, Isaac lit a gas lamp, connected the propane cylinder to the stove, and set a pot of water on to boil. Tonight's plan was spaghetti and a salad from a bag. The sauce and salad were two less things that had to go in the cooler for the night. For the first time, I understood why winter, in a place like this, had certain advantages. You had to produce heat, but making things cold was taken care of.

Once the stove was lit, I instructed Isaac to sit while I fixed the rest of dinner.

I could cook a pot of spaghetti and dump a salad out of a bag. But I wished I could light a lamp. Hook up the stove. Do all the other things.

We ate at the table with the gas lamp between us. Isaac's face was made for lamplight, the gold in his eyes flashing, those wonderful, mobile brows accentuated by shadow. Out in the rest of the world, he could pass as an ordinary man. Here, he was beautiful.

I didn't exactly know where to sleep until he showed me the nook on the far side of the fireplace. The place where we built the fire faced the larger partition of the single room. But on the opposite side of that big plaster edifice, a narrower portion of the room held a platform with a mattress.

"He had a horsehair mattress when I first came up here," Isaac said. The blankets were folded neatly on a shelf. He shook them out. "It was right around when I first met you that he got a regular bed. I helped him carry it up the hill."

Isaac extinguished the gas lamp, and we arranged ourselves in the blankets and pillows as full darkness descended. Once my eyes adjusted, I could see a single blade of moonlight through the front window.

"I've never used an outhouse," I said.

"Oh fuck, I'm sorry. I meant to show you. You only really need it for number two. There's a flashlight by the door." He shifted onto his side and worked his left hand under the blanket and under my shirt. "Why are you wearing all this stuff?"

"Number one is easier for you. You're a guy." I rested my hand on his upper arm. Smooth. Muscular and lean.

"Just squat in the meadow," he said.

"Is that what you say to all the ladies?"

He pulled my leg over his. "Only you, babe."

The light dawned a pale gray across the cabin floor. On waking, my mind snapped reflexively to Frieholdt's until I remembered the current arrangement of things. Safe. After that momentary startle, I thought about it for a while as Isaac slept. I had never been this distant from it, either in body or in mind, and I wondered if it would have helped, all those years, to have gotten a little more distance.

I shivered, pulling up the blanket, and Isaac rolled over.

"What happened?" I said, shifting closer to his warm body. "It was summer yesterday."

He coughed and rubbed his face, then pulled me closer. "But it's almost fall. Yesterday was a fluke."

"When did you grow a beard?" I combed it with my fingertips.

"A few years ago. Do you like it?"

"I do." Something about it kept me grounded.

He hauled himself up to sitting. "I don't know about you, but if I don't get coffee pretty much right away, I get a pounding headache."

He scooted himself to the end of the bed, pulled on his pants, and hopped over to the stove. With a quick flick of a match, he lit it and set the water on before I could watch how he did it. I wrapped myself in the scratchy wool blanket that lay on top of our bedclothes and found my way in the dim light to my bag.

"Meg?"

I looked up. Isaac leaned against the counter that was built into the back wall. The stove glowed blue next to him as the pot hissed quietly over the fire. He motioned me over.

He wrapped an arm around my waist and buried his face in my hair. "I can't stop myself from thinking how little time we might have together."

"Shhh. We only just got up. Don't think about that yet."

But I thought it too. I rested my hand on his hard hip bone. Every fraction of a moment felt fragile. It could all collapse.

"I want to say something before I come back to reality and chicken out."

"What do you mean *reality*?"

He turned to face me. "When we first met, that first year... we had...feelings for one another back then."

I nodded. My body filled with warmth but also the burning of fear. I had done something wrong. Whatever we had back then, I had failed in some way, and now it was too late. It made no sense. I forced down a sudden urge to cry. This was very old training at work—looking for love, expecting love, and finding a void.

He looked in my eyes. "What's the matter?"

"Nothing."

"It's not nothing." He stroked my hair away from my face. "But listen—don't cry. Why are you crying?"

"I'm not crying." I pulled the blanket tighter around my body and stepped back.

He sighed and looked at the ceiling. "Okay. Postulate three requires me to say this, as little hope as I have, and as much as I think I'm an asshole for getting you involved in my train wreck of a life. But that's the whole point of postulate three. Okay. Jesus. This is harder than I thought."

I crossed my arms. Gripped the blanket hard in my fist.

"Just say it. Whatever it is. Please."

The color drained from his face, and he looked like a man about to get shot.

"I love you."

I opened my mouth, but he stopped me.

"You don't have to say it back. You don't owe me anything."

"Isaac—"

"With the risk you're taking, I had to. It wasn't fair for you not to know—"

"I love you too."

For the first time since I could remember—since I was a child, before all the conditions, before I had to fight and perform and achieve, before my whole life became about being better, pushing beyond everyone else—for the first time since I was young enough to love what I loved just because, at last something was stronger than fear.

I stood there in that cold cabin, wrapped in that scratchy, musty-smelling blanket, thirty-eight years old, with the stove hissing, and the water beginning to boil. With Isaac Wells and his messed-up leg and his arrest warrant. With a proof that would change the world locked up far away in the basement safe. With all my flaws and all my history and all my pain.

And I loved. And was loved.

I almost laughed, almost cried, tried to breathe. He reached out both arms, and I leaned my head against his chest and counted the beating of his heart. One hundred. One-twenty.

"Meg?" I felt his voice more than heard it.

"Hm?"

"You should get dressed. We've got work to do."

A cold front moved in from the west over the course of the morning. We closed up the doors and windows, but the damp chill got in through the floorboards. Isaac went out back, and I heard him grunting and struggling with something. My phone pinged—there was spotty but passable cell service, surprisingly. I checked it.

Lizzie.

Want to go on a hike at Great Falls today?

Shit. What to tell her? Vague evasiveness wouldn't do it. If I said I had a cold or didn't feel like going out, chances were she'd offer to come over, and if I outright told her not to come over, she would be suspicious, and I would never hear the end of it.

So I told a version of the truth. I'm out of town. Took a drive into the mountains for the weekend.

This I had done before, though always alone.

A minute later she texted back, Lucky you. Drive safe!

I hoped I wouldn't have to keep this whole thing a secret from Lizzie for too long. She had always been the person who knew everything about me.

Isaac cursed a few times outside, then the door opened. He stood there, breathing hard and scowling.

"We need a fire, and I cannot fucking manage an axe on one leg," he said. "You're going to have to split the wood."

"I don't know how to split wood."

He turned back to the outside. "I'll bet you can learn. All those brains've got to be good for something."

I followed him. "So this is what you're like when you're grumpy? Good to know."

He shot me a look over his shoulder, frustrated but not without a humorous twitch of the eyebrow.

He leaned on his crutches. "Get a log out—not that one, the grain's going to give you trouble… That one's good. Now, set it on end on the stump."

I did as I was told.

He took a pair of safety goggles out of his pocket. "You should wear these."

They were ancient and scratched. "Do I have to?"

"Unless you want a splinter in your eye."

I took them. I did not want a splinter.

Isaac hobbled over and picked up the axe.

"Hold it like this." He couldn't do much of a demonstration, but he was able to show me the arc of the swing in slow motion.

I took the axe and placed my hands as he showed me. "Like this?"

"That's good." He hobbled back a few steps. "Legs wide. Left foot forward, right foot back. And bend your knees a bit."

I gripped the axe handle and eyed the log in front of me. There was something deeply calming in knowing that I was about to commit a minor act of violence. Axe. Log. Impact. Breaking. I dropped immediately into the kind of deep focus I always strove for when I was working.

"Step back a bit," Isaac said. "It seems like you want to be closer, but you forget how long the handle is when you really give it room to swing. Hands a little wider."

My first blow missed, but not by much. The axe hit the stump and jarred my arms. Isaac started to speak, but I held up my palm.

"No. Let me try again."

He stepped back. I took it slower this time, testing the angle and impact. Principles of arc and momentum were at work here. The axe-head was a point on a circumference, the handle the radius. I lifted and swung. And missed again. This time Isaac said nothing.

My next swing glanced off the edge of the log and knocked

it over. I muttered *damn* and set it upright. I swung again. This time it struck true and drove the axe-head into the wood, but not far enough. I struggled to get it out.

"Take the log off the axe. Not the axe out of the log," Isaac said.

I did. And set it up again.

"Use the torque of your body." He sat on the back stoop, leg extended. "And on the downstroke, use the weight of the axe. You want to almost pull it down through the wood."

My shoulders and arms tightened, and I swung again, a perfect, round sweep over my head. I hit the same spot, only this time the log sprang in half, only a few pale fibers holding it together. I yelped and jumped and looked over at Isaac. He nodded approvingly. I laughed at myself, then pulled the pieces apart with one hand.

I set up another log. I was not as physically strong as some women, but I fully understood how to exploit mass and gravity. I split the second log in three tries, and the third one in two.

Isaac broke into a real smile. "Well done."

He showed me how to split the smaller sections. Aim for a good spot on the grain. Swing out in front of yourself. Don't put a foot where it might get hit.

I pulled a log from the pile and set it with a dull thump on the chopping block. Then I set my feet and aimed. *Crack* went the axe as it found a path through the grain. The exercise took on a meditative intensity. Sweat trickled down my back. The small pieces clopped together in a pile to my right. Isaac went inside and returned, handing me a mug. Water had never tasted so good.

"You're going to be sore tomorrow," he said.

"I'm getting it, though."

"Of course you are." He smiled at me and went inside.

Log on block. *Thump.* A shuffle as I set my feet. And *crack* as the wood split apart. Way more wood than we would probably need, but I kept going. I could have gone on all day, surprised at my own stamina.

A drizzling breeze picked up, and I set the axe under the shed roof that covered the woodpile. Brushing the chips from my clothes, I gathered an armload of wood and took it inside, dropping it by the hearth.

Isaac sat in the leather armchair, holding *The Blacksmith's Companion* close to his face in the low light.

I stood in front of him and held out my hands.

He examined them, holding my wrists. "Ouch."

In the crook of each thumb and forefinger were shiny, angry blisters. Along the center of my palm, smaller bubbles had risen and burst, leaving raw, pink spots.

"I didn't even notice until now." I took his hands and pulled him up. "Come see."

With the rain clouds so close overhead, the light had a diffuse quality, throwing no shadows. I showed him where I had stacked the wood neatly under the shed roof.

"Not bad," he said.

"I'll do some more tomorrow."

"If you can still move."

A million therapists had told me to exercise. That it would be good for me. And I had ignored them.

But, I thought, this is what they meant. This feels amazing.

"Show me how to light the lamp," I said.

He did. It wasn't hard.

"Now, how do I make a fire?"

Isaac laughed. "You're going to have me teaching you to shoot deer with a bow and arrow by the time we're done here."

"Really?"

"No. We shoot deer with a rifle."

He laughed at the look on my face, but suddenly a whole new world seemed possible that had not seemed possible before. As I think he had known it would.

14

The rain grew steadily heavier into the afternoon. Wearing a rubbery old raincoat from a hook on the wall, I walked out to the well twenty paces down the meadow. The metal pump handle screeched and stuck, but I wrestled it into compliance, and the cold water splattered into my jug.

We lay down on the bed, a loose tangle of arms and legs. My fire popped and sparked. Rain shushed outside, and at one end of the roof it tapped in big drops off the needles of a tall pine.

"You hear that?" I shifted my shoulder. "I had a professor once who wrote really fast on the chalkboard. Like *tap-t-t-tap-t-tap-tap*. Reminds me of him."

"It's amazing, you know, everything you can do," Isaac said. "I suck at math."

"No, you don't."

He laughed. "Tell that to my tenth-grade teacher."

"Maybe your teacher sucked."

"That's entirely possible. But how do you know I don't suck?"

"I don't. But that's what I say to everyone because everyone thinks that. And they don't suck. I mean, not everyone is going to devote their life to it, but saying 'I suck at math' is like saying 'I suck at breathing.' Math is patterns. It's detail. It's understanding how things relate to one another. In a way you're doing high-level math just by existing in the world. You just don't know it."

Isaac was quiet a minute, his thinking-face on.

"Was the breakdown really bad?" he said.

"What breakdown?"

"When you came home to Lila's. When you left the college."

I lifted myself up on an elbow. "I didn't break down."

"That's what she told me."

I had always assumed it was only my father using a supposed breakdown as a cover story for why I left academia. Looking back, I could see why Lila would have used that story too. Higher learning was revered in my family. Better for everyone to think the problem was with me.

Isaac looked at me with those big cinnamon eyes and rubbed his fingertips on my forehead.

"Stop scowling. What actually happened?"

"I hated it. So I left."

"Wait, you hated what? You don't hate math."

I dropped back on the mattress and put my hands behind my head.

"Where do you want me to start? The meetings, the interruptions, the competition, the covert and overt misogyny. The snide comments about my research. And—oh god—the teaching. I hated it."

I told him about the privileged man-children who made up nine-tenths of my class. How they complained the entire semester. They challenged me in class. Or ignored then challenged me. I had no qualms about exposing their ignorance, swatting it away like the distraction it was. But then the petty drama began. They went over my head to the chair. *Dr. Brightwood was mean to me. Dr. Brightwood has favorites.*

Even the smallest insects begin to wear on a person if they never fucking go away.

"There was not a single other woman in the department, and I felt like some Darwinian freak of a mutation that would never survive."

The breeze blew a spattering of raindrops at the back window. It was painful, with his bad leg, for Isaac to lie on his side, but he turned his head and shoulders as much toward me as he could.

"Was it also hard being so pretty?"

I laughed out loud. "That sounds like a pickup line."

"No, I'm serious. I don't know math people, but I know guys."

I climbed off the bed and placed another log on the fire. Why had I not had more fires at Lila's house? It was fascinating, the physics of airflow and combustion.

"What about guys?" I said.

"I hate to say it, but the prettier a woman is, the harder it is for a lot of guys to notice, you know, other stuff."

"Other than her looks?"

"Exactly. Plus they get all confused and threatened."

I sat on the end of the mattress. Isaac shifted his foot over to touch my leg.

"Yes," I said. "It was hard being pretty."

"So you just walked away."

"Yes. One of the very few times in my life I made a decision for myself alone. I hated it, so yes, I walked away."

"But you don't hate math."

The new log popped loudly. "Why do they do that?"

"The wood's not all the way dry."

"Water expanding into vapor." I placed my palm against the plaster of the fireplace. Still cool. "I don't know. I kind of do hate math. I can't help it. I lost so much more than I gained."

Isaac shifted himself so he could lie on his back and look up at me, which involved getting his head from one end of the mattress to the other. It involved a lot of huffing and the obligatory complaint about the leg brace.

"I don't know if I believe you."

If he didn't look so unbearably hot with his hair all a mess, and his thin T-shirt lying over his firm chest, and looking up at me with those eyes, I would have been more annoyed than I was.

"What do you know about it?"

"I can see the way you look at things. Like splitting the logs. And the fire. You understand something I don't. You see in a way other people don't, and it lights you up."

"That's physics, not math."

"Math. Physics. Whatever." He put his hands behind his head. "Teach me something."

"Why? What if I don't want to?"

He reached over and stroked my leg. The knee. Then the thigh. The inside of the thigh. A long, slow shiver loosened all the bones in my back.

"Because I don't know shit. Teach me one thing that you know."

My neck became so loose, my head leaned to the side. "As long as you keep doing that."

"But no more. Not until you teach me something."

At that moment, he could have asked me for anything, and I would have said *yes*.

"Okay, okay. Speaking of Darwinian mutations, you know the seventeen-year locusts?"

He nodded. "I stepped on one in bare feet when I was seven years old. I'll never forget."

"And you get the concept of survival of the fittest?"

"I do."

"So why seventeen years? That's a weirdly specific number, right?" I looked around the room. No paper. Obviously no chalkboard. It would be so much easier to explain if I could show.

Isaac sat up. "What?"

"Do you have something I can write with?"

"In my bag. There's a pencil."

I found it, but *The Blacksmith's Companion* was the only paper in the entire place. I was about to start on the inside of the back cover, but he snatched it away.

"Hey, that's from the library. Just write it on the hearth. It'll wash off."

He came around and brushed the dust from the ledge in front of the fireplace, and I used the whitewashed plaster to explain the prime. A number divisible by only one and itself. Isaac stood up and watched as I scratched numbers in the light of the fire.

I explained the concept of factors—numbers which divide evenly into other numbers. I only got slightly tangential about the infinite other ways that factors are important, but I startled when he said my name.

"There was something about cicadas?"

"Right. So with a life cycle that's a prime number—and a larger one like seventeen—the cicadas stay out of sync with the life cycles of all the other animals, and every time the other animals see the cicadas, they're like 'What the hell is that?'"

Instead of being like 'Oh, there's those bugs we see at these regular intervals in our life cycle' and turning into specialized cicada-killers. Isn't that amazing?"

Isaac's eyes grew wide. "Totally."

He limped across the room and took my phone from the table. "Would you unlock your phone?"

"Why?"

"That was amazing. I want you to see it yourself."

"Do I have to?" It was a token protest—I wanted to say it all again. It fascinated me.

"I'm going to withhold sex until you do."

"I'll talk fast, then."

As promised, Isaac quit withholding sex after I went on video about the cicadas and prime numbers. When he was done with me, I was so stupid with pleasure that I let him set up a TikTok account for me and watched, only half paying attention, as he clipped and edited the video, added some hashtags.

I nestled closer against him. "How do you know how to do that?"

"I got high with this kid on a job site once." He swiped and tapped. "There. It's up. Anyway, this dude was funny as shit. He showed me."

"You can barely see me."

"It doesn't matter."

I closed my eyes. The room smelled dry and woody, and the rain fell hard outside. "I could stay here forever."

That was hyperbole, of course. Three nights was what I agreed to, and having a boundary around this little adventure was what made it work. I might not want to go home the day after tomorrow, but knowing I would was part of what made it possible to relax.

★ ★ ★

The cabin faced west with a high ridge behind it, and un-like the beams of sunset, morning came on indirectly. I woke to the clunking of Isaac's crutch by the propane stove as he fixed coffee and oatmeal. The fire was out, but when I put my hands on the plaster, it felt warm like the iron radiators at Lila's house. I got dressed and opened the front door to the meadow under a misty but clear sky. Isaac came to my side and handed me a hot mug, and we watched as the shadow of the ridge behind us grew shorter, sunlight rising up the hill toward us like a tide.

Amazing how it cleared the mind.

"You up for a walk?" Isaac said.

"Walk where? You shouldn't be walking around in the woods on that leg."

He bumped me with his hip. "I know *Dr.* Brightwood. But I have something to show you."

He didn't take the path down to the car. Instead we fol-lowed a path that led past the outhouse. It was a longer walk, but more level and less rocky, making it easier to manage on crutches. After half a mile or so, the road appeared through the trees, and soon a building came into view.

A long rectangle just off the road's edge, with a metal roof, it was larger but simpler than the cabin and built of the same logs. Isaac took a key from his pocket and undid the padlock on a big door that hung from a track. It stuck at first, and I watched Isaac's shoulders as he worked it open. I loved his shoulders. Sometimes they were more expressive than his face.

Finally the door gave way and slid open with a squeal.

"Take your shoes off," Isaac said as he went inside. "We don't want to track mud in."

In his sock feet, only the crutch creaked on the floor as he walked the room, opening the shuttered windows.

Two long metal tables ran half the length of the room. The walls were lined with hooks holding dozens of iron tools. Some looked like tongs. Some like hammers. Some of them I couldn't begin to tell what they were. The place was cool and dust hung in the columns of grayish light from the windows.

Isaac beckoned me from the far end of the room. "Come here."

He was taller in this room, shoulders straight and square, standing beside an anvil which was mounted on a massive section of a tree trunk. An honest-to-god anvil, the kind I had only ever seen in cartoons. I could almost feel its mass just looking at it.

At the very end of the room, set off from the wall, stood a black metal box on legs with a square tube going up and through the roof.

Isaac pointed to it. "That's my great-uncle's forge. This is his smithy."

"*Smithy.*" I looked around the room. "I don't think I've said that word in my life."

He smiled. "The cabin's nice. But this is what really makes it heaven. I'm not going to light it. Not yet. But come see."

His voice had never sounded so animated as when he talked me through all the workings of the forge. Walked me down the long walls, naming the tools and what they were for. Lifting them from their hooks and setting them back on. Tongs—square-nose, box jaw, scrolling, offset. Hammers—three-, four-, five-pound, ball-peen, Swedish pattern. Jigs and rasps. Shears and brushes. We startled a nest of mice out from under a bench, but other than that there was not a leaf or twig to litter the floor.

"What's it like?" I said. "When the forge is going and you're working."

Isaac took a broom and swept up the few pine needles we had tracked in from the outside.

"You put on goggles and hearing protection, and you have to really focus. You can't be off in your head." He set the broom against the wall and leaned against the table. "It's calming. It's about the only time I don't think I should be someone else."

"Do you have anything you made here?"

He shook his head. "None of it's very good."

"Well, show me anyway."

He went over to a cabinet and checked the lower shelves.

"Oh, here." He gave me a knife in a leather sheath.

It balanced on my palm, stout and solid, about seven inches long, the handle silky and butter yellow.

"Careful. It's sharp." He looked slightly worried. "Wiggle it a little to get it out."

The inscription, *Wells*, and the sharpened edge were bright against the dark gray of the blade.

"The handle's pretty good. It's birch. But the blade…" He came closer and looked at it with me. He frowned and shrugged. "It works okay as a utility knife."

I couldn't see a solitary flaw, and I understood curvature, angle, and balance.

"Isaac, this is beautiful. Is this the kind of thing you were making when—you know, when—"

"You mean before I shot that guy?"

I nodded.

"No. I was working construction. I was making some custom door hinges and fence work and stuff like that. But not knives. Knife-makers are serious. I'm not that good."

I handed him the knife, and he returned it to the shelf. Then something softened in his back, and he reached deeper in the cabinet. When he turned around, the look in his eyes had softened too. He held out his hand, and lying on his palm was a narrow strip of black metal curved in the shape of a heart. It was smooth and gracefully curved with a little curl at the end.

"I made this for you."

It was heavier than it looked and cool to the touch. "When?"

"Before I left for my apprenticeship. On a weekend trip down here. But, of course, I was too scared to give it to you then."

He looked a little scared now, and I closed my hand over the little heart. "I'm keeping it."

A car rumbled by on the road, and we both held our breath. When the crunch of wheels faded in the distance, Isaac leaned his forehead against mine and heaved a heavy sigh.

"Let's go back to the cabin," I said.

He kissed my forehead and nodded. I tucked the heart in my pocket and we locked up the smithy.

I wanted to light another fire, but the day warmed up, and Isaac worried that without the cloud cover and rain it would be too easy for others to see that we were here by the smoke from the flue. He busied himself fixing a few chips in the fireplace mortar, oiling the door hinges, and cleaning windows, but he refused my help.

"I've got to feel useful," he said. "I was fucked up enough to get myself in this mess—" he gestured to his injured leg "—so I might as well do what I can."

I walked out into the woods. The paths were so narrow and forking that I stayed near the meadow for fear of getting lost, but one trail led in a switchback up the hill in such a way that I could see the cabin roof. I followed this one. Wild shrubs grew taller than my head, curving and winding their branches toward the sunlight. Between the rocks in the path, little green plants bloomed with tiny white and yellow flowers. Isaac would know all their names.

The afternoon grew hotter, wrapping me in a humid blanket of still air. My thigh muscles burned from the climb, and sweat tickled my back. All my life, other people had told me what was important to know and what was not. And I had learned a great deal about a very few things. But it wasn't the fault of my professors that what I knew was so narrow. They were teachers of a very specific range of knowledge. It wasn't their job to ask a girl *What do you think is important? What do you want to know?*

That was my father's job. And he had not done it.

The path suddenly opened on top of a rock outcropping, the cabin roof just visible below. From that height I could see across the next ridge to the flowing crests of the range beyond. I stopped. The trees all had names. The shrubs, the vines, every tiny plant in the path. They all had names.

Those names were important.

Mountain laurel. There. I remembered one. The leggy one with the small white flowers and dark green leaves. I plucked a leafy twig from a tree, then a bit of a pine with long, silky needles. I would look them up. I would ask Isaac.

All those years—*your friend, that book, the pony, they aren't important. Don't waste your time on that.* I had forgotten. I had focused year upon year into the keyhole which led to the center of the universe. But I had forgotten how to look out. How to wonder. How to dream. An unbearable weight sank in my heart, and I sat down and wept.

The rock under my right hand, rough and striated—it had a name, as did the dynamics of my own heart, the nature of my feelings, the clouds. I looked up. I knew some of them. *Cirrus, nimbus.* The blue sky extended into eternity.

Maybe the Beckett Prize didn't matter. Maybe Frieholdt's didn't matter. What mattered to me? I didn't even know. But if I knew how to do one thing, it was how to learn. So I would learn.

"Meg?"

Isaac's voice from far below. I lifted my head.

"Where are you?" Growing more urgent.

"Up here," I called back, but my voice came out too soft. I stood, took a deep breath, and yelled down the mountain. "I'm here. I'm up here."

He waited at the bottom of the path and held out his free arm.

"Oh, thank god." He held me tight. "Those paths—you can get lost so easily."

"It's okay. I'm okay."

My cheek rested against the shoulder seam of his shirt, my face against his neck. I could have wept again, but this time from an overflow of joy. This mattered. Isaac Wells mattered.

I reached in my pocket.

"What is this?" I showed him the pine needles, still standing close by his side.

"What do you mean? It's a pine twig."

"But what kind?"

"Eastern white pine."

I took out the other twig, pale with broad green leaves. "How about this."

"Sycamore. Why?"

I spun the twig between my fingers. From the tree with the white bark in the high branches. It felt so good to say.

"Sycamore."

Night fell. We lit the lamp, and as I heated soup from cans, Isaac made another TikTok of me talking about the Draper point—the moment at which a heated solid begins to visibly glow. Something we barely think about, but the physics of it are astounding. We sipped the bourbon with watery ice. As the evening grew cooler, we put on warm clothes and pulled two chairs together on the porch to watch the last of the sunset.

Isaac grew quiet as the sky darkened. His eyes distant, brows lowered. I took his hand, but even the touch felt far away.

"Back to real life tomorrow," he said.

I looked up at a shadowy thing flitting through the air. "What's that?"

"A bat." He sipped his drink. "I don't know what kind."

Irritable wasn't totally out of character for Isaac. He was human, after all. But this seemed like a strange time for it.

I emptied my glass and shifted to get up, but Isaac held on to my hand.

"I can't believe…" He breathed as if to start again, then stopped. Then dropped my hand. "I cannot believe… I know I'm not supposed to decide what's good for you. But with everything I… I cannot believe that I am."

I shook my head. My heart pounded. It sounded like what a person says when they're breaking up, which we clearly weren't. It didn't make any sense.

Isaac turned suddenly toward me.

"I am poor." He began to count out his fingers. "I am stupid. Uneducated. Fucked up in my head and my heart. And

I am a wanted man. You are brilliant, beautiful, you're going to make history, you're going to have plenty of money, and I just, I can't believe…" He leaned his forehead in his hand. "I should never, never have done this to you."

I felt it—my body trying to go into panic. The short, fast breath. The burning skin. The stiff neck. But it couldn't cross that boundary into the self-perpetuating spiral. It was a strange feeling, and I noticed it even as I felt it. This was anger. Regular old, normal-person anger.

"Look at me. Pick your head up and look at me." I gripped the metal heart in my pocket.

"What. Okay. I'm looking. What?"

"Fucking quit it. Just quit it. Stop with all the *I'm such a fuckup* business. You're the one who can split wood, and light a fire, and build a house, and make a knife—which is perfect by the way—and fucking…TikTok videos. I could tell you all the ways I'm a burden and a liability, but since we're talking about you—" I stood up and counted on my own fingers "—you are strong and smart and capable and loyal and also beautiful. It's so obvious. Why do you insist on thinking you're not?"

He stood, grabbed his crutch, and walked with heavy steps to the end of the porch, his head and shoulders a dark silhouette against the deep blue sky.

"Why, Isaac?"

He spun around, dropping his glass, which rolled off the porch into the grass.

"Because I'm…because no one…fuck." He looked up and sighed angrily. "Because no one ever told me."

"Well, I'm telling you now."

His shoulders began to shake. He was a little drunk. It was necessary. It was a thick hide to break through.

"My grandmother, who raised me and Kate, was not a nice

person," he said. "When I was fifteen, I came up here to live with my great-uncle Kimmo, and he taught me how to use the forge. He said I would make a good blacksmith. It might have been the first time anyone said I would make a good anything—and I just wanted to be like him."

I nearly held my breath, I was listening so hard.

"But you know what my grandmother said?" He shifted into parody, a sarcastic snarl. "'A blacksmith? In case you hadn't noticed, it's the twentieth century. Jesus, Isaac.' You know what? She said 'Jesus, Isaac' so often that Kate started calling me Jesus as a joke. It went on for months. 'Can't find a spoon? Maybe you better go out back and make one, mister blacksmith. My pastor's got a son working for Intel, and I've got a spoon-maker. Go on, Thor, go make me a spoon.' I am damaged, Meg. I am angry and mean and—"

I grasped his hand and held on hard. He startled and stopped talking. I was so out of my depth. So angry. At his horrible grandmother, at him for stubbornly insisting I had this great life he was going to wreck, at the world for all the crap it had thrown in our way, and at myself for being angry in the first place. One thing I knew—we both needed contact, each the anchor to the other's faltering ship.

My back felt rigid, my face tight. "I got my first chalkboard when I was seven years old."

Standing on its end, it was as tall as I was, which at the time seemed immense. And it was heavy. Still, I dragged it from my room up the stairs to my father's study whenever he worked at home. He would look up and nod at me as I entered the room, as if I were a trusted colleague, a peer, and we would both work in silence.

One evening, he put down his book and strode over to observe my childish scribbles. I had propped the board against the wall in my accustomed spot, and I sat on the floor. My father towered over me for a few minutes, rubbing his chin. Then he knelt down.

He reached for the ledge and collected all the pink chalk, his fingers slender, almost feminine. He held the little pile of stubs out in his palm.

"This will be my color, okay?"

I nodded. "Okay."

"Leave the board in here when you go to bed." He looked serious, but with a glimmer in his eyes.

The next morning, I sprang awake at dawn, hopped from my bed, and tiptoed down the hall, woolly carpet under my bare toes. My father usually closed the door to his study, but that morning he had left it ajar, and I peered in.

Pink marks on my chalkboard. I scrambled to my spot on the floor to see. Two places he had struck through and corrected. And at the bottom, *See Nowakowski, page 917.*

Nowakowski. I scooched the few feet over to the low bookcase where my father kept his textbooks. *Nowakowski.* They were roughly in alphabetical order. There.

I dragged the heavy book from the lower shelf and opened it on the floor. Page 917.

Peering at the text on the silky-thin paper, my skin prickled. My eyes opened wide. I joyfully rubbed out the pink with my thumb and corrected my work.

Yes. I understand.

That evening, after he reviewed my board, my father handed me one of his own erasers. "Only you can use this on your own board. No one else can erase it but you."

Satisfied with my comprehension of that day's problem, I

erased the board and started a new one. When I was done, I left
the board in his room, eager for tomorrow's messages in pink.

"This went on for a few weeks," I said. "But I was seven.
And one day I realized that here I had this board and colored
chalk. I could do something other than math with them. So I
drew a unicorn, and me and our house, and a rainbow. I was
going to show him."

The pressure nearly choked me. The shame. So many years
of poison getting coughed up.

Isaac's shoulders softened. "I'm sorry."

"My father saw it, and you know—" the tears came now
"—he didn't say, 'Oh look at your nice picture, Meggie.' He
didn't say, 'Is that our house?' He didn't say anything. He fucking picked up the eraser. *My* eraser. And he erased the whole
thing. Real fast and hard, and then he picked up the board
and turned it to the wall. And I never used that board again."

He made the slightest move to turn toward me, and I
wrapped my arms around him.

"I need you." Tears formed rivulets down my jaw.

"I need you too."

His body felt new that night, as if making love for the first
time. It hadn't been easy to talk, but we had, and now I knew.
This was it. He was it. I loved Isaac Wells, with all his flaws
and all his beauty, and I would never stop.

"Meg." His voice was muffled from under the blankets.

"What?"

"You're thinking. Quit thinking."

"Sorry."

He laughed, which was an amusing sound from down there,
like a small creature nesting in a burrow.

We needed a little practice. I hadn't gotten laid in years—and not more times in my life than I could count on one hand. Until Isaac, that is. So yes, I needed to relax and quit thinking. He, on the other hand, had had enough sex but precious little intimacy, so his job was to be present.

"You still with me?" I said.

He nodded, and his beard tickled my thigh.

Whatever our issues were, he had patience, and so did I, and at last my body released into that marvelous moment of escape when the brain went fully offline.

The gas lamp flickered on the table across the room as Isaac emerged from the nest of blankets. He lifted my knee and let my leg fall outward. We had to go a little bit sideways to keep him off the injured leg. I was still gathering up my ability to move as he glided into me with a low, satisfied groan, but I managed to bend my other knee and reach for him, the muscles in my arms protesting from their overwork.

Propped up on his arms, he looked down at me. "It's really almost painful how beautiful you are in this light."

Reaching my arm above my head, I braced against the wall, to better feel him as he moved in me deeper and harder, until he closed his eyes tight and gritted his teeth.

"Hold my hand," he said.

There was something about the hand. Even if it meant merely gripping his wrist where he held up his own weight on the bed. Something about touching hands kept him with me.

Then my second-favorite part—when he came and everything went warm and loose and we rolled together, heaving and sweaty and happy.

We were quiet a long time, watching the lamplight. There

again was turbulence. It was everywhere. The way the air moved the flame and the flame moved the air.

Isaac rested his head on my arm. "Did you ever want a family?"

I watched the light flickering across the ceiling.

"That's the weird thing," I said. "I just never got to know what I wanted. Or trust what I wanted. Even when I did want something, it was always, *Oh, you just want that because everyone else does. You'll get over it.*"

"Do you now?"

I lay there and remembered Lizzie's wedding. I thought about when Sharon's boys were little. The way they bumped around the house, all their energy, then their soft arms around my neck as they fell asleep while we watched a movie.

"I might. Maybe. What about you?"

"I always thought I would be a shitty dad. But now? I don't know." He lifted his shoulder. "Maybe."

I watched the light. The thin stream of gray smoke rising from the tip of the flame. Rising smooth and straight, then breaking apart.

Isaac touched my cheek, turning my face toward his. His hand trembled.

"I don't know what's going to happen. How I'm going to get through...what I need to get through. But if I do—if I can somehow get to the other side—" His focus tried to move, but he brought it back. Made himself stay. "Could you imagine a life together?"

"Yes." I was able to say it once looking in his eyes before I had to hide my own face. Arms around his neck, lips against his skin, I said it again. "Yes."

As we lay together, I thought of the priceless object in my grandfather's safe. The Impossible Theorem wasn't just for me anymore. It was more than a way to vindicate my lifetime of work. It was a bridge to the life I really wanted. It could buy us a way out.

15

I had never noticed how truly enormous Lila's house was until we came home. You could have fit the cabin into the foyer with ease. It would have fit twice over in the garage. I appreciated the electricity and indoor plumbing and took a long, hot shower to prove it. But all the extra space oppressed me. I realized it wasn't just for the sake of privacy that I occupied the third floor. The rooms were smaller. Built to be lived in, not to impress. The maid's quarters were too cramped, and everything else too gaping. The third floor was the Goldilocks zone of the house.

The third floor was still mine alone, though, because Isaac refused to sleep anywhere there wasn't an exit. And granted, it was hard for him to manage those stairs on crutches. He liked the maid's bedroom. It was five feet from the side door and had a window to the garden with only a short drop to the ground.

Up in my little bedroom, I emptied my bag. My clothes smelled smoky and shed a few blades of grass and flecks of bark onto the floor. In the pocket of my sweatshirt I felt something heavy.

The heart. I tested it, gently tried to bend it, but it didn't give. And it was a little bit sharp at the lower point. A heart that had gone through the fire and come out strong.

High up in the top of Lila's house, I felt like I was standing at the edge of a precipice, having just pulled myself up over the rim and finally able to see the huge distance I had climbed.

I had the window open, and the early fall air reminded me, as it always did, of the bottom of that gorge. The worst moments of my life.

My first year of college, my father pulled in some favors and tucked me away with room and board in the home of a member of the engineering faculty. I was only fourteen years old, after all. Not exactly ready for dorm life.

They were people who had never had kids. The Magnusons. I remember them. He was awkward and seemed to avoid me, but she was kind.

What was her first name? I couldn't remember. I only ever called her Mrs. Magnuson. She had hair so blond it was almost white. She knocked on the door of my room after I'd been at their house a few days.

"What do you like to eat, Meg?" she asked, opening the door.

I sat on the bed with a book in my lap. So startled I could hardly speak. She walked in and sat on the end of the bed.

"Do you need help unpacking?" She looked around the room. "Look at all your books. You're quite the collector."

"It's okay. I can do it."

"I haven't really asked what you like—for dinner."

I shrugged and kept my eyes on my book. Outside the window, a maple was just beginning to turn from green to yellow. The afternoon light angled low through the branches. Summer at an end. My life at home as well.

Mrs. Magnuson smiled. "There must be something. Pizza?"
I shrugged again. She wore a pink sweater. Very soft-looking.
"We want you to feel at home here," she said. "We're very excited to have you. It gets a little boring, just me and Karl."

She didn't mean to, but it made me think that in addition to facing a new home, new school, life on my own before I was ready, I would also be expected to be interesting. I needed to be invisible, and my first classes had already satisfied that need. I got stared at then promptly ignored, but at last the subject matter was at my level.

I wished I could just survive on air and math and not need food. Not need other people.

Mrs. Magnuson tilted her head. "It's okay. I'll make something or other."

She stood up and walked to the door.

"Hamburgers?" I said.

She smiled. "And fries? Do you like homemade or takeout? There's a place nearby I love."

I shrugged. Again. It seemed the only movement my body was capable of.

She did her best. Got takeout and put it on her china plates around the table. Karl joined us, staring at his laptop the whole time. And I did my best, but my mouth was so dry. I sipped a Coke and managed a few bites. I knew she was watching me, expecting something. Expecting me to be happy.

There was nowhere I fit in. Too strange and quiet for Mrs. Magnuson. Too young and female for my classes. Distant in every conceivable way from anyone my own age.

I thought about how it might feel to disappear completely, and I wished for it, in my darkest moments. For a release from consciousness. A release from *me*—the only vessel I had available to navigate waters far too deep.

Things got better, but the darkness of that first autumn never left me.

But now, everything was different. My room grew dim as clouds blanketed the sky outside. I switched on a light, and there was my own face in the mirror. The same face I had seen in the mirror before we went to the cabin—but there was something different underneath. I couldn't place it. Something freer, with the smell of smoke in my hair and muscles sore from splitting wood. A woman who knew the names of trees. Could identify a bat in the evening air. Knew that sycamores grew near water and how to sharpen an axe-head with a stone.

I lifted the heart up to the mirror and laid it flat against my reflection, near my own heart.

And I whispered to the woman in the mirror, "I release you."

Isaac slept in and came to find me the next morning in the parlor. I sat cross-legged in my grandfather's armchair, blank notebook in my lap.

"What are you doing?" he said.

"Figuring out how we're going to pay for a lawyer. Go get your crutches. You're not supposed to be walking on that leg."

He rolled his eyes. "It doesn't hurt that much. And the brace is giving me a rash."

"Oh no. Poor baby, not a rash." I rolled my eyes back at him.

"Lawyer for what?"

I looked at him, incredulous. "To get you cleared, that's what. What else would we need a lawyer for?"

"To keep you out of jail for protecting me. You don't need to get me a lawyer."

"Yes, I do."

Going back to my notes, I tried to indicate that I had had the last word.

Lila had left me the fifty thousand dollars and two years to live in her house. About thirty-five thousand was left after eight months. Sharon might still pay me something to move out early, but probably not as much now. The Beckett Prize was one million, but even if I submitted my proof immediately, the prize money wouldn't come until it had been reviewed, and that could take years. Then there was Anne MacFaull's offer. She had left two messages during our weekend at the cabin. Vague call-me-at-your-earliest-convenience messages. Following up, I figured.

Thirty-five thousand may seem like a lot, but I didn't want just any lawyer. I wanted the biggest, baddest criminal defense attorney I could find. I wanted someone who would go to that small town, and that small-town prosecutor, and that small-town judge, and eat their lunch. That kind of attorney would be expensive. Plus Isaac was right. I probably needed a lawyer of my own in the meantime. Not to mention something to live on. That's why I had the notebook and pencil in hand. I had real-world math to do.

When I looked up again, Isaac had me on video.

"What are you doing?"

"Making a TikTok of you looking smart and sexy at the same time."

"What's so special about that? Women do it all the time," I said. "Would you be willing to run an electric line up to the cabin?"

"Willing? I've wanted to do that for years. Why?"

Good. No power was fine for a weekend, but not for every day. I had even researched composting toilets. I'd been up a while.

"Sit down."

He limped over to the ottoman in front of me and sat, cradling his coffee in both hands.

"Here's my plan." I sat up straight and set my pencil down. "I use the money I've got left in the bank to get a badass lawyer on retainer, and we pretend I only just found out you were a wanted man. I get some more cash to pay said lawyer. They get a self-defense ruling, and you go free."

"Meg—?"

"No. Not yet. While we're getting you cleared, whatever money you've been sending your mom I'll send in the meantime. Then, once it's all done, we go live at the cabin. You start your blacksmithing business, I do whatever the hell I want, and we both live happily ever after."

He reached for my hand and kissed my knuckles.

"I love your optimism, but it's not realistic."

I snatched my hand back. "Didn't I already tell you not to patronize me? Why isn't it realistic?"

"How is a lawyer going to get me off? There's no evidence that I didn't just shoot DeVries. There's no way to prove it was self-defense."

"Yes, there is. Your truck is full of bullet holes."

He shook his head. "That's not going to be enough. They'll just say I fired first."

"Then, let your sister help you. You know she would want to."

He stood and walked to the window. "No. I'm not going to let this all be for nothing by bringing her right back to that snake pit she was living in."

"You're not. Just because she testifies doesn't mean it all falls apart."

PRINCIPLES OF (E)MOTION   165

He sighed. Frustrated to the point of anger. "I don't want to talk about this anymore. I already told you, I won't do it."

"You're making decisions for her."

He tossed back his head. "Of course I am. Look where her decisions got her."

"They got her clean, safe, and in school."

I glared at him. He glared at me.

"No, they didn't. I did that. It's not happening. I'm not bringing her into it."

"Violation of postulate three."

"Postulate three doesn't apply to addicts. I can't trust what she thinks she wants."

My shoulders dropped. "It seems like you don't even want to fight this."

"I can't." He turned away. "It's like my fucking fate. If I ever go back to Blind Fork, I'll wind up in jail. They all know me, and they'll find some way to put me in my place."

"Your place? Do you hear yourself? That's ridiculous."

"You don't know fucking small-town politics. Small-town people."

"Maybe they're just people, Isaac. Maybe your grandmother filled your head up with a lot of lies about the way the world works, just like my dad did to me."

"Maybe. Or maybe not. But whose freedom depends on the answer? Not yours." He limped back across the room, brows low, eyes dark, and took the notebook from my chair. "Holy fuck. Fifty thousand? You're going to pay a lawyer fifty thousand dollars?"

"I would pay a lawyer fifty million dollars. I would pay five hundred million dollars. I don't want money. I want *you*. I want a life with you where we're not hiding, and we're not scared, and we can turn on the lights and let smoke come from the chimney, and just be free. Together. I would pay anything for that."

He dropped the notebook on the floor and took me in his arms.

I pressed my cheek against his, hard against his jaw and his beard to feel the roughness, the realness, and stop the shaking in my chest. "I'm hiring you a lawyer. And I'm in charge of what I want. Not you. You can't tell me *no*. You can refuse to show up or refuse to talk to the lawyer or refuse to let Kate help, but you cannot tell me *no*."

He held me tight, one arm around my back, his hand pressing my head to his, breathing short little breaths. The kind that only go into the very tops of the lungs. I knew that kind of breathing well. It was for moments of crisis. I managed to turn my head enough to kiss him, high on his cheekbone, and take a deep breath next to his skin.

He exhaled in a long shuddering sigh. "It's just so hard to believe it's possible."

Anne MacFaull's card sat on my desk where I had left it the day she came to my house. I looked at it before touching it. Our ticket out. Hers was the most ready money. She could have her exclusive access for two years. Enough to give her a head start before I made the proof public and let every other engineer in the world have at it. In exchange, I would ask for a large sum of money up front and a yearly retainer for consulting.

I can't say it didn't grate at my conscience. Climate change wasn't going to wait. But maybe with her exclusive access, Anne would be able to throw the kind of R & D money at Frieholdt's that would turn it into something actionable. I didn't know what it would take to bring its promise to reality. No one really knew. But I did know that I needed money.

I settled in my chair facing the front windows looking out at the worksite across the street at the General's house. How strange that Isaac had been there all that time. That I had watched him at work and not known. I picked up Anne's card, actually looking forward to talking with her. She had said she thought I needed an equal, and she wasn't wrong. I could see becoming more familiar with a person like her. And the mint copy of *Discourses on the Loading Hypothesis* hadn't hurt the first impression.

I announced myself to her secretary as Dr. Brightwood.

"I'm sorry, Dr. Brightwood, Ms. MacFaull is... *Brightwood?*"

"Yes," I said. "Dr. Margaret Brightwood."

"Just a minute," she said. "She's in a meeting, but please stay on the line. She'll want to talk to you. Please don't hang up."

I laughed. "I won't hang up."

Hope is an amazing feeling. It has lift and energy. It reverses the gravity of history and gets a person to look forward. Midday sun shone through my front windows as I waited on the line. The old, curved glass broke the rays into ribbons on the floor, almost the way sun reflects off water. There was a very good chance that ours was a problem that money could fix. And once we were in the lawyer's office, maybe Isaac would come to his senses about letting Kate help. Maybe the lawyer could persuade him. Maybe there was some way to keep her anonymous, or off-site, or something. Anything. This was a solvable problem.

"Dr. Brightwood?"

"Yes. Call me Meg, please."

"I'm so glad you called."

I felt like I was a teenager on a date. Awkward. Excited.

"I'd like to discuss your offer."

She paused, and something in that silence stuck like a needle deep in my chest.

"I'm delighted to hear it, but…didn't you…. I'm sorry. I spoke to your father on Saturday."

"My father? What did you talk to him about?"

"About Frieholdt's. I tried to call you."

My neck grew rigid, and my skin burned. "What did my father say?"

"It was about the proof you're going to publish together," she said. "He said you were submitting it for the Beckett Prize, but he offered to consult with my team."

The room seemed to lose focus, then lurch to the side. I gripped the edge of the desk, yanked open a drawer, and snatched a pencil. I pressed the tip of it into my palm until it hurt, and the pain kept me in my body. *Stay here. Stay now. Breathe. Do not panic.*

"Are you okay?" Anne asked.

"I'm fine." I was not fine.

"I'm sorry," she said. "When I came to your house, I didn't know you had worked on it together. I would have waited to speak to both of you."

I slid off the edge of my seat and knelt carefully on the floor where I could reach the edge of the rug. The fringe, woolly and rough. I raked my fingers through it, pulling the threads through a tight fist until the scabbed-over blisters burned.

"Did he give it to you? The proof?"

"Yes. I was just meeting with my top engineers when you called. Is there… Dr. Brightwood, is something wrong?"

I could no longer speak. I could barely breathe. A hand that didn't feel like my own touched the red circle and cut off the call. My head felt like a hundred-pound weight, and I let it drop to my knees, to the floor. I pressed my forehead against the rug, palms out flat. If only it had been the ground, the dirt in the garden, if I had been outside. It was always better if I could make contact with the earth. But instead I was perched up in this ridiculous tower. I felt detached from gravity, as if I would fall upward forever.

Thinking was for later. At that moment I had to will my heart not to stop.

The door clicked open. Footsteps receded, then returned, slowly, across the room to my side. How long had it been? I opened my eyes and stared hard at the patterns on the rug. Isaac's socks and the tip of his crutch. He sat. I took a short breath, then blew out as long as I could. And again. The way one of my many therapists had told me to do. The stabbing pain in my chest retracted ever so slightly.

"I have your meds, if you want them," he said.

Whenever people had to deal with me in the middle of an attack, no matter how sympathetic they were, they always seemed a bit like they wanted to get away. Even, at times, Lizzie. I scared people. But not Isaac. I couldn't yet see his face, but his voice sounded so normal. Concerned, but in a going-about-his-business kind of way. As if I had twisted my ankle or something.

I lifted my forehead and touched it with my fingertips. The rug had left an impression. Then I rose up on my elbows, slowly so I wouldn't throw up. So I could get back in agreement with gravity somehow. I held out my palm toward Isaac, and he put a pill in it. It dissolved slowly on my tongue, vaguely sweet.

He scooted close and began to rub my back gently and slowly with one hand.

"Panic attack?"

I nodded and managed a moment of eye contact.

"Want to sit on the couch with me?"

I nodded, and he helped me up, steadied me by the elbow. He sat in the corner, and I sat next to him, feeling like a wooden doll with joints that didn't move.

"Here." He put a cushion on his lap and guided me to lay my head down. "Put your legs up on the couch."

I curled into a fetal position, fists tucked under my chin. He stroked my hair, and for a long time we stayed just like that.

"How come..." my throat loosened as I spoke "...how come you know what to do? Nobody else does."

He kept stroking my hair, letting it fall through his fingers all the way to the ends.

"You mean with a panic attack?"

I nodded.

"I don't know. My mom used to get them. Kate had a few. Seems like half the people I know have had a few."

The exhaustion that followed an attack was crushing. I could barely keep my eyes open. But I also couldn't let go.

"I need to get the safe open." The moment the words were out, the tears followed. It was all I had left. I dragged myself to a sitting position and put my arms around Isaac, trying to pull some strength from his solid, calm body.

"Right now?"

"Yes."

He nodded. "Okay, then. Let's go open it."

We went down to the basement. I had the combination memorized, but I didn't need it. The door was open. And the safe was empty.

Deep in the part of my mind where obvious things lived, I had known it would be empty. Lila had told me no one knew the combination to the safe—no one but she and I—but how well did she remember? Of course, of all people, my father would have it. And he knew me well enough to look here.

I had been so cautious. I had made no other copy.

So obvious. My brilliant move to lock Frieholdt's up here kept it safe from everyone but the one person with the balls to steal it. My own father had been the only threat, and to him the safe was just a big, heavy box.

"I can't believe it. I can't believe he did it."

I sat on the bottom step and stared at the safe, hands in my lap, face slack. Even through all my self-recrimination, I felt genuine shock that he had actually done it.

"Who did it?"

"My father. He stole it. He lied. He said we did it together." I told him everything. My conversation with Anne. Suddenly a sense of urgency propelled me to my feet. "I need to look something up."

I climbed the basement steps, went through the center hall to the big stairs. Everything was so far in this house. Isaac started to follow me up the stairs to my study.

"Don't," I said. "Don't walk on that leg. Why don't you ever listen? I'll be right back."

The first place I looked was in my desk drawer where I had put Anne's letter. And there it was. I hadn't been particular about how exactly I placed it, so I didn't know if it had been moved, but of course he would come up here. Of course he would look in the drawer. How did I not see this coming?

I returned with my phone, having already looked on the math community's message boards on my way down the stairs. My arms hung limp at my sides. My feet dragged on the floor.

Isaac stood—he had retrieved his crutches. "What happened? Come here."

It was all over. Dr. Brightwood had sent a proof of Frie-holdt's to the Beckett Institute. Dr. *Henry* Brightwood. Maybe my name was on it. Maybe I would even get half the prize money, but that wasn't what was important. It was my work. Mine alone. The one solitary thing that I had accomplished in my life. It was the thing for which I had sacrificed any sense of normalcy, for which I had traded my childhood. All those years he had driven me into that higher and higher and smaller and smaller space, and finally I had found the hatch that opened to the sky. Me. Me alone.

I dropped into a kitchen chair and leaned my forehead on my crossed arms. There wasn't energy enough in my body to summon any more freak-out. I thought, and not for the first time, it's a good thing breathing is involuntary, because if it were something I had to choose to do, I would just stop.

Isaac got up and put a hand on my shoulder. "I'm going outside. I'll be back in ten minutes."

Even in my state of collapse, it seemed odd to me that he would walk away.

The house around me seemed to have a heartbeat of its own. I would move out. I would hope Sharon would still pay me some extra to clear out early. All those years I lived with Lila, I hadn't been thinking. I had been avoiding. But I had also been doing a job. A job that got harder and more consuming with every passing month and year. And that was caring for the very woman whose death left me with space I couldn't afford and freedom I didn't know how to use.

Not that I thought any of those things as I sat with my head on my arms, the edge of the kitchen chair digging into the backs of my thighs. All I thought then was how badly I wanted to sleep and forget.

The side door opened and closed, and Isaac crutched himself through the back hall to my side.

"All right," he said. "Get up."

"Why?"

"Just do it. Come on."

"No."

"Yes. I need your help with something. Come outside."

"No."

"I googled defense lawyers."

That got me to look up.

"I'll tell you about it," he said. "But you have to come outside."

We crunched across the first few dry leaves along the path that wound between rhododendron and azaleas back to the garden shed.

Isaac picked up an axe and held it out.

I took it and nearly dropped it with my weak grip. "Is this the answer to everything now?"

"Yes. It's as good an answer as lying there with your head in your hands."

He led me farther from the house, and I hefted the axe and followed.

I had been a good caregiver for Lila, but not so much a caretaker of the house, and the places I didn't go often suffered from neglect. None more so than the back fence. Weathered to a splintery gray, it leaned and warped, more like a stiff ribbon than the straight, wooden wall it should have been. Narrow trees grew in a straggling row along the fence line, and in their shade the undergrowth did not thrive.

"Tree of heaven," Isaac said, looking up. "What's that word when a thing is the opposite of what it's called?"

"Irony? Oxymoron?"

"Well, this is the tree from hell. It's invasive. Kills the other plants. Plus it smells bad."

"There's a lot of them. Can't we use a chain saw?"

"No." He gave me a sarcastic smile. "*We* can't use a chain saw. I can use a chain saw, but *we* don't have one. So you can get to work, or you can go cry. It's up to you."

Part of me wanted to sit down on the prickly ground right where I was and do just that. Cry. Sleep. Disappear.

But I gripped the axe instead. "You're lucky I'm still trying to impress you."

He came to my side and laid his hand on the small of my back. "You don't have to impress me. Just give it a try. I used to have anger issues, and it always helped if I busted the shit out of something."

The nearest tree was about twenty-five feet tall, with a trunk about as big around as my upper arm.

"Right here." He pointed to a spot low on the trunk and stepped back.

I swung the axe, and it lodged in the trunk, jarring my shoulders. I rocked it back and forth and swung again, making a small notch. The wood was soft and pale under the thin layer of bark. It felt different to drive an axe into living wood, and my arms burned, still sore from splitting the dry wood at the cabin. I felt weak and ineffective, but the axe-head was good and sharp and each swing took another chunk out of that trunk.

Soon I could feel my heart beating. I leaned the axe against my leg and pulled off my hoodie.

Anger issues.

This didn't feel like anger. Or at least it hadn't started out feeling that way. Anger was not an emotion that worked properly for me. It tended to contort inward, and it was painful. When it did flare up, it would turn almost immediately to tears. Anger meant the withdrawal of love. From my father, of course, but even from my mother. There was a reason they had been married in the first place.

The axe-head struck deep into the trunk, and I yanked it free.

We were the Brightwoods. We were not average people. We were wealthy, smart, and above all, self-controlled. I don't remember my mother once raising her voice. She would just press her lips together and lift her chin and wait me out.

And I didn't get angry with my father. I learned so early I had forgotten that I even learned—anger got me nowhere. It only got me alone in my room clutching my arms around my knees.

A Brightwood might cry alone in her room. She might swallow the weight of bitterness and disappointment. But a Brightwood, a Dr. Brightwood, did not lose her temper.

My throat grew tight, but I had to breathe, and breathe hard. Sweat ran in a rivulet between my breasts. One more swing.

This was not misery. Though I wanted to cry, and I sort of did through the exertion, this was not sadness or grief. This was anger. And I was entitled to it.

The tree suddenly let loose a loud snapping sound, and the trunk above my notch shifted.

"Okay, now stop," Isaac said. "Step over to your left and give it a good shove toward the notch."

I did, but the top of the tree only swayed. I already knew what to do and swung again, making the notch deeper. The tree leaned. I swung again. It leaned farther.

He stole my work, slapped his name next to mine as if it were in some way *his*. As if he owned it because he owned *me*.

"Okay, okay, Meg, pay attention."

I stepped back, and the tree creaked, leaned, and then came down, its crown thrashing nearly to the ground, snagging one tenacious branch along the top of the fence.

"Now you cut through the other side and free it up," Isaac said.

This was nearly as much work as felling it in the first place, and by the time I was done, I was soaked with sweat.

There were still ten more. I dropped the axe.

"This is crazy. I can't do all these. I can't even get this one off the fence."

"It's all right. That one's probably enough for your purposes." He rested his weight on his good leg, looking totally at home. "I'll come out and clean it up later."

"What do you mean? Why are you smiling?"

"You do have a chain saw."

16

I hadn't even washed my hands as I sat at the kitchen table, email open, composing a global get-your-hands-off-my-work email, as well as a long list of people to send it to.

Then I remembered. "Hey, you said you googled defense lawyers."

Isaac looked up from across the table. "What?"

"Did you lie about that too?"

"I didn't lie about the chain saw. I said *we* didn't have one. I didn't say *you* didn't have one. But yes, I did lie about looking for a lawyer."

"It worked. But let's not make it a habit, okay?"

He stroked my calf with his foot. "Of course not. I promise."

I closed the computer. My physical and emotional energy finally spent, I felt the shame that lay underneath it all, bitter and inescapable.

"I'm so fucking stupid." Leaning my elbows on the table, I rubbed my forehead hard with my fingers.

I had no backup copy of the proof. It was my own fault,

my own paranoia, my own delusion born from nearly a lifetime of living with a brain that couldn't properly calibrate fear.
Nothing on my laptop. Nothing on my phone. I could have
just taken a picture, but no. I thought it wasn't safe. What if I
lost my phone? What if I got hacked? It never once occurred
to me that my own father would make off with the paper
original itself. It should have. I wished it had. But it hadn't.

Gravity pulled me down. I wanted to succumb, but where
had that ever got me? Still energized from busting the shit out
of that invasive tree, I handed Isaac my phone.

"Make a TikTok."

He did as directed.

Anonymity no longer equaled safety. Anonymity was vul-
nerability. If no one knew who I was, if everyone forgot Dr.
Margaret Brightwood, it made my father's theft that much
easier. Plus I had gotten used to the video thing. Editable. De-
letable. Where I had been nervous at first, I now felt at ease. I
could be exactly as I wanted to be, and if it didn't look right,
no one ever had to see it. If I could have conducted my entire
career like this, people might still know my name.

Isaac reached over. "You've got a hair sticking out right
here."

I fished a Sharpie out of the kitchen drawer and looked
around. Whoever bought this house would paint it. They
would probably knock out walls and replaster. Whatever I
did now, short of burning the place down, wouldn't matter.

So I used the wall. I wrote, $\{a\} \cap \{b\} = \emptyset$.

"If you use set theory, then this says there are no common
elements between sets a and b. The sets are called disjointed."
I cupped my hands and held them up. "Two sets of things,
conditions, whatever, that don't go together. Don't have any
of the same elements. Separate. These two things remain what

they are. It's a static system. But look what happens if you change just one symbol." I rewrote the line, replacing the $\cap$ symbol with a plus sign. "If you change the principle to addition, then *a* and *b* are separate things, but *a* combined with *b* equals something bigger."

I wrote out another line.

$$\{a\} \bullet \{b\}$$

"The principle of multiplication. Now the result is even bigger. It's *a* times *b*. Now let's do this—"

$$A^b$$

"Even bigger." I paused. There was more. I looked at the wall, then straight at Isaac. He smiled at me, riveted.

"But here's the thing," I went on. "*A* and *B*, *by themselves*, have to be bigger than one. If they are each just one thing, nothing happens. It's all one, one, one, no matter what you do. You have to be able to believe that you can be more than just one thing."

My father did not answer his phone, so I left him a terse message. A few minutes of research on the message boards yielded the name of the journal he had submitted to for publication. I fired off an email, read receipt required, high importance, stating that it was my work, and that to publish it with his name on it would constitute fraud. Another email went to the Beckett Institute asserting essentially the same thing.

I hadn't even changed my sweaty shirt from chopping down the tree, sitting at the kitchen table with a cold beer, glaring at my laptop. They might well decide to publish anyway. And the Beckett Institute had no reason not to review a proof from Henry Brightwood. But maybe this would slow them down.

My final email went to Anne MacFaull.

The next day I drove to my father's house. I hadn't been there since Lizzie's wedding the previous spring. The leaves on the Japanese maple in the front yard were starting to curl. I tried the door, but it was locked, so I pounded on it with the brass knocker and waited.

When I was up for my professorship, he'd told me outright, "Don't let them know about your research on the Impossible. It won't look good."

The Impossible was a glamorous puzzle, and if solved, the wonders would never cease, but serious scholars knew it was a fantasy. It didn't look good for Henry Brightwood's daughter to be interested in such a fringe problem. Especially now that she was *unaffiliated*.

And now—now Henry Brightwood would astound the world. After shaming me half my life, he would take the credit and the glory.

The moment he opened the door, I marched past him into the slate-tiled foyer. He was clearly not expecting me.

"Give it back," I said.

"Excuse me—"

"Where is it? Give it back."

He turned toward the living room. Damn. There was someone over. My bravado wavered.

"Dr. Hwang, this is my daughter, Meg." He gestured toward me. "Meg, this is—"

"You can call me Dr. Brightwood," I said. It had been a long time, but I had learned to play this little game of professional manners.

Dr. Hwang stood, ready to smile. A roundish man with narrow shoulders, he would have gone unnoticed in a crowd. But not a crowd of mathematicians. He was a senior fellow at Princeton. His work on topology was groundbreaking. But I did not have time for him.

"I'm sorry," I said to Dr. Hwang, not to my father. "Would you excuse us?"

I started toward the kitchen through my father's pristine dining room, gleaming as if dusted yesterday. On the far wall hung the best painting from Lila's house, a portrait of her own grandmother, a hundred years old. My father did not follow.

"Dr. Hwang and I were just discussing the proof."

I turned toward him and for once—for once, thank god—my body gave me fight instead of flight. Instead of freeze. This was how a person feels when she is about to attack. Thrilling.

"What on earth—?" I strode back to the foyer. His brazenness kept me strangely calm.

Dr. Hwang collected his jacket. "I'll just take a brief walk? It's a lovely morning? Give you time to talk?"

"There's no need for that," Henry said. He placed himself in an alignment with the door so that he wasn't blocking it, but it would be awkward for his guest to leave.

"Yes. All right." Dr. Hwang put down his jacket and backed into the living room again. "It's remarkable work, Dr. Brightwood. Quite remarkable."

This was addressed to me, not my father.

"Thank you." I turned my back to him. Gave the poor guy a break. He didn't need to be put in the middle of this. I whispered hard to my father, "Give it back. It's my proof. You stole it—physically stole it from the safe, and I want it back."

"I know you're upset," he said, straightening up his back as if he were the upset one, "but I can't let you accuse me of theft in front of my own colleague. In my own house. I was going to give you coauthorship as a courtesy, but if you're going to act so unhinged, I'll take your name off it. You don't have to be involved at all."

It was dizzying absurdity. I laughed like a machine gun. "*My* name?"

"For bringing in the Loading Conjecture."

"More like for writing the whole fucking thing."

"Meg, please."

I was still laughing. The nerve to lie to my face like he did. I didn't think he had it in him. Dad looked plaintively at Dr. Hwang. Two men. Old men. Men with bank accounts and nice houses, careers, respect, settled futures. After all those years of my life, what did I have? I had a half-empty house and enough money for food and heat for another year. I had the love of my life hanging by a thread. But I had done the Impossible. No one but me.

No wonder people had so-called issues with anger. I didn't get to experience it like this very often, and it was a strange kind of high. I felt powerful. Invincible. Like I could smash through anything in my way.

"So you are saying…" my breath came fast, hands on hips "…you are saying you did it all yourself—"

"No one does anything all by themselves in math." He looked over at Hwang again. "You know that as well—"

"Shut up. You are saying you did not steal my handwritten research out of the safe in Grandma's basement?"

"Of course I didn't. I don't know where you—"

"Well then, who the fuck did? And how are you suddenly the guy who solved Frieholdt's? You haven't worked on it in twenty years."

"Perhaps we could talk this over later." He turned to his

colleague, while herding me out the door. "I'm sorry, Peter. If you'll just excuse me a minute."

I was never wise to his tactics. That had been the root of the problem since I was a child. It wasn't until he had already won that I realized we were playing a game. And here I was again. I saw. The esteemed professor, surrounded by all the accoutrements of his professorness, forced to defend himself against his *unhinged* daughter. I could already hear Dr. Hwang gossiping about me to his colleagues. *Disturbing the way she laughed. And something about a safe? She's been unaffiliated since she left Halberstam. Yes, fifteen years. It's a shame. She had such promise. But to accuse him like that?*

It was a perfect morning. Perfect house. Perfect trees. Perfect stairs. Like a doll's house in a doll's neighborhood. All the perfectness money and status could buy. But it wasn't real. No twigs littering the walk, no dirt, no vines. Just a bunch of plants stuck there to look pretty.

The fight response died like the flimsy matchstick fire it was. I looked in my father's eyes and was shocked to find no turmoil. They registered inconvenience, nothing more.

My hands felt limp at my sides. "Dad, don't do this. Give it back. It's not yours."

He stepped out and closed the front door. His voice dropped, but he shifted his stance and his intensity. I took a small step back.

"Do you ever think of what I sacrificed for you?" He leaned in, his face a mask of disdain. "Do you ever think of anyone but yourself?"

I took another step back. My heels touched the wall at the edge of the porch.

He pointed a finger in my face. "All the camps, the tutors, the presentations. All the people who were so impressed by *your* genius. I saw what you were capable of, and I made it happen. If it weren't for all the time, all the money, all the strings I pulled for you—if I hadn't done all those things you'd be a goddamn English major working at Starbucks. *Not yours,*" he mimicked me. "I gave you every possible advantage, and you gave up. I got you a position when you were twenty-one that grown men would kill for, and you just quit. You embarrassed me."

I froze. I couldn't help it.

"My colleagues, my friends—it's been fifteen years, and they are still asking me, 'What about that daughter of yours, Henry? What happened to her? Wasn't she supposed to be a big deal?' Even Peter Hwang." Dad pointed toward the door. "But you know why I did it? Because I knew you had the mind that would make history, not me. I knew since you were five years old. And you know what? I was right. Everything I did brought us to this exact point, because I was right. So yes, Meggie, it is *ours*, and I have absolutely no problem putting my name on it, because we did this—" he grasped my head between his hands "—together."

He let go. My skin felt as fragile and hot as ash where his hands had been. I wanted to lash out, but the defense of silence was so strong from years and years of use that it imprisoned me. To turn my back on him was as much defiance as I could muster, and it was a lot, given how long I had desperately tried to hold on. And with anxiety like mine, spontaneity is not a strength.

It was all I could manage to move one foot, then the other, descending the steps carefully and climbing in my car, not fully balanced. Not fully in the world. But I will say this—once I closed the car door and Dad disappeared into the house, once I was alone again, the silent spell broke. It left me weak and weary, but not without my faculties. I had heard every word, and now I knew the truth. Now I knew who I was really dealing with.

Before Isaac, I would have gone home alone after a conflict like that and collapsed. I would have slept for two days, then burrowed into my research until it all blew over. There had been conflict when I quit my professorship and moved in with Lila. Dad had been angry and resentful, and I had waited it out. I had gone into a crouch, and the storm passed.

Now it was different. I had someone to talk to. And not with the filtered, reasonable, three-days-later version of the event I might tell to Lizzie. I had someone right there, in the house, in the moment. Even so, it was hard. My father spent nearly my whole life building a finely tuned sense of shame deep into my machinery, but Isaac had walked me through a panic attack as if it were no big deal. He knew my unreasonable parts, the odd-shaped bits of me that didn't make sense. And he loved me anyway.

Postulate two: Meg is a head case. It was built-in. Nothing about me being a head case would be any kind of revelation to him.

I divulged the whole scene to him, legs tucked up sitting at the end of his bed in the maid's room, and not in a cool-headed manner.

He sat up, leaned toward me, and as I spoke, his interjections grew in intensity and profanity. *He said what? You have got to be shitting me.*

When I concluded, he looked past me with a dark scowl and wrapped it up with *Motherfucker*, the *m* and *f* drawn out slow and slightly menacing.

Something about his emphatic swearing drained some of the

fuel from my shame and left me feeling paradoxically stronger
when I finished than when I started, as if I had been through
a great trial and survived.

"Do you want to go break some shit?" he said. "I'll teach
you how to use the chain saw."

I even laughed. "No. It's all right."

He sighed. "Probably better. You shouldn't use power tools
when you're upset. Maybe we should go fuck up his car."

"Isaac, be serious."

"I am serious." He reached out and pulled me into his arms.
"What else can I do? I want to help you."

For a person who had lived such a rough life, he had amaz-
ingly soft skin. I loved the place where his shoulder met his
neck. Leaning my head forward, I felt the big vessels pulsing
below the surface.

"You are helping."

My phone rang. Sharon.

"Meg, is it true?"

Sharon didn't usually register surprise, and it threw me off.

"True that Dad stole my proof? Yes."

"Wait. You seriously think he stole it?"

"What do you mean *think he stole it*? He did steal it."

Isaac looked at me. I shook my head and put Sharon on
speaker. What was happening?

Sharon paused and then sighed. "This is going overboard."

"Overboard?"

"It's one thing if you want to live this weird life all by yourself, but Dad's got a reputation."

"Reputation?"

There is a psychiatric disorder where a person echoes the
last word spoken to them. I noticed it happening. Add that
to my diagnoses.

"Yes." She sounded angry. "Reputation. The opinion of other people. You can't just go throwing around accusations like that."

Anger corroded my brain so I could barely think. But Isaac poked my arm.

Fuck you, he mouthed and raised his middle finger.

"Fuck you." It sounded so weak, but so much better than whatever else I could have said. "It's not an accusation. It's the truth."

And I hung up.

Isaac nodded. "Well done."

Beyond what I had already done, emailing out my denials everywhere he had sent the proof, I was at a loss. I did still need a day or two to recover from such a direct conflict with my father, and I spent that time in my study, drinking coffee, staring at my board. I started getting responses to my emails. They were serious and promised investigations of my claim but were far less satisfying than the horrified outrage I wished for.

Each day, Isaac would make me come downstairs and teach something to my minuscule TikTok following. And each day, at least once, he made love to me. Thus fortified, I lost less ground than usual.

My inventory arranged itself.

Lost: proof, notes.

Retained: board, mind, work ethic.

Reconstructing the proof would be like rewriting an entire novel from memory, only worse because every word had to be exactly right. But I began to think it was maybe just possible.

One evening, after spending most of the day in my study,

I came downstairs. As I reached the first floor, I heard Isaac in the kitchen.

A cabinet door banged shut. "Fuck." Loudly. Then another one, softer. "Fuck."

He had started taking care of the cooking, but until that night he had seemed to like it.

By the time I reached the kitchen he had crutched himself through the dining room and out to the back porch. The French doors stood open, and I closed them behind me. He stood at the end of the porch, looking out at the garden, smoking a cigarette.

I walked up to his side. "I didn't know you smoked."

"I don't. Not very often."

It's bad for you, is what I wanted to say. Don't do it. I want you to live to be an old man. But it wasn't the time or place for scolding. I could see that on his face. Tense, restless, avoiding eye contact.

"What's the matter?"

He took a long draw off the cigarette, then stubbed it out against the aluminum crutch that leaned against the porch rail.

"I'm bored."

"That's fair."

"I feel like a freeloader."

"You're not."

"I can hardly even work on your house because there aren't any tools." He gestured toward the garage. "I mean, there's hand tools, but the table saw in there is a hundred years old. And it was a shitty one to begin with."

"Okay, what's one tool I could fit in my car, that's not too expensive, that would make you feel like you could be useful?"

"I'm not a fucking charity case."

"Oh, come on. If I say you can work on the house as bar-ter for rent, does that make you feel better?"

He rolled his eyes. "Actually, it does. Okay, a circular saw."

The porch rail flexed under his weight. Everything in this house needed fixing.

"I can't even fucking walk," he said, finally looking at me, and it wasn't with the anger I expected. It was something sad-der. More like shame. "I'm a liability, and I hate it."

"I would like to wax poetic about your *asset* right now, but I know that's not really what you're talking about."

His grip loosened on the rail. "I feel so fucking useless."

The way he said *useless*, it sounded like it had a kind of life of its own. It was pointed, like a finger at his own face.

The next night, the doorbell rang. This was a crisis, under our current circumstances. Isaac rushed to the maid's quarters, opened the window, and closed the door. I put on my best neu-tral face and took several slow breaths. We had a signal planned out. I would always carry a heavy book to the door. If it was the cops, I would accidentally drop it. That way Isaac would know to run.

It wasn't the cops. It was Lizzie in scrubs, hand on her hip, unsmiling.

"Why haven't you been returning my calls?" She walked in as soon as I opened the door. "I've been really worried."

"I'm sorry."

"So what's the truth about your dad?"

"Who told you?"

"Sharon told me."

"Told you what?"

"Jesus Christ, why are you being so secretive? What is going on? Sharon said that Henry said that *you* said he stole your proof, but she doesn't believe it."

"Are you on your way to work?"

"Yes. I got called in for an eleven-o'clock shift. Don't change the subject."

"He did steal my proof."

Her mouth hung open. "You mean he actually— I can't believe it. I mean, I do believe it, but—"

It felt better, knowing that I wasn't the only one.

"He literally stole the physical paper original out of the safe in the basement. It was the only one I had."

"The only what?"

"The only copy. I know." I held up a hand as she opened her mouth to speak. "I was paranoid. It was stupid. I didn't make a copy."

"I'm going to make his life hell. You know that. He can't just say it's his and have everyone believe him."

I sighed. What would it be like to inhabit a mind like hers? With that much fight?

"He *can* say that, and he did. And everyone—besides you— may very well believe him. But I would appreciate it if you made his life hell."

She eyed me shrewdly. "I'm glad you're okay, but we clearly need to talk. We need a plan. I need to go to work, but I'll come over tomorrow morning with bagels."

"Sounds great." I hugged her tight and wished I could tell her everything. "I'm sorry, Lizzie. I didn't mean to worry you."

She tilted her head and looked at me as she opened the door. "You look different. Why do you look different?"

I evaded. Shrugged her off. "I don't know."

"There's something you're not telling me."

"You're right."

★ ★ ★

"I would trust Lizzie with my life." I leaned against the kitchen counter.

Isaac leaned next to me, arms crossed, shaking his head. "It's too much of a risk. And that puts her on the hook too."

"We need help." I passed him the beer we were sharing.

"How's she going to help?"

"I don't know. You have to know Lizzie. I mean, you put any problem in front of her, and she's like—" I waved my hand like I was holding a wand "—and it's done. I don't know how she does it."

"This isn't your average sort of—"

"I know, I know. That wasn't very persuasive, but…" I put my arm around his firm waist. He was wearing his pajamas. It seemed odd to me that a person who lived his whole life from a backpack would use some of that very limited space for pajamas. But a person has to be comfortable sometimes. And they were light and soft. Probably packed up small. They let me get a feel for his hip bone leaning against mine.

"What if we give her your fake name?" I said.

"How's she going to help if we don't even tell her what's wrong?"

"I can tell her…part of it. But not your real name, so she can't look you up. Fuck, I don't know." I leaned against his shoulder. "All I know is that Lizzie has fixed so many things for me. She's the only one I would trust with this. She's the only one I trust with anything. And I do trust her with anything."

He kissed my forehead and pulled me an inch closer.

"My friend Darrell—we've been friends since like fourth grade." His chest lifted and fell. "I would trust him with anything."

"Why don't you ask him for help?"

"Because he would try to help, but he wouldn't be able to do anything. And then he'd be in trouble too. He lives in that community. He's got kids. I don't know if DeVries's brother would go as far as actually hurting them, but he might."

"So the only people you'll let help you are the ones with nothing to lose. But that's nobody."

"True."

I turned so I was facing him, our bodies close, feet touching. "What if you don't have to actually meet Lizzie? She'll have deniability. She can say she didn't know anything about you. Just let me talk to her. I won't do it without your consent."

Dusk had turned to night. His eyes glinted in the light from a single lamp in the corner as he cradled my face in his hands.

"Okay. If you trust her, I trust her." He kissed my lips.

Relief flooded through me. Relief from the weight of this secret. I could ask for help. I could talk to one other single human being in the world about it, and that was enough. More than enough.

I whispered against his cheek. "Thank you."

He pulled me closer in, lifted my hair, and kissed my neck, breathing deeply, gently encircling my breast with his hand. I felt his erection growing and lifted it with my fingertips through those wonderful pajamas. Everything so warm and real.

He kissed my jaw and whispered gentle and low.

"I trust you."

17

I finally had to do a real shopping trip. We had been subsisting on convenience-store fare and takeout for several days, and I, for one, was ready for some regular food. So I got up early and went out before Lizzie came over. She was bringing bagels, but I would buy some fresh-squeezed orange juice. And then for that night, just Isaac and me, I would actually cook. There was something about cooking a meal that placed a flag in the ground. This is my home. These are my people.

I drove to the good market a couple of miles north of the house and bought T-bone steaks. Lila had a charcoal grill that hadn't been used in years. Isaac would love a steak, and he could show me how to light the coals. Beer. The local kind they didn't sell at the convenience store. I even put a bottle of prosecco in the cart for no good reason. Lizzie liked prosecco. Maybe she would go for mimosas with the bagels.

On the way home, I stopped at the hardware store and bought a circular saw. Looking at the box on the back seat as I pulled out of my parking spot, I almost wanted to put a bow on it. The first gift I'd bought for Isaac. But that would have drawn attention, and Isaac was like me in that making a production out of something only made him uncomfortable. Still, I was excited to carry it in. I would leave it in the front hall while I got the groceries and just tell him, *Hey, I got you something.*

I made the turn onto my street, pulled into my driveway, and carried the box and the bottle of prosecco to the front door.

The moment I stepped inside the house, I knew it was empty. Empty through and through. All its twenty-one rooms. I immediately scolded myself for such magical thinking, put down the box, rushed to the kitchen, and called Isaac's name. The house responded with silence. I held my breath. Nothing but air gliding from room to room.

"Isaac?"

I went to the maid's rooms. Empty. Made up as he left them every morning. As if no one's back had touched that mattress in fifty years. The window was closed. I searched the room, the kitchen, the hall, everywhere for a note or a message. Nothing. Nothing was different, except that everything was.

My body began to betray me. My muscles grew weak, my heartbeat irregular, and a hot heavy blanket of dread pulled at my neck and shoulders and burned down my skin. I checked the garage, then back through the house to the back porch. I stumbled down the stairs, dragged my feet through the dry leaves along the garden paths. My voice would no longer make a sound as I searched through the white oaks, silver maples, through the leggy azaleas, broken twigs, and fallen limbs. The garden breathed for me. Silent.

And yet I kept walking. Kept searching. I began to dissociate from the space around me, as if my body existed in a parallel universe to which I had access only through a kind of invisible control panel from far, far away.

I looked in the garden shed. I shoved open the back gate, pulling vines and weeds along the ground, and looked down toward the park.

My throat closed up, my body offered only two options: weep or suffocate. So I wept. And once I began, I was lost. Great, heaving, strangulating sobs like coughing up barbed wire, snagging, pulling, releasing. I dropped to my knees and gripped the long grass. I realized I wasn't actually looking for Isaac himself anymore. He was gone. All that I could look for now were his tracks.

Walking back to the house, I felt like a ghost in my own garden, wavering with every movement of air. Inside, all those rooms surrounded me like a great pile of empty boxes. Half-furnished, dusty, empty. I took the bottle of prosecco from the bag and made for Isaac's bed, where he had made love to me less than two hours ago.

I opened the bottle. If I drank, I could sleep. If I slept, I could escape.

The front door opened. Lizzie called my name. Then called again with greater urgency. I followed the sound of her foot-steps as they went upstairs, came back down at a run, then out into the garden. I tried to call out "I'm in here," but my voice was too faint. I got up and opened the window. She turned, ran inside, and in a moment threw open the bedroom door.

"What happened?" She sat on the bed and hauled me up into her arms. "It's okay, honey. It's okay. I'm here."

Those arms. The smell of her shampoo. A thousand times Lizzie had comforted me exactly like this. *It's okay, honey. It's okay.*

So many times I had been in this same arrangement of arms

and hair and cheeks. Knees bent up, and hands—mine gripped tight, Lizzie's stroking my back. It's okay. Whatever it was, it was okay. There could have been a nuclear holocaust outside the window and Lizzie would have put her arms around me and said, *It's okay.*

Words formed and struggled out of my throat.

I whispered, "There was someone."

"Who?"

I pressed my forehead hard into Lizzie's shoulder. A firm, stable bone. I rolled my brow back and forth against it.

"I loved him."

Lizzie's body softened, and she pulled me closer in.

"Oh, sweetheart. Meggie. Really?"

"Yes."

It was the only word I could say. Yes. Yes, I loved him. Yes. Yes. Yes, he loved me too. Yes, he was here. Yes, it was wonderful. Yes. Yes.

"And now he's gone."

"What happened?" Lizzie asked.

"I don't know."

Lizzie took a drink of the prosecco from the bottle, then lay down beside me, arranging my body and hers.

I released the story. Beginning to end. My mind was made by nature and trained by mathematics to be orderly and logical. To relate a sequence of events was no great challenge. Falling in love was linear. It was logical, even. Preliminary conditions: Isaac was hot. I was lonely. The one plus the other resulted in more complex but still rational sequelae: in spite of my genius and my anxiety, he was not afraid. He possessed both discernment and a high tolerance for deviation. Love was the easiest part of the story to explain.

The wanted-for-murder part I left out. He had given me

permission, said he trusted me. But his vanishing felt like a revocation of that trust.

Everything went adrift. There were too many non-primes. It was all big numbers with thousands of factors. They swam in my mind. The cruel grandmother, my proof, my father, the guy Isaac shot at, the smithy, the axe-head, eastern white pine, bats, steak, house, lawyer, prison, Kate, the broken leg, a life together. Which ones were important? Which ones canceled out?

I wanted so badly to lay it out in a logical string. Reduce it to one variable and then identify. Solve for x. But I couldn't do it. My mind wouldn't function under the crushing weight of his vacancy.

Lizzie got me to eat a little and helped me to bed up in the third-floor bedroom, just as we had so many times as children, padding back and forth to the bathroom in our socks. Only it was noon. But she had asked me what I needed, and I said I needed to go to sleep.

"Something must have happened," she said. "People don't just up and disappear like that."

The pragmatic way she persisted in being alive in spite of the absence of Isaac Wells set a good example. One I tried to follow.

She sat on the bed, knees tucked up. "There must be something we don't know about. Why would this be your fault? Don't think like that."

Something we don't know, indeed. But I couldn't tell her his secret. I wanted to, but the words wouldn't come out. I needed his permission with this secret, and now I wasn't sure about anything.

"I'm here for you," she said. "But I don't want to go barging around your life like I'm the boss. That wouldn't be fair. You're a grown woman."

"Thanks."

It was no small thing, having a woman like that in my corner. I hugged her and mumbled goodbye.

The veil began to fall. My thoughts grew gray and gauzy.

It was my fault. Somehow. It had to be. Why else does a person withdraw their love? I had done something. Or not done something. Failed at some test I didn't know I was taking.

I am thirteen years old, curled into a warm corner by the radiator. So absorbed in my book, I do not hide it quickly enough when my father approaches.

"What are you reading?"

"Nothing."

"Let me see." He holds out his hand, and I give him the book. He sniffs and looks at me with scorn. "A person of your intelligence. Why would you waste your time?"

He crosses the room and drops my book in the wastebasket with a metallic bang.

Met with my silence, he says, "No, seriously. Why? Are you still trying to be like the other girls?"

The worst offense: to want to be normal. The radiator clangs. I slide up the wall to stand. Direct cold eyes back at him and walk away. I do not retrieve the book, a novel, *A Wizard of Earthsea*. There would be no more reading that night. No more thinking. No more being.

Yes, I had been to this place before where cognition shut down. It was more like death than sleep. My body was just a body on a bed, doing the involuntary things bodies do, like breathe. There was no *I*. My consciousness recessed to a vanishing point, safe and infinitely far away.

★ ★ ★

It wasn't death, of course. Eventually a living body needs to pee. The room and the hall were dark when I rose and shuffled to the bathroom. I crept back into bed and lay there awhile, but though I resisted it, consciousness slowly revived, and I found myself fully awake and bored. The time on my phone was 3:12 a.m.

I wrapped myself in the blanket and dragged it with me to my study. I flipped on a lamp. There was my big red rug. My empty desk. The old sofa. I pushed open the balcony door that Isaac had fixed all those years ago, poking at my consciousness to see if I could feel anything. He had built the frame. Installed the latch. With his own hands.

No. Nothing.

Outside, the cold asserted itself, impossible not to register on my skin. The tops of the trees still held their leaves, but above, the sky was clear and black and full of stars. I had never seen so many stars in the city. Usually the lights from the street dimmed all but the brightest ones. But with no moon, dry air, at three in the morning, I could almost have been in the country.

It was impossible, knowing even rudimentary astrophysics, to look at a night sky like that and not feel a disoriented sense of wonder. To behold something so vast it could not fit inside a human mind, no matter how I tried. To look straight at something so fully incomprehensible wasn't a happy kind of wonder, though. It spooked me a little, and I couldn't bear it for long before I pulled the blanket tighter and went inside, closing and latching Isaac's door behind me.

I stared at my board, standing alert and at ease in the middle of the room.

Dissociation. That's what my psychiatrists called it, and I had been here before, operating my own body as if I were an engineer running a sophisticated machine. Input came in from the outside and was processed to produce a response. It was the complete triumph of the mind. Feelings—even sensations— were easily dismissed.

Again, I took inventory. Assets: my mind, the notes on my board, a roof over my head. Liabilities: anxiety, inability to present, my father. In the absence of all that turbulent emotion—in the absence of Isaac—my mind returned to its familiar patterns. To claim credit for my proof, I had to *have* a proof.

I pulled a fresh spiral notebook from my shelf, sharpened a pencil, and pulled Fenty's *Discourses* from its box. I had done the Impossible once—I could do it again.

Among the many advantages of dissociation, I did not need to eat. Working from memory, I reconstructed the opening of the proof. That part was easy. I had done it a hundred times over the years. It was always the middle that was the problem. Around six in the evening I got tired and slept. Waking at ten at night, I worked some more and made more progress than I expected.

Sometimes I pried at the idea of loss. When I went downstairs for coffee, I even looked into the maid's quarters. It elicited no feeling. Or, possibly not nothing—just a vague sense that something ought to matter. That there was more of a void in that one place than I was entirely comfortable with. It had its own gravity, and I didn't like it. Didn't want to get too near.

Lizzie called the next day. Or was it the third day? Time wasn't relevant. No one cared when or where I did my work, ate my meals, breathed my breaths, so I did them whenever and wherever I felt like it.

"Are you okay? Have you heard anything?" she said.

"I'm fine. Anything about what?"

She paused. "About Isaac."

"Oh. No." I worked my earbud in and put my phone down on the desk.

"Meg?"

"What." I only half paid attention.

She sighed. She knew. "Are you eating?"

"Um…"

"Go get something to eat."

I was trying to remember the part about a third of the way into the proof. It was right there, but I couldn't focus if I was on the phone.

Lizzie pulled my attention back. "Are you going to get some food?"

"All right." It wasn't worth arguing. "I'm going now."

"I'll be there tomorrow."

I snapped on the overhead light in the kitchen. Got a piece of bread and chewed on it for a while before I decided it would be better with some butter. Poured water from the tap. Snapped off the light. Eating done.

As I crossed the foyer to the main stairs, something caught my eye on the table by the door. A book. Black. Thick. Coming closer, a library book. *The Blacksmith's Companion*. I carried it upstairs with me. Sitting on my sofa, I opened the book. It began with a short glossary.

Creep: This is the slow yielding of metals under a load. This yielding may take months or years as in furnace and steam boiler parts. Creep takes place more often at high temperatures, but soft metals such as lead, tin, and zinc suffer from creep at room temperatures. The lead sheets on church roofs thicken toward the eaves.

I slouched against the back cushions and continued to browse.

Ductility: The property which enables a metal to withstand mechanical deformation without cracking, particularly when being stretched.

Shear Strength: The ability of a metal to withstand the action of two parallel forces acting in opposite directions.

Interesting. Pragmatic. The pages were thick but brittle. The light quickly grew dim. Must be a storm bringing in clouds. Would have to turn on the lights. I felt a lump under my hip. I shifted over and felt between the cushions for it.

A shirt. Flannel. Worn and crumpled. I shook out the wrinkles. Isaac's shirt.

It smelled like him. No one thing in the entire world smelled exactly like that except him, and with the second breath of his scent something crimped down tight in my chest.

No, no, no. No.

It led to so many things. Beautiful things. Pleasurable things. Sweet, funny, day-to-day things. He was gone. It was my fault.

I folded the shirt and took it to my bedroom, where I hung it in the closet. Then I readied my bed to sleep in. If I could get to sleep... Who knew what time it was? Who cared? But the narrow end of the wedge was in. After lying in bed awake for who knows how long, I rose, took the shirt from the closet, then climbed back under the covers. Holding it to my face, I breathed deep. A button brushed my cheek. My breath came fast and light as I touched between my legs and, closing my eyes, it was almost as if I could have reached out and found him there. I could feel his upper arm, his rough jaw. I gripped the shirt in my fist, and my own naked longing startled me back into life.

I lay there for a long time, eyes wide open in the dark.

18

Early the next morning, before it was fully light and before I
even got out of bed, I made a TikTok.

Come back.

That was as far as I could get without crying, so I stopped
and saved it as a draft. Crying wasn't going to help anything.
I sat up, wiped my face, and called Lizzie. She was at work so
I left a message.

"I need help, Liz."

Six o'clock. I had been dissociated for about forty-eight
hours. That was better than the first time it happened, when
it lasted for four days, but still there was always a recovery pe-
riod when I came back. A kind of hangover—my head cloudy,
thoughts sluggish, my body still not feeling quite real.

Dressed again in my softest, grayest clothes, I went to my
study. Not quite ready to look at my proof, I tried another video.

"Please come back, Isaac. I miss you. I can't do this without
you. Whatever happened, I don't care. I only want you back."

That, too, went into the drafts folder. I didn't know what
I wanted to say, and that was the problem.

I'm not sure why I hadn't set myself up to make coffee in my study in all the fifteen years I'd been at Lila's. Sometimes it was the only thing that got me to go downstairs. Then again, when she was alive, it was something we shared. The ritual of preparation in the creaky old kitchen reminded me of her.

A cold rain tapped against the windows. Birds fluttered to a low dogwood branch where a feeder dangled, empty. I would have to fill it. Poor hungry things.

He was out there somewhere. Maybe hungry. Definitely in pain. That knee was never going to heal right. My thoughts rattled around like a loose wheel. It was my fault because I had pressed him about Lizzie. No, he was out there violating postulate three, thinking he was doing the right thing. No, he had lied to me, didn't love me. No, something terrible must have happened—DeVries's brother. No, it was my fault.

I searched the internet, looking for some sign that he had been picked up by the police. Nothing. And all the while that loose wheel cranked away, somehow always coming back to my fault, my fault, my fault. I wanted him back so badly it physically hurt, right in my stomach, like hunger.

I didn't feel like eating, but I did anyway. Part of me didn't feel like doing anything, but I took my coffee and toast to the parlor and found my notes. Under the large figure that I estimated for legal fees, I had made a list of names. Now it was time to make phone calls. I hated making phone calls, but I hated almost anything less than the gnawing pain and that rattling, rattling wheel.

Lizzie came after work. Once she looked me over and ascertained that I was not in any of a half-dozen possible states of crisis, she relaxed her shoulders and kicked off her shoes.

"I ordered Thai. It should be here in a couple of minutes."
I was trying so hard to do and say the things that a normal
person would do and say. "How was work?"

"We delivered twins." She smiled. "I love multiples. We
had them in the same bassinet—we're not supposed to do that,
but it was only for a minute—and the one is rooting around
and he finds his brother's nose and starts trying to nurse on
it. It was so freaking cute."

That was my Lizzie. Disarming, funny, and not afraid to
shed a little sunshine into the darkest corners.

Our dinner arrived, and I unpacked it on the counter. Lizzie
was a grounding presence, and with her there, the postdisso-
ciation fog burned off more quickly.

I spooned green curry into a bowl. "Will you help me pick
a lawyer?"

Lizzie looked up, eyes bright. "To sue Uncle Henry?"

"Maybe that too, eventually. But no." I took a deep breath.
It was a risk, but I needed help. "Isaac is wanted for murder."

Lizzie set her fork down on her plate without even a clink,
eyes wide. "Please keep talking because you're kind of freaking me out."

I told her the whole story, exactly as he told it to me. No
embellishment, nothing left out. In that moment I suddenly
understood how that secret had distorted my world. As the
distortion cleared, I began to see it through Lizzie's eyes. A
problem to be solved. A very big, very serious problem, but
one of normal, real-world dimensions.

"That's why he left," Lizzie said. "I knew something didn't
seem right."

"I'm sorry. I should have told you."

"No. Whatever. But that's why. Someone probably came to

the door, and he got spooked. Or maybe it was even the cops. He had to run. He didn't have time for a note or anything."

It all sounded so rational when she said it. Everything always did. She had a mind that went to the rational place first. Not the most painful, most frightening one. Still, mine was the mind I had to live in, and it didn't tell me he'd had to leave. It told me he wanted to. I picked at my food.

"You don't have any way to contact him?" Lizzie said.

"He never let me have his number. And I don't think he even has an email. He deleted his social-media accounts when he went on the run. So no. Except for my TikTok videos."

Lizzie jumped like I had poked her with a stick.

"TikTok videos? You've been making TikTok videos?" She slapped both hands on the table and leaned toward me. "Who are you? And what have you done with my cousin?"

"Isaac made them on my phone," I said. "I just talked about math, and he did all the other stuff."

"Meg. He's going to be watching your account."

"Maybe. I don't know. I don't even know what to say."

"You say 'Get the fuck back here, you idiot. I'm hiring a badass lawyer.'" She shook her head, seeming almost irritated. "Okay, I know that's not quite your style. But don't waste time agonizing over it, okay? He could be in trouble."

"What if he's not? What if he doesn't want to come back?"

Lizzie stared at me. "Do you hear yourself? Jesus Christ. If everything you told me is true, which I know it is, then he has zero reason to leave you and every reason to run from what either might have been or what he thinks might have been the police. Be rational."

I dropped my fork, and it clanged on the table. "I'm trying."

"Good. Keep trying, because right now you're being ridiculous."

"What if he thinks it's better for me that he left?"

"Then make a fucking TikTok and tell him it isn't."

Lizzie angry wasn't a thing I'd seen much in my life. At least not since we were kids.

She finally attended to her meal again, twisting up a forkful of noodles. "So this is why you've been ghosting me."

"I'm sorry."

"You've got to trust me. When have I ever not had your back?"

I looked for a quick retort, but she was right. We may have fought as children. We may have had an issue or two over the years, but bring a third person into the mix, and Lizzie was always, always on my side.

I poured her another glass of wine.

"Make a video and post it," she said. "Tell him you want him back."

"Okay. I'll try."

"Do or do not—"

"There is no try. I know, I know."

"Also, I thought of a job for you." She pointed her glass at me. "Tutoring. Online."

She pulled up a site on her phone and passed it over to me. The pay for a tutor with a doctorate wasn't awful.

"Low commitment," she said. "Totally freelance. Work when you want to, and not when you don't."

So many times I had wished I could bottle up her pragmatic optimism. I would have taken it daily.

Over the next week, I regrouped. Sleep was not my friend, and mornings found me scared and unstable. But if I spent an hour in the garden hacking down vines and hauling dead branches into a pile, the sweat and dirt and scratches on my arms pulled me back into the real world and held me there long enough that I began to feel I belonged. After a shower and putting on makeup and a decent shirt for my first tutoring session, I stared at my TikTok account: 412 followers. I figured that wasn't bad for the handful of videos we had posted. But now I was performing for an audience of one, and he didn't even have an account.

"I won't use your name. You know who you are. I don't know why you left, and I'm trying so hard not to think it was my fault. And I'm so worried about you. I love you. I miss you. There has to be a way."

No. This one went in the drafts folder too. None of it felt right. It was all me, me, me. And I didn't even have a lawyer yet, though Lizzie and I had scheduled a call.

Finally returning to my inbox, I found the early responses to the emails I had sent about Frieholdt's, as well as several that had come through in the days since. The *Journal of Number Theory* said they were holding publication for review and would contact me. The Beckett Institute said essentially the same thing. And Anne MacFaull said something I didn't quite understand in corporate-ese about pending contracts on hold. I took it to mean they weren't going to pay my father to consult until this cleared up. I had succeeded in gumming up the works, at least.

The tutoring site had come back to me with a list of potential students that was longer than I expected. Most in high school, some in college. I didn't care. I would teach Algebra 1, I would teach addition to a five-year-old, as long as they paid me the PhD rate.

My first session went reasonably well. My student was nerdy and awkward, doing math three years above his grade level. I felt for him. Back when I was his age, the further ahead I got, the more people looked at me funny and wondered why I was so *different*. As I closed the browser window, I felt a tiny grain of solid ground under my feet that hadn't been there before. Maybe I could do this. And being in this slightly stronger place, I checked the math message boards. I couldn't afford to ignore them, but they were too charged to browse without thinking.

A few threads about a breakthrough proof in algebraic geometry which I clicked past. I used to read everything. It was all so interesting. But now I mined through the forums for one thing and one thing only.

There. Someone posted anonymously about the *Journal of Number Theory* pulling the Frieholdt's proof. The responses were skeptical.

brightwood family drama? i thought we were over that.

is margaret brightwood even active anymore? she hasn't published in ten years.

meg brightwood could run circles around her father. you all know that. why do you think it's any different now?

I shifted in my seat. That one was gratifying.

why don't they post it on arxiv? let us all review it. what's the big secret?

I stopped. Why not? My father was doing whatever he wanted with it, but for some reason he had not posted it in the one place where serious mathematicians shared their work.

The habit of secrecy had been with me so long, I hadn't even thought of it.

Why not?

The only reason I could think of that he didn't post it there was that, just like I had been, he was afraid of plagiarism. He wanted credit.

But now *I* could post it. I had already lost control. If I finished reconstructing it, I could post it. Then whose proof would it be?

I went to the website of the American Mathematical Society, thinking I was almost done for the day, and there I saw this:

Dr. Henry Brightwood, Professor Emeritus of Mathematics at Georgetown University, to present a complete proof of Frieholdt's Conjecture at a special session sponsored by the Distinguished Alumni. Healy Hall, Georgetown University, October 25, 2 p.m.

My neck shivered and grew stiff, and my breath crowded the tops of my lungs.

Two weeks. It had taken me twenty years to solve Frieholdt's. Now I had two weeks to rebuild it from memory. My heart stumbled, caught itself, and stumbled again.

Fuck. No.

My father would be right in the comfortable center of his power, in that big stone building, in that hall, where everyone thought he walked on water.

My skin flushed burning hot.

I felt it coming. The freeze. The flight. Then the inevitable collapse into depression and isolation. It was exhausting. I stood. No. Not again. I was so tired of this shit.

I fought it. Pacing, shaking out my fingers. What did my therapist used to say? What was I supposed to do? Why hadn't

I been to see her? How long had it been? Jesus, fuck—what was wrong with me? Did I really think I could hide out the rest of my life with nothing but math and benzodiazepines to get me by?

What did she used to say? What was the rescue remedy?

I remembered. I could almost hear her voice.

A quick state change.

I ran out of the room and down the stairs, but it wasn't enough. I needed to get outside, but when I got to the foyer, I confronted the circular saw. The box on the floor, pushed to the side. I had been purposely not-seeing it, but now it assaulted me. A visceral reminder of what I had lost. Not just my proof. Not just my career. But the one love of my life.

No. I would not fall to my knees. I would not crouch until I dropped into a half sleep. Not this time. This one time would be different. This one time, I found myself perched on a tiny hill built from small victories, decent sleep, and good sex. This time I would fight it.

What else did my therapist say?

Exercise.

I nearly ran out of the house that second, but it did occur to me that if anyone saw me outside, running in full makeup, a dress shirt, and no shoes, they would probably call the cops. So I dashed back to my room, changed my shirt and put on sneakers. I took the stairs down by twos and threes.

Cool. Sunny. Dry leaves under my feet. I hadn't been running in who knows how long, and my body felt jerky, my gait slow and uncoordinated. But I ran. Down the block to where a trailhead dipped into the park. I stumbled over a root, caught myself. And good god, it was beautiful. Sun pouring through the autumn leaves, a sparkle on the creek.

Even if I were sitting still, my heart would be pounding from anxiety. My cheeks would be flushed, my breathing heavy. Even if I were on my knees, as still as a turtle in its shell. At least out here all that effort could be good for something.

The trail reached the paved path that ran along the creek. Another runner passed me, nodding, as if I was doing the most ordinary thing in the world, and I wanted to shout, *No, look at this! This is extraordinary. This is different.*

My lungs burned, my knees ached, my bra dug into my ribs. Absolutely the wrong bra. I touched a fingertip to my cheek, and it came away black from my eye makeup. I almost laughed at how ridiculous I must look to these appropriately dressed fitness enthusiasts out for a run on a brisk fall afternoon. A woman, no longer young, with jiggly parts improperly supported, running like a toddler.

I did laugh. At myself. At everything. That's right, motherfucker, I thought. You might be on mile twenty of a marathon, but what I'm doing is a hundred times harder.

Then again, who knew? Maybe that guy with the cap and sunglasses and perfect stride who smiled as we passed—maybe he struggled too. Maybe he had cancer or a heartbreaking divorce. Maybe I wasn't alone.

At a spot where the creek came close to the path, I stopped, stumbled down the rocky bank, and splashed water on my face. I'm sure it was polluted with any number of urban toxins, but it felt like heaven. With my sleeve I wiped the mess off my face as best I could, and with the clarity of cold water I realized it was probably time to turn back.

The run home was less desperate, but no less driven. I could have walked up the steep trail that led from the paved path to my street, but I didn't. I ran. I forced myself to run, muscles burning, grunting and gasping until my body had forgotten whether this was a panic attack or just a desperate attempt to stay on its feet.

The last block, I at last slowed to a walk, twisting my torso in the torture chamber that was my bra.

I had to have a decent sports bra somewhere. This was ridiculous.

In the foyer, I laid eyes on the circular saw again and took out my phone, sweaty face, smeared makeup, and all.

"I've got a call with a lawyer," I said to the camera. "We're going to get you cleared. It was self-defense. This can work. I swear it can. You deserve to be free. You have worked hard and tried hard, and you deserve freedom and happiness. Please let me find you."

I watched my own video as my heart rate slowly dropped.

Closer, but still not there. I wasn't sure what I was after. With all of the videos that had gone into my drafts folder, I could imagine Isaac watching. He would be struggling with postulate three, I was sure. He would be thinking of the danger to me, the danger to Kate, how no one would support his mom if he came forward. And he would be thinking that he wasn't worthy. That all the shitty things he had been told all his life were true and everyone was better off without him.

If only, if only he was okay. I had to find a way to get through.

I struggled with postulate three myself. I wanted to track him down. To track down Kate. To take charge and impose my version of what was right.

As I walked back to the kitchen for a drink of water, I felt a whisper of exultation. I beat it. This one time, I didn't succumb.

My next thought was *Now call your therapist.*

★ ★ ★

That night was the first really decent night's sleep I'd had since Isaac disappeared. The next morning I took a long, hot shower. Back in my robe, I checked the tutoring site. There were more than twenty requests. I would have to turn some down.

I was dressed by the time Lizzie arrived for the call with the lawyer. She was dressed for work, take-out coffee in hand.

"You look better," she said as she walked in and kicked off her shoes in the hall. She spotted the circular saw. Confused at first, then understanding registered in her eyes. "Should we put this in the garage?"

I hadn't wanted to touch it. But today it didn't feel as charged. More of a friend than a tormentor.

"No. Just leave it."

We put in earbuds and sat at the kitchen table on a three-way call. The lawyer, Erin O'Keefe, was a friend of a client of Lizzie's. Sometimes I thought everyone in the world was a friend of a client of Lizzie's. When a person is as extroverted as she, the network gets very big. And when your network is the wealthy and well-connected childbearing women of Washington, DC, those people do not mess around.

I had never hired a lawyer before, and though she made almost no small talk, she was warmer and more human than I expected her to be. She asked pointed questions, some of which I could answer and some of which I could not, and questions which surprised me. What was Isaac like? Did he have family to support? What would his employers say about him?

She explained some things. Juvenile record, not important. A long record of hard work and supporting his mother would make him a sympathetic defendant. The sister wouldn't make it a slam dunk but would definitely help. Likewise the truck. We would need all available tools.

Her retainer alone would erase one-fifth of my bank account, but I did it without hesitation.

Lizzie hugged me as she left for work.

"I made an appointment with my therapist," I said.

"Good girl." She kissed my cheek. "Now, how about getting your meds sorted out?"

I sighed and rolled my eyes. "I know. I'm getting there."

Tutoring turned out to be the perfect work. The students were like me—advanced thinkers, hungry, and nervous. It wasn't the first time I'd thought of doing it, but I'd always thought it would be torture. A lineup of overprivileged, entitled mediocrity. It was anything but. And if I didn't like one of them—which hadn't happened yet—I could just say It's not a good fit and cancel. It felt good. Productive. And seeing the numbers in my bank account go up instead of always down was going to be nice.

Full makeup and two sessions later, I stood staring at my board. Nearly the first half of the Impossible Theorem lay on loose-leaf paper, spread out on my desk. When I'd solved it in the spring, this part had come through so clearly, but now the crucial pivot in the middle seemed obscured. Like trying to see through a glass that would not get clean no matter how hard I scrubbed at it.

I pulled the armchair into the center of the room, scraping its old legs over the floor, then sat and tucked up my legs. Maybe it was fatigue, mental, physical, emotional. All were present from my exertion over the last few days, but at that moment when I thought of Isaac it wasn't with fear; it was with only the most normal, familiar feeling. I just wanted to talk to him.

Holding up my phone I started the video, showing him the board, panning from one side to the other.

"I'm working again. Trying to rebuild this thing, but I'm a little stuck right now." I turned the camera back to my face. "We've got a lawyer. She's a badass and thinks you'll be a sympathetic defendant. She says the juvenile stuff doesn't matter. I've got her on retainer. And I went running. I'm going to go to my therapist, and maybe even my psychiatrist. It's all stuff I should have done years ago, but I was stuck. And it's all for you. I mean, it's for me, but it's because of you. It's because you made me believe…"

I hit Pause, unsure of what came next. Bogged down as I was with the proof, a year ago I would have turned on myself. Berated and talked down to myself. A year ago I would have thought, *If you can't do this, then what are you good for?* It wasn't that such feelings were gone. But they weren't the only ones anymore.

"It's because you made me believe that you love me—and that I mattered. And that it didn't matter whether I had solved Frieholdt's. It didn't matter whether I had a job. It didn't even matter if I went to my psychiatrist. Not that those weren't all good things, and maybe things I should do. But I didn't have to *do* anything."

Stop. Save as draft.

As long as I could remember, crying had been painful and bitter—the only way to release unbearable amounts of stress. But as I sat in that armchair, hands loose in my lap, tears rolled down my cheeks and splashed on my wrists in a cleansing flood, as if some force was flushing the blight from inside of my brain. These weren't tears that made me clutch my fists and drive them into my eye sockets, or kneel, or hold my head as if it would explode. My muscles draped over my bones, relaxed and pliable, my head dropped back.

And it didn't last long either. I dried my eyes on the corner of the throw blanket. It was over for now, but I knew these tears would be back. They needed to come back. There would be more cleaning out before I was done.

I stood and collected *Discourses* from my desk, then climbed into the chair again. This time I let my mind wander gently, slowly through the winding paths. I didn't seek that bright, straight rail, though I knew I'd have to find it eventually. The beauty of the Loading Hypothesis and Frieholdt's Conjecture made a sort of dance in my untethered consciousness. I saw a hundred ways it was all likely to work. But *likely* is not what mathematics is after. We deal, in the end, in absolute certainty.

But if certainty is all one seeks, it will be a hard road, and not one that is likely to lead to anything new. One must seek ambiguity, fluidity, release.

I rose and went to the front windows, looking out at the big house across the street. The crew was hard at work on the windows. Maybe trying to get it sealed up before winter. The foreman who had come to my door that day could be a character witness, I thought. I'd have to tell Erin.

The light from outside made my freckles stand out on the phone camera. My eyes were still red-rimmed and a little puffy, and my voice, though strong, felt tired and raw.

I hit Record.

"Five people may see this video, or a million. But I only care about one. I'm talking to one person. You know who you are.

"I want you to know that you are enough. You are worthy of love and happiness exactly as you are right now.

"It was wrong, what they said to you and did to you. All the times you should have gotten love, all the times they *said* it was because they loved you, but it really only caused you pain. It was wrong, and it wasn't your fault. But you know what's also wrong? Holding on to it and letting it control you now. Letting it stop you from finding happiness.

"I know it's hard. All those feelings are still there. All the ones you didn't get to feel when they actually happened because it wasn't safe. You weren't safe. You were a kid, and you did what you could to get through it.

"They didn't care what you wanted or how you felt. They said, *You are who I say you are.* And yes, when you're a kid, it's so hard to fight.

"I couldn't fight it, and I didn't. But that was then. That's in the past.

"Listen to me. Please, please, listen. As much as it feels like it's still with us, it's not. Now we get to choose. We get to say who we are. So I challenge postulates one and two. You are not a fuckup. And I am not a head case. We are human beings, worthy of love." I gazed out the window and began to lose my sureness.

"Maybe I'm just talking to myself," I said. "Maybe you're not even there."

Pause. This was my last one. I couldn't stop. It was all I had. *Record.*

"But I am not violating postulate three. I desperately want you back. I have a lawyer on retainer, and she thinks we have a case. If you come back—if you *want* to come back—I will do everything I can to keep you safe and get you free. And if you don't…" I took a breath, dried my eyes "…you are in charge of what you want. Not me. I love you right now, exactly as you are, and I always will."

This one was not a draft. This one was for keeps.

19

The few comments people left on my math posts had never interested me, but for this post, I read every single one. Within twenty-four hours it had been viewed more than fifty thousand times, and there were hundreds of comments.

Thank you.

You may be talking to one person, but all of us hear you.

Beautiful. I needed to hear this.

I hope you find him.

you r a fuckin freak. is that a rash?

And more—better, worse, some heartbreaking, some incoherent. So many crying-face emojis. I scrolled through them all. For the first few hundred, my adrenaline surged, but as the numbers mounted with no reward, it became routine.

Lizzie called in the afternoon. "That post is going viral. I mean, crying on TikTok? Since when did you become the social-media expert?"

"Since never." I laughed. "I didn't know crying on Tik-Tok was a thing."

"It's totally a thing," she said. "If this doesn't reach him, nothing will."

"That's what I'm afraid of."

"You're up to three hundred thousand followers." Her voice distorted. Probably wind. Or traffic. She was walking from work. "But I didn't mean it like that. If this doesn't reach him, something else will. We'll hire a PI. We'll make this happen."

It became a full-time job, digging through the comments. Digging through my direct messages. A baffling job that made no sense to me, but it didn't matter. I wasn't there to interpret people's motives or plumb the zeitgeist of the age. I was there for one thing—a message from Isaac. Sleep found me that night before anything else of value did.

The next morning, before getting out of bed, I opened up my phone. 1.6 million views. Thousands of comments. Hundreds of direct messages. Some so beautiful. Some so ugly. Even with my training, my attention to detail, my ability to filter out insignificant data, it was nearly overwhelming. I brought everything I had to bear, combing through the comments and messages, but still—what if I missed something? I shuffled to the kitchen, still scrolling, made coffee, shuffled back toward my room.

Halfway up the narrow back stairs, scrolling my direct messages, I froze.

woodwitch6594: where are you? and where is my brother?

I stopped breathing, hand to mouth. It couldn't be. Farther down, another one.

woodwitch6594: Please, please, please. I remember you. I don't mean to sound stalker-y, but I can almost remember where you live. I used to drive him to your house when his bike broke down. It was a long time ago. Please contact me.

And there was an email address, written-out so it couldn't be picked up by bots. Barely breathing, I went to the TikTok account of woodwitch6594.

About my age. Dyed blond hair with dark roots growing out. Her videos left no doubt in my mind. The way she cocked her head. The twitch of her eyebrows. The accent. She didn't look much like him, but she moved like him. She talked like him. I swiped from one to another to another. It was like seeing his shadow.

This was Kate. There was no question. I remembered her, and it looked like the intervening years had been hard.

Putting my coffee mug on the stair, I emailed her. I didn't send anything. Just my address. She emailed me back within minutes with her phone number and the name Kate Wells.

I texted her. He told me not to bring you into it. I promised.

Then my phone rang. My actual phone, which I had to choose to answer or not. Of course, I did.

"Meg Brightwood?" Her voice was hoarse, like she had been crying.

"Yes." I gripped my phone like a lifeline, terrified she might vanish.

"Oh, thank god. What happened? Is he all right?"

Kate pulled up to my house alone in an unremarkable but new-looking sedan. She sat a minute, and I watched her a minute before she got out and walked purposefully toward the house. I opened the door before she reached it, and we both stopped, three paces apart, and just stared for a second, unsure of what to do.

She was shorter than I had expected and looked older in person than she did on camera, hair pulled into a tight pony-tail, wire-rimmed glasses.

"I remember you," I said.

"I remember you too."

I was anxious, but she was—something else. I couldn't place it. She stepped forward. Stopped. Then stepped forward again and hugged me. After a moment of startle, I hugged her back. She felt wiry and tough, kind of like Isaac, and familiar, even though we'd seen each other so briefly, so long ago.

"Is he okay?" she said.

"I don't know. He left eleven days ago. I haven't heard anything since."

She let go and stepped back again, as if embarrassed. "I'm sorry—"

"It's okay."

"I'm just so glad it was you."

The big, deep front porch made for a comparatively personal space, without me having to invite her in before I was ready.

"You're glad what was me?"

"That he came to you. I mean, it took him long enough." A sisterly roll of the eyes. "But that he finally came back. That he picked you."

I took a deep breath. "He didn't, exactly. He kind of tried not to."

She had deep creases in her forehead. Regretful ones. "Meg, please tell me everything. I haven't heard anything since the day he rescued me, and I've been so worried about him."

It occurred to me to mistrust her. Isaac had mistrusted her, in his way. Not Kate herself, but her addiction. But what did

I have to tell? Nothing that would compromise him any more than he already was.

"Can I take a stab at what you're thinking?" Kate said.

"Go ahead."

"You don't know me, and you don't trust me."

"Sort of. I'm sorry."

"I know. I'm used to that look, and I don't blame you. All I can do is try." She took out her wallet and showed me her driver's license. "No, please. Look at it. I want you to be sure. I'm Kate Allison Wells. I live in Philadelphia now. I'm in school for social work. I haven't taken drugs for seven months. Except for cigarettes—I know, it's awful, and I'm going to quit those too. I haven't been in contact with any of Danny's people since the day I left, and I never will be again if I can help it. There's a guy I'm seeing in Philly, but it hasn't been very long, and nobody knows about Isaac or what happened. I have been totally silent. You don't have to tell me anything you don't want to. I'll stand right here, or go away, or do whatever you tell me to do. It's just... Isaac is all the family I have. He saved my life when he got me away from Danny, and I'm scared for him. I miss him."

I had thought I was the one who needed Kate. Clearly she felt just as strongly that she needed me.

"Why don't you come in."

Kate looked up and turned in a circle in the foyer. "This place is amazing. I never got to come inside before."

"It's beautiful." I led her back to the kitchen. "Much too big, of course."

She walked slowly through the dining room and the parlor as I made coffee, then we went out back. Sun shone through the red and gold leaves while squirrels skittered from branch to branch and in spirals up the tall gray trunks.

"See that little birdhouse?" I pointed to the trunk of the nearest maple.

Kate nodded.

"Isaac put that up, back when he worked for Lila. It's about a couple of feet higher now than it was then."

Kate sat cross-legged on the sagging couch. In profile, she looked even more like Isaac.

"He told me about you back then." She looked out into the garden, cradling her coffee mug close to her face. "About how smart and pretty you were and all that. He kind of went on and on about it for a while. I remember, we'd be getting up in the morning—I was trying to get through nursing school at the time—and he'd be getting ready for work like he was getting ready for a date. You know, everything clean. Showered and shaved."

I listened in rapt attention.

"And I was finally like, 'Why don't you say something to her?' I remember, he laughed at me and said, 'There's no way, Kate. No fucking way.'" She sipped her coffee. "Did you know? Did he ever say anything?"

"He never said anything. Not until the day he left, and even then he just said, 'I'll miss you.' But I knew. We both knew."

Kate looked at me, her brown eyes deep and serious. "You should know—you probably do know—our grandmother, who raised us, was a terrible, cruel person. She made it her mission in life to make sure we hated ourselves as much as she hated herself. That's what I meant when I said I was so glad he came back to you. If Isaac could believe for one second that he deserved you—"

"You don't even know me. I might be a horrible person too."

Kate laughed. "Yeah, no. I mean, I already knew from all the things he told me back then. But I can take one look at you—and also your video—no, you're a good person. It was only a matter of time before the ghost of our grandmother caught up with him. There's no way he could bear to be loved that much."

A knot formed in my throat. "He didn't come back to me. It was an accident. Well, mostly an accident."

I told her the whole story, from the fight in the street to the day I came home with the circular saw. She asked a few questions, shed a few tears, but mostly listened fiercely, eyes fixed on me.

"We had a deal," I said, finally slowing down. "My whole life, other people have decided what was right for me. What was good for me. And same for him. The only way I got him to stay in the first place was by refusing to let him decide that leaving was better for me. And by promising that I won't decide what's good for him. I can't do something for him that he doesn't want just because I think it's right. And he flat out refused to ask you for help."

Kate put her hand on my arm. "That's beautiful. If everyone lived that way, the world would be a better place."

"So I can't ask you for help," I said.

"Meg, one—you didn't ask me for anything. I showed up here all on my own. And two—that's a lovely philosophy, but this is my only brother we're talking about, and if I know him at all, which I do, he has gone down a deep, dark hole that our grandmother dug for him, and he can't get out by himself. You do what you need to do. But I am going in after him. What day is it?"

"October fifteenth. What are you going to do?"

Her eyes lit up. "Perfect. Give me your phone. I want to make a TikTok on your account."

I opened the app and handed it over.

"I promise I won't hit Post unless you say okay." She looked at the screen and smoothed down a few stray strands of hair. "You don't have to be in this one. In fact, it's probably better if you're not."

"He'll recognize the porch, I think."

"That's fine." Kate tapped Record. Her tone changed from warm and questioning to a firm and directive. "Jesus, I know you're watching. Meet us at the Good Place on Muddy's birthday. That is all I have to say."

She hit Stop and looked at me.

"That's it?" I said. "What did that mean?"

She smiled. Her eyebrows so much like his, letting me in on a secret.

"The Good Place is Uncle Kimmo's cabin," she said. "Muddy was a bullfrog we found there once when we were kids. We threw him this ridiculous birthday party on October seventeenth. Even Kimmo got into it. He went down to town and bought us sparklers and hot chocolate. Probably because we never got birthday parties. Anyway, for years after we used to send each other messages on Muddy's birthday. He'll know."

"Well, that's convenient. That it's this weekend."

Kate sighed. "We had twenty different special occasions that we made up over the years. Grandmother never celebrated anything with us, so we had to kind of make do."

Birds fluttered to the empty feeder hanging at the other end of the porch. Sweet little things. Bright yellow ones, brown ones with white breasts. I would have to feed them. And learn their names too.

"Where are you staying?" I asked.

She shrugged and sat up, as if taking it as a signal to leave. "I figured I'd just drive back. It's not that far."

I waved her to sit. "Why don't you stay here? There's clearly plenty of room."

That night I shuffled in circles around my study, scrolling through the comments and messages on my post. There were some on Kate's post too—people were following this now—but not as many. I still read through all of them, unable to sleep. Nothing. Nothing at all that seemed remotely like it could be him.

I scoured my list of bookmarked sites—the papers local to Blind Fork, the local police, the crime pages. Nothing. The thought that I might actually find him stirred up the visceral fear I had been trying so hard to keep down. He said Danny DeVries had a brother. A brother that could have found him. The absence of news could mean he was safe, or it could mean he was dead.

Kate seemed so sure that we would see Isaac in one piece at the cabin the day after tomorrow. I was anything but sure and scared to my core that we would see his name in the newspaper at last.

As the hours of night passed, my attention wandered, and I put down my phone. It was a fluid, past-midnight state of mind, my heart weary, hands restless. The figures and diagrams on my board seemed to float free of the surface and rearrange themselves. I sat on the floor and covered my lap with the blanket. *Discourses on the Loading Hypothesis* lay within reach, and I picked it up, turning to the page near the end which had drawn me in ever since I lost the proof. It pulled my mind away from the reeling thoughts of Isaac.

There was no controlling my father. I couldn't stop him. I had done everything I could. And there was only money enough for one lawyer. That money would go to Erin O'Keefe and to Isaac's freedom, not to some intellectual-property claim on a proof no one had ever heard of.

But if I could reconstruct it—get the proof back in my hands by rebuilding it from scratch—then I would have more options. I could at least confuse the issue. If my father had the only copy of the proof, then he could dismiss me as a failure at best, and a fraud at worst. But if I could produce my own, then the *Journal of Number Theory*, the Beckett Institute, Anne MacFaull, and the fucking Distinguished Alumni of Georgetown University would all have to ask themselves, *How is it possible that they both have it, yet Meg Brightwood is claiming sole authorship?* It wasn't much, but it wasn't nothing. And I had less than two weeks in which to do it.

My attention moved from book to board and back, like a child on a playground swing.

It had been so clear before. I remembered that bright rail which shot me straight through to the end, but now all I could find were paths forking and winding, leading to nowhere, or circling back to the middle again.

20

We took separate cars. Kate led the way along the same route Isaac had taken me before. Leaves fell and blew across the road, and as we drove up the first ridge the forest spread out below in all the colors of fall under a bright blue sky.

I had barely been able to eat breakfast, but Kate persuaded me to take a banana and a piece of toast in the car. She was motherly, warning me of low blood sugar and saying things like *You have to keep your energy up*. It wasn't much use.

In the two days she stayed with me, she set up shop in the parlor with her laptop and books, doing remote school, while I tried to figure out what to do with my mind, which circled and circled the center of Frieholdt's, and my body, which couldn't seem to be still. The day after she came, I went out and bought proper running shoes and a decent sports bra.

"Don't overdo it," she said, looking up from her books as I got ready to go out. "You're not twenty anymore. You'll strain a tendon."

She was only two years older than me, which should have made us peers. But something about Kate Wells made me feel like a child in the way I often felt with Lizzie. Cared for. Looked after.

Kate turned down the gravel lane that led to the cabin. She took the turns with ease, while I crept along, heart pounding, hands sweating, staying as far from the steep drop-off as possible. She had shown no doubt. He would be there. And she would have a talk with him. I could almost believe her she seemed so in command. But I also couldn't believe. If he was going to come out of hiding, why hadn't he done it before? Why hadn't he come for me?

Kate was already out of the car and stretching her back when I pulled in to park beside her. I texted Lizzie and told her where I was. She had worried enough. When I got out of the car, the breeze through the dry leaves sounded like rushing water.

Kate hoisted her bag over her shoulder. "Ready?"

I nodded. Unable to speak.

It was a noisy walk up the path, ankle-deep in dry leaves. If it weren't for the exertion of the walk, I would've been reaching for my Klonopin. It might have been happy anxiety—the anxiety of anticipation—but still, there was only so much I could take.

"Look." Kate pointed to the left of the trail. A wild turkey scurried through the twining branches of mountain laurel, followed by three chicks. They looked so silly with their long necks and fat bodies.

"What if he's not here?" I said.

"He'll be here."

The path led into the meadow, and there it was. Just as we'd left it. Kate stopped for a second, brow furrowed, then resumed her climb up the grassy hill to the porch.

He would be there. She said he would. We reached the porch and clomped up to the door.

Kate opened it. "Isaac?"

Nothing. It was one damn room. There was nowhere to hide. Nowhere he might be that we wouldn't see him. There were no bags. No shoes on the floor. No embers in the fireplace. I dropped into the spindly wooden chair by the door, fighting my racing heart.

He wasn't there.

"Come on, man." Kate held up my phone, recording. "We drove all the way here. I'm missing school. Where the fuck are you?"

She scowled as she finished and posted and handed the phone back to me.

Even I believed he was watching. It wasn't that he didn't know where we were, it was that he'd persuaded himself that a miserable, lonely life was all he deserved. But reasons didn't matter. I ached in every single bone for him, and he wasn't there.

Kate sat in the chair opposite me, staring out the window. She was not a person I knew well, but still her determination surprised me. She did not seem dejected, only pissed off. But I couldn't say the same for myself. I was slipping, and fast.

"I'm going to climb up the ridge," I said, standing.

"Do you know the way? Those paths are—"

"Yes, it's okay. I won't go far."

She pushed her water bottle across the table. "Drink some water first."

The path behind the cabin cut steeply upward, and I took it in big, fast steps, thighs burning, trying again for the pounding heart that came from exertion to overcome the one that came from panic. Looking side to side, I said the names out loud. Eastern white pine. Silver maple. Spicebush. Sycamore. The clouds forming high above. Cirrus. Stratus. I mapped the topology of the ground on a grid in my head, creating formula after formula to describe the curves. Anything to drown out the voice that said, *If this didn't work, nothing will.*

At the rock outcropping I stopped, looking out over the hollow and the ridge beyond. The sweat on my back grew cold, and I shivered. When I lost Lila, I still had my work. When I lost my work, I still had Isaac. Now what was left?

A bird floated in lazy circles high above. An updraft. Air movement. Flow and turbulence. What would it feel like to live it? To be it?

A sound broke through the wind and the leaves. Voices. I leaned forward to hear. Definitely voices. Kate's, raised. Maybe arguing. I turned and ran.

She was alone. She could be in trouble.

Or it could be him.

I tried to silence my feet, running through the fallen leaves. I stopped, listened. Ran some more. Then gave it up. Whatever it was, I didn't want to just listen. I wanted to be there.

Twenty yards from the cabin, I nearly wept with joy.

"She could be lost. Fucking—Kate, how could you let her just wander off?"

Footsteps across the front porch.

Kate, annoyed. "I didn't *let* her do anything. She's a grown fucking woman."

I willed my feet to move. Touching the trees for balance, I stumbled down the hill. I could have floated the rest of the way. There. There he was.

It had only been two weeks, but he looked thin. And for a

moment so angry, his brow deeply grooved. He dug his hand into his hair then rubbed his forehead. Everything fell into slow motion. I thought if I moved too fast I would scare him, and he would run and disappear again. If I even spoke. If I even stirred the air too much, he might blow away like a leaf.

Beams of light shone low through the branches, sun sinking into evening.

He met my eyes, as if looking across miles and miles of empty space. Those cinnamon eyes. He tried to shut me out. I saw him try, but he couldn't. I walked forward, never looking down, never letting go, until I was close enough to hear him breathe. Then I gathered him in my arms.

How was this the same man I had held in my arms only two weeks ago? Where had all his strength gone? The solid realness that had brought me back to earth? He wouldn't hold me. His body was there, but he was far away. I took tiny gulps of air. My heart broke and broke again, but I didn't let go.

The bones of his spine felt hard under my fingertips. He lifted his hands from his sides. One on my hip. One touched my hair. He leaned his head against mine.

Kate gently drew his attention and said, so softly it was almost a whisper, "I didn't mean to pick a fight."

Isaac turned his head, arms still around me, and said, "Yes, you did."

Kate shrugged. "Okay. Fine. But I don't now. I'm sorry." Something relaxed in his body with her there.

"It's gonna get cold," she said and winked at me. "Why don't you come in? You look like you haven't eaten in a month."

She mothered him, just as she probably always had. Kate Wells loved her brother in a take-no-shit, take-no-prisoners kind of way. No conditions. No *I love you, but…*

The way Lizzie loved me.

She fired up the propane stove, and Isaac slumped into a chair. I stood behind him and stroked his hair until he leaned his head back against me.

Something bad had happened to him. Or else he was finally feeling the effects of all the bad things that had ever happened to him. Or both. And we had traded places. Even though he had a broken leg and an arrest warrant, he had been the solid one when he hopped up my driveway last month. I was the one about to fly to pieces. At the time, it would have seemed impossible that he could be so shaken and I could be so comparatively stable.

The presence of Kate helped. She seemed to know just what to do, as if she'd been here with him in this fragile state before.

I looked around the room. Apparently, their great-uncle had never thought to bring a sofa to the cabin, so there was nowhere that two people could sit and be close. Except the bed, of course, and who would sleep where was still an open question. Kate worked away at the counter by the wall as if dinner for three with a two-burner propane stove, no running water, and no refrigerator was something she did every day. I got the feeling she had a lot of practice making a home out of very little. It's no wonder she'd succumbed to drugs, I thought. She must have shouldered so much in their family.

She looked over at us. "It's cleared up outside. You all should go look at the stars."

So Isaac and I put on our coats and took two chairs out to the porch.

"Can I?" I pulled my chair close to his.

He nodded.

"How's the leg?" I asked.

"Not too bad. Aches sometimes." He took a pack of cigarettes from his pocket and shook one out. "You mind?"

I shook my head. Even though his touch was still fresh on my skin, he felt far away. Unreachable. Better cigarettes than narcotics, than meth, than heroin—than any of the things he could have chosen to numb the pain in his leg and in his heart. A slight breeze tumbled the smoke as soon as it emerged from the glowing ember. He held it so it moved downwind and away.

"Where have you been staying?" I said.

"On the street for a few days," he said. "Then a shelter. Then someone from the job."

"Did I do something wrong?" I asked. I couldn't help it. That was the first place I always went when someone who had shown me love withheld it.

"No. Cops came to the door."

I waited for more, but that was it, and I was still a little afraid to push too far. "I'm sorry. I didn't mean to bring Kate into it."

He took a drag of his cigarette. "She straightened me out about that pretty quick. And I saw your TikTok. I know you didn't go looking for her. Once Kate's got it in her head to do something, no one can stop her. Not even you."

He had seen the video. The questions screamed in my mind. What about the lawyer? What about us? What about everything?

But I waited. And waited. A pan clanked inside.

"You've lost weight," I said.

He nodded. "Just haven't been eating much."

"And you seem depressed."

"I'm always depressed."

"No, you're not. Not like this." I couldn't stand it anymore. The pressure I felt inside shoved upward and cramped my throat. "Please say something, Isaac. Anything. You saw my video. And now you're here. What happened? Were the police looking for you?"

"I don't know. I was already out the back door."

I hated the clipped way he was talking.

"They never came back," I said. "It was probably nothing. Someone's car alarm going off."

"There was some kind of an alarm going off. I couldn't tell where. Next door."

I stared at him in the dark, a burning feeling in my chest. "Why didn't you come back? I don't understand."

He took another long drag of the cigarette, then crushed the butt under his heel on the porch. "Once I was out of the house with my bag and I got across the creek to the parkway and looked up at that house—that fucking giant mansion—it was like the spell broke."

Grief constricted my throat. "You escaped."

"No." He shook his head. "You did. You escaped. I realized I didn't belong within a mile of that house and you and your family."

"My family? I don't understand."

"Hey, Kate?" he called inside, and she came out on the porch. "Would you mind getting me a drink? Anyway, I'll talk to your lawyer, and I'll turn myself in because you're right, this can't go on forever, and then I'll go to jail, and you need to just get on with your life— Thank you." He took a glass of bourbon, neat, and Kate went back inside.

"No."

"What you mean *no*?"

"I mean no, I'm not going to get on with my life, if by that you mean leave you behind and forget about you and go... do something else. Give me some." He handed me the glass, and the bourbon warmed my throat, immeasurably helping indignation to win over sorrow. "You can try and break up with me. You can act like you don't care, but you can't make me stop loving you. And that's the part you can't stand, isn't it? That you don't think I *should* love you, but I'm going to anyway."

He took the glass back and drained more than half of it. The sky above was black and ablaze with stars in the dry, mountain air. The Milky Way arced over the cabin.

"Lila paid for my apprenticeship," he said, eyes fixed forward into the dark. "Did she tell you that? She found it and paid for it."

"I thought you said it was someone who knew your uncle."

A derisive little sniff. "Every blacksmith on the east coast knew my uncle. So it wasn't hard for her to find someone nice and far away."

I saw what was coming into focus, and I hated it. But I hated obscurity more. I hated secrets.

"Are you saying she did it to separate us?"

He made that dismissive sound again. "Don't you think? She saw what was starting to happen. How we were together."

"And she thought you weren't good enough." I leaned elbows on knees, head in hands, not from distress but from the sheer exhaustion of a truth so long suspected and so long withheld. I loved Lila like a mother, but I knew her well. She was an old-school American aristocrat, cognizant of her position and her power, and not above managing the affairs of others to her concept of right. More than that, she would have considered it her duty to the family. I remembered how assiduously she erased Isaac once he was gone. A person who had been nearly a daily presence, who I believe she really cared for. She didn't talk about him. Didn't keep in touch. Once he was gone, he was gone.

I loved her and was grateful. She had supported and protected me, gathering me into her private sphere with a kind of matriarchal authority. We had had many happy days together. But she was my father's mother and, like my father, had a very different conception of my autonomy than I did.

I took the glass back from him and finished the whiskey. "Why didn't you tell me?"

"Because I didn't want you to think badly of her." He sighed heavily. "And because I loved her. I wasn't angry. I was grateful. She probably thought she was doing right by both of us."

"That's why you never came back."

"Part of why. It was enough, on top of everything else in my life. When I came back after…what happened, I was sure you'd have moved out or gotten married or something. I never thought you'd still be there."

I couldn't bear his flat tone, the way he didn't look at me.

"Isaac, what are we even doing here? I love you. You love me. Lila was wrong. She was an old-fashioned snob, and she was wrong."

He took out his cigarettes again. My eyes ached at the match flare in the darkness.

"You only love me because you're starved." He tossed the match into the meadow. "Your father is such a fucking stingy bastard that you're starved enough to think just because we wound up together again, I'm the one you should love."

I sat up straight. "Don't fucking patronize me. I waited for you. I waited fourteen years for you. I didn't know I was waiting, but I was. And now here you are. This is bullshit. It's all just obscuring the truth."

He rubbed his forehead, like he had before. Like it was a habit.

"I meant it when I said I'm a fuckup," he said.

"I meant it when I said I'm a head case. But we were both wrong. Postulates one and two are invalid."

"Who says?"

"I do."

The only light came from the sky full of stars, a faint glow through the front window, and the ember of his cigarette. He did not—would not—look at me.

"But I don't get what you're saying." I leaned forward, but he still didn't turn his head. "You're no more of a fuckup than you were before."

"I will be when I'm in jail."

The creeping flaccidity of grief and the resilience of anger vied for dominance as my body stiffened. At least that stiffness would keep me upright. Keep me here in this chair.

"It doesn't matter. Postulate three is still valid—"

"I knew you were going to bring that up." He stood suddenly and turned toward the meadow. "I knew it."

Lifelong habit told me to retreat. Hide. Disappear. I fought it.

"It's still valid. You can act in your own interest without asking anyone's permission. But if you're going to try and act in my interest, you need consent."

"Fine." He turned to face me. I could hear the tinge of sarcasm in his voice. "May I please have your permission not to fucking ruin your life?"

"No. And you also do not have my permission to play amateur psychologist with me about what I want and who I choose to love."

"Fuck's sake." He edged farther away. "What am I supposed to fucking say?"

"You're supposed to *fucking* talk to me like I'm an adult. Not a child."

"I'm not talking to you like you're a child."

"Yes, you are. That's what you're doing when you decide what's good for me. I'm done with it." My voice grew hoarse. "I'm getting the idea that you are trying to break up with me for good, and I'd like to run down to the car and lock the doors and cry right now, but I'm not doing it. Because that's what a child would do. It's what I've done practically my whole life when someone who says they love me acts like you're acting now. But I'm not going to do it because I am not a child anymore."

The door of the cabin opened, and Kate stepped out into an arc of lamplight. She had her coat on, and a bag over her arm.

"Sorry to interrupt," she said. "But I'm going to the hotel down in Bristow."

We both stared at her.

"It's the middle of the night," Isaac said.

"No," Kate said. "It's eight o'clock. There's one bed so I've got to go somewhere. There's food inside. I'm taking a serving. The rest is for you."

She hugged me. Then Isaac. Then flipped on a flashlight and climbed down the porch steps. "You know how to reach me. I'll see you in the morning."

"How can you be leaving?" Isaac said.

I went after her. "Kate, wait."

She turned around, and I met her on the grass.

In a soft voice, that Isaac might have been able to hear, or not—Kate didn't seem to care—she said, "Listen. I've had a lifetime worth of the kind of fight you're having. Sometimes you've just got to eat dinner and go to bed."

Her eyes looked tight. Her lips a thin line. It was the first time I saw a crack in her formidable strength.

"I'm sorry—"

"It's all right." She adjusted the bag on her shoulder. "I just know my limits. If I get too stretched…it doesn't go well."

I hugged her again, and she disappeared into the dark woods.

21

The porch was empty, and the door stood open when I turned back from the meadow. I climbed the stairs and went inside. A fire flickered in the fireplace. The oil lamp glowed from the counter along the back wall. Kate had even put a regular candle in a wrought iron candlestick on the table.

Part of me felt like I should leave too. This wasn't my house. But in spite of the roiling emotion, I was famished and getting light-headed. I would eat, then decide.

Isaac and I sat opposite one another and ate spaghetti with Alfredo sauce from a jar and a salad of sliced cucumbers and dill. We did not speak.

When we finished, I rose and took the dishes to the washbasin, where Kate had already warmed the water. Isaac got up to help but winced on his bad leg.

"I'll do it," I said. "Sit down."

I watched him limp out to the porch and light a cigarette, then turned my attention to the dishes. The warm water felt good on my hands, stinging my palms where they were raw from doing yard work at home, and it was a relief to have something to focus on. Soap bubbles, dishes and utensils clinking together underwater.

Maybe I would sleep in the car. Maybe find the hotel where Kate went. But I wasn't going anywhere until Isaac sent me. Until he told me directly that he wanted me to leave. For better or worse, I had learned to fight for what love I could get, and this wasn't so different from all the times I had to suffer for the crumbs that came from my father.

Only, it was completely different. My father was my father—a god to a little girl, until he wasn't anymore. Isaac was Isaac. Only himself. And I loved him, not like a little girl loves the people who biology tells her she must love. I loved him like a grown woman—the way he walked, his intelligence, how he could build anything, how easy it had been to make him laugh.

My throat cramped, tears rolled down my cheeks as I set the dishes on a towel to dry and began on the silverware. The soapy water, the smell of the fire, the rustle of night creatures in the wood. Everything felt so perfect and real and yet so horribly indeterminate, as if it could all be gone any second.

I withdrew my hands from the basin and reached for a towel. The door opened and closed behind me, and Isaac's steps crossed the room. I could not turn around. I wasn't ready to show him my tears. I stood, drying my hands, listening to the creak of the floorboards. His uneven steps.

Then he was behind me. Then his hands were on my shoulders, on my arms. I set down the towel, trying to steady my trembling. He smelled of cigarette smoke. Clothes still cold from the outside air. His touch was unsure, but so familiar in spite of everything.

He leaned his head so his lips were nearly touching my shoulder.

"I'm sorry. Will you please stay?"

★ ★ ★

Isaac fed the fire. The cabin grew warm and snug as the night grew colder. We closed up the shutters to keep out drafts, and I carried the oil lamp to the shelf beside the bed where we both changed into sleeping clothes, backs turned to one another.

"You're right," Isaac said as I climbed into bed. He lay on his back, arm up under his head. "I do feel worse than before. I'm so fucking tired all the time, and it's like I don't have any fight left."

I curled onto my other side and looked at his profile in the lamplight. I had spent a good portion of the last fifteen years in silence. A bit more wouldn't hurt.

He went on. "When I left your house—you know how it feels when you get something you wanted so badly, and then you lose it again?"

"I do know."

He turned his face toward me. "What's happening with your proof?"

"Nothing different. I'm trying to reconstruct it, but I'm stuck. I don't know if I can do it."

This had never been allowed. Failure was a death knell. Even doubt was weakness, and I had learned early on what happened when I said *I can't*. The frown. The freeze. And suddenly I would be alone in a universe I didn't understand. Even saying it now, I shrank inside and space expanded vast and empty around me.

Isaac rolled to his side and reached for my hand.

There it was. A lifeline. I wove my fingers through his and said, "You never lost me."

"I know. But I knew I would lose you. Even if you persisted in letting me fuck up your life, I would eventually go to prison, so…"

He tried to withdraw his hand.

I didn't let him. "I don't care if you go to prison. I mean, of course I care. I don't want you to go, but it doesn't change anything."

A profound weariness washed over his face. He pulled my hand to touch my knuckles to his forehead.

"Please help me," he said. "I'm scared, and I'm struggling. I've got all this baggage, and I feel like I can finally see it. I'm trying, but I need help."

He yawned and tried to hide it.

"I need help too." I unwound my fingers from his and brushed back his hair, short and uneven, like he had cut it himself. "I have baggage too."

"I know. I'm sorry—"

"No, it's not that. It's just… Our history might come up again and again, and we might both need help for a long time. Maybe forever. We might not be the easiest partners for one another. But sometimes I think, if we could be with other people, we would be. But we're not. We're together."

Isaac sat up and extinguished the oil lamp. Then he reached out and pulled me in, and it had never felt so good to feel so exhausted.

He kissed me gently, full of love and relief and on the brink of sleep.

Morning light pierced the cracks between the shutters. Even lying close alongside Isaac's body, the cabin felt cold, so as little as I wanted to rouse him, I got up to feed the fire. It required new kindling and small logs. Almost a whole new fire but not quite. The hearth was warm, and the flue was drawing. A few embers still glowed under the grate. When it was crackling and hot again, I went back to bed.

Isaac lay on his back and looked up at me. "Thanks."

I hesitated. Should I get dressed? Back in bed? I crossed my arms.

But he reached out. "Come here."

I nestled into his shoulder. "You sleep okay?"

"Mmm-hmm." He stroked my back and kissed my shoulder and neck, slowly, almost meditatively. Birds chattered outside. The bed creaked as he shifted closer and reached under my shirt. My heart sped up and sent blood out to my skin, tingling and warm.

In spite of everything, he still felt strong. And somehow, so did I. In a way I had never noticed before. Not a head case. Not the girl who had panic attacks, who everyone had to tiptoe around. Not the highly guarded woman living a highly circumscribed life, but a woman who could split wood, and light a fire, and stand her ground.

He lifted my shirt and pulled it off over my head, held my breast, rolled my nipple until it was hard, and I felt the deep pull and lift in the center of my chest.

"I'm sorry I fell asleep on you last night," he said.

"It's okay. Sleep was perfect."

He kissed my breastbone. Took my nipple in his mouth. An involuntary sigh eased past my lips.

"I dreamed about this," he said, kissing my other breast, breathing harder.

I pulled his shirt over his head. He extricated me from my underwear and ran his hand over my skin, waist to knee.

"Parabola," he said.

I laughed. "What?"

"Just remembering some high-school math." He ran his hand up and over the curve again. "Isn't this a parabola, right here?"

"Sort of. A parabola is U-shaped. That's more a minor segment of a circle."

"Whatever you say." He reached behind my thigh and drew my leg over his, reaching in to touch where I was already flush and wet. It almost took my breath away, and I pulled air into the tiny upper apexes of my lungs. Like during a panic attack, only this wasn't fear. There was no fear in it at all.

"All last night, even when we were in bed together, I had no—" His voice grew low and rumbling. "Everything felt so damped down."

A literal ache grew low between my hips, that could only be soothed by one thing.

He entered me with his fingers. "And now all I want is to fuck you into next week."

"Oh god, let's please do that," I said, gasping for breath.

"It was scary," he said, "feeling so weak. I don't ever want to feel that way with you."

"You weren't weak." I pushed his pajama pants down, and he kicked them off. "You were stronger than ever."

My body shuddered. Isaac drew his fingers out slowly, cock rigid against the soft lower part of my belly, then rolled me under him. We tried to slow it down, to enjoy it a little longer, but the moment took on a force of its own. I braced my arms against the wall, elbows locked, and wrapped my legs around him. Nothing was missing.

We lay together, drowsy and loose, Isaac's arm looped over my waist, for a long time. But it was morning, and a person does eventually feel the urge to move.

I sat up and opened the shutters on the little window beside the bed, watching the dust motes float in the white morning sun. It was as if time had slowed for us, to stretch out this moment of peace.

Time. Motion. Peace. Time. Something shot through me so suddenly my heart skipped a beat. I scrambled out of bed.

"What's the matter?" Isaac sat up.

Cool air bathed my naked skin. I dropped to my knees and dug through my bag for my notebook and my copy of Fenty's *Discourses*, safe in its box. I tugged them both out and sat down at the table. A cold wind blew my mind clear. Utterly clear. I didn't even feel my body until Isaac came over.

"Stand up a second," he said and wrapped me in a blanket.

"Thank you."

The Impossible Theorem was like pulling apart a great knot of string, and for years I had been picking at it from the outside. A knot can be pulled apart that way, but it's not until you find the center that everything comes loose. The center. Begin at the center. The middle is the beginning.

The beginning. It doesn't need to be the answer to everything.

I'm not sure how much time passed before I heard a clink and a creak and a mug of coffee appeared on the table in front of me. Steam rose from its surface. The laminar flow as it rose straight in the still air, then it reached its Reynolds number and swirled into turbulence. There was no straight line through the Impossible. There was a fork in the path. Right at that moment, I couldn't see the way, but I knew without a doubt that it led through. And I knew that *Discourses on the Loading Hypothesis* would lead me. I lay my notebook and *Discourses* side by side and paged slowly through them. Perhaps Bonnie Fenty had known too. Perhaps if she hadn't had to fight so damn hard just to be who she was, if she hadn't had to literally pretend she was someone else, maybe Frieholdt's would have been solved in 1860.

The front door opened and closed. My pencil wore down.

"Isaac?" I called. "Isaac? I need help."

He appeared at my side.

"Do you have a pencil?" I held mine up.

"No, but hang on." He took it and, after a minute, returned it. Sharp. But not sharp in the perfect round manner of a fifty-nine-cent pencil sharpener. Sharp as in sharpened by hand, by a knife.

He left me alone. As if in a trance, I peered as hard as I could to see around that bend in the path. I climbed one way, then another in my mind, but the steps ahead remained obscure. What I did see was the ghost of my old straight line. The old path which, I now realized, did not lead straight through but instead stopped at a kind of cliff wall.

It was wrong. I had been wrong. The Loading Hypothesis was not just tangentially related to Frieholdt's. It was critical scaffolding. It was not optional.

The proof as it was currently written—the configuration my father held in his hands—was wrong.

My coffee was finished. My mug was cold. My feet were getting numb. I couldn't believe it, and yet it was so fully real that my heart felt light. My body prickled with joy. My proof was wrong. That's why I had been stuck all this time, trying to reconstruct it.

I closed the book and stood, shook out my hands, walked a few circles around the empty room, blanket clutched at my breast. I couldn't see the way yet, and I felt some disappointment— more like disorientation—at finding myself working again on a problem I thought I had already solved. But more than that, I felt the invigorating brightness of clarity. If my last proof had been wrong, no amount of feeling one way or another about it would make it right. And now that I knew *where* it was wrong, I was that much closer. It would take time to figure out *how* it was wrong and how to make it right. It might take a good deal of time, but I had no doubt at all that I *would* get it right. I was ready to start on a new proof that very second, but I had paused long enough to realize I was starving.

The fire still burned in the hearth. On the counter at the back of the cabin, someone had left a ham sandwich on a plate and a tin cup of well water. I ate and drank as if I hadn't had a meal in a week. Then I got dressed.

Outside, I found Kate and Isaac. They had carried the porch chairs down to a sunny spot in the meadow and were sharing a cigarette. They both turned as I walked through the grass.

I stopped and stretched my back, arms over my head, bright sun on my face. "Jesus Christ, I could murder someone for another cup of coffee. What time is it?"

Kate laughed. "It's one in the afternoon."

"No wonder I'm so stiff."

"What have you been doing?"

Isaac reached for my hand and drew me into his lap. The sun warmed my cheek. How to explain?

"I was wrong."

They looked at each other, then back at me.

"The proof is wrong. I'm almost sure of it. It's not going to work." It was like sharing the most wonderful secret.

"But that seems like bad news," Isaac said. "Why do you seem so happy?"

"I'm not exactly happy, but it's the opposite of bad news. Because now I know the truth. It's like when you give up some long struggle. When you've been feeling all along that something was off, and now you know what it is. I was holding on to this proof so tightly because I thought it was right, but also because I thought it was going to fix something. Like I was finally going to prove something about myself. And now it's wrong, and I don't need it to prove anything, and it's okay. I'm still here. I'm still—" I laughed, looking out into all that clear, open air. "I don't know if I'm making any sense."

Kate nodded. "You're making a fair amount of sense, actually."

"And that means what your father has is wrong," Isaac said.

"Exactly. Provably wrong."

"We'll have to come up here more often. You'll probably win the Nobel Prize if we stay for a week."

"There isn't a Nobel Prize in math," I said, "which pisses me off, but that's a separate issue."

Kate stood. "It seems like a strange thing to celebrate, but let's make this woman some coffee already."

22

It was dark when we got back to Lila's, just Isaac and me. Kate was on her way to Pennsylvania to retrieve the truck. So many times the click of the heavy front door behind me had meant safety, both from the outside world and from myself. It had meant home. But this time it rang tinny in the empty foyer.

We had spent the afternoon at the cabin on the phone with Erin O'Keefe. Isaac sat, his back hunched, head down, saying over and over, *Yes, ma'am. Yes, ma'am.* Telling her the story, covering his eyes with his hand. The whole, ugly, painful story.

But Erin had been warm and disarming and called him Mr. Wells. She took names of character witnesses, of which it turned out there were many. And she told him he had a very good case, but he should turn himself in as soon as possible. It would be a good-faith gesture and would make a difference.

"I know you're probably scared," she had said at the end. "But you're doing the right thing. I'm optimistic."

I flipped on the lamp on the table by the stairs. Isaac looked at the box on the floor. The circular saw.

I opened my mouth to speak but was immediately choked up. He took one look at me, walked over, and wrapped me in his arms.

Ever since Kate had messaged me through TikTok, I had held the sorrow at bay. Fear and anxiety I could handle, but sorrow would have drowned the tiny seed of hope I had. But the circular saw... I had taken such time and care picking it out at the hardware store. I was so excited to give it to him, and I had come home to emptiness.

"Was this for me?" he said.

I nodded and sobbed into his shirt.

He nudged the box over with his foot. "Good choice. I like this kind. You have a saw like this and a hammer and nails, you can build some shit."

I dried my eyes on my sleeve. "Whatever happens, I'm holding on to it for you."

"Of course you are," Isaac said, putting on a little more bravery than I imagined he felt. "We'll use it when I get out."

I was restless from the long drive, so even though it was dark, I changed into running clothes.

Isaac looked me over as I headed for the door. "You look hot," he said. "Like an ad for Nike."

"Thanks. Promise you won't run off while I'm gone?"

He smiled and kissed me. "Promise you'll let me take those clothes off you when you get back?"

Cold air filled my lungs as I headed for an easy four-mile loop up the avenue and back down the neighborhood streets. My muscles eased through the burn and resistance, and my breath dropped into a steady rhythm. As I ran past the storefronts and apartment buildings and turned onto the tree-lined residential streets, I began to release the strong grip I had on loss. When I'd first recognized Isaac out on the street in front of my house, a part of my soul grasped on and never let go. I had hoped and dreamed for so long and then given up. And then the impossible had happened. He came back. I held on tight in the face of his arrest warrant, his readiness to run, and the deep doubt we both harbored that things could ever work out. It was exhausting.

As I ran, I literally felt my hands and knuckles creak open. I didn't need to hold so tight anymore. I didn't need to hold on at all. He wanted to be with me, wanted to stay. And postulate three would keep him from doing anything stupid out of macho self-abasement.

The side streets were quiet. Light glowed from porches and dining rooms, the flicker of a TV. A diffuse scent of woodsmoke from a fireplace somewhere. I nodded to a woman walking a small white dog. My shoes made a rhythmic *chiff-chiff-chiff* against the pavement. The road took a turn and dipped down the hill, and I saw Lila's house at the end of the block. I slowed to a walk. I had forgotten to turn on the porch light. One tiny light glowed deep in the back of the first floor. Isaac must be in the kitchen, I thought. The rest of the rooms were dark. While the other places around me looked like homes, Lila's looked like a great, dark hearth with a single ember of warmth within.

Half the furniture was gone. The floors were nearly bare. Time and change had erased the habits and routines Lila and I had gone through for fifteen years. With the exception of my beautiful tower study and my blackboard, this was just a house.

Stopping in the street, I looked at it.

Just a house.

Nothing about it had changed, which meant something was different inside of me. My body began to feel the October chill, and I hugged my arms to my chest.

If I could never again be shoved into that vast, loveless void which had terrorized me my entire life, then everything else was management. My anxiety wouldn't just go away, but it could be worked with. There might be many things I wouldn't like to do, or wouldn't choose to do, but very little that I could not do.

Including proving my father wrong.

"I'm back," I called as I walked in.

At the creak of a chair in the kitchen, my apprehension vanished. Still here. It seemed impossible, but there he was, walking toward me through the center hall. He looked purposeful and picked up his pace as I slid out of my shoes.

"What?" I said.

Something mischievous glinted in his eyes, and as I nudged the door closed with my foot, he slammed it shut with the weight of his body and mine. He kissed me like he'd been waiting his whole life, not just the last hour, and it sent a wash of heat right to my core. He put one hand behind my neck and the other on my ass.

He stammered, surprised. "You're not wearing—"

"No, they chafe."

I loved when he tried to kiss me and smile at the same time. He slid his hand up my shirt. "You did promise."

I laughed. "Yes, I did. But I'm sweaty now. I feel like I should clean up."

"If you want to," he murmured into my neck. "I don't care."

He steered me toward the couch in the parlor.

"No, that thing is awful. The upholstery feels like sandpaper."

"Maid's quarters?"

"Perfect."

I was spent and naked, and it was nine at night when I wrapped myself in the sheet, instructed Isaac to be quiet, picked up my phone, and called Sharon.

I skipped all pleasantries. "Twenty thousand. I'll be out a week from today."

"Where have you been?" she said. "Are you okay?"

It wasn't what I expected. "I'm fine."

"Why didn't you answer your phone?"

"I was busy."

"Are you ignoring my calls?"

"Yes."

I thought I heard the pop of a cork in the background. "I can't say I blame you."

"Excuse me?"

"Lizzie came over and read me the riot act." Her screen door squeaked open and closed. She was probably going to the porch to drink where her family wouldn't hassle her. "She's been watching you do this research for years. Plus she gave the names of five people who were at your presentation at NES, and the direct line to Anne MacFaull at Nautilus."

"I don't know why she bothered. Plus you could have just believed me instead of having to get proof from Lizzie."

"You haven't exactly been credible at times."

"So are you trying to apologize or just piss me off?"

"All right, all right. I'm sorry. Let's talk about the house."

It was the best I was going to get. But I would rather have Sharon with me than against me, no matter how unwillingly.

Isaac and I slept in the most comfortable second-floor bed in the room with the big windows that looked out over the garden. In the morning I woke to the tickle of his beard against my neck.

"Meg?"

"Hmm?"

"I'm sorry." He brushed the stray hair from my face. "This is going to be the last chance for a while, so—"

Still half-asleep, I wrapped my arms around him. Within hours we would be in the car to Blind Fork to meet Erin and walk into the police station. After that, we didn't know. She said bail was unlikely, but it wouldn't take long to build his case. Days. Weeks. Months maybe. Erin said definitely not years.

"When do we have to leave?" I croaked from a still-waking throat.

"Eleven."

"What time is it?"

"Six."

I rubbed my face and whined, "Six? Isaac. You know I'm not a morning person."

But I didn't mean it. Dappled sunlight fell on his bare shoulder, and he looked at me, smile crinkling around his eyes. He reached around my back and pulled my hair over my shoulder, smoothing it down over my breast.

"You're even beautiful when you're grumpy and just woke up."

I grumbled and buried my face against his chest, sleep still pulling so hard on my consciousness. But Isaac was stubborn. He ran his fingers through my hair until my scalp tingled and pleasure washed down my back. Then he said the only three words that could possibly make six in the morning worth waking up for.

"I'll make coffee."

This bought me ten more minutes of sleep, and I can't say I didn't enjoy them. But what I enjoyed more was sitting up against the headboard, cradling my coffee mug in both hands as Isaac nudged my knees apart. An entirely pleasant thing to wake up for. Pleasant enough that I had to put the mug on the bedside table and grip the sheets, then Isaac's hair as my body shuddered and clenched.

It was exquisite torture, how slow and gentle he took me, turning up the intensity bit by bit, stretching it out as long as he possibly could, eyes shut tight. Then suddenly he opened them wide, looking for me.

"Meg?"

"Right here." I forced my hand beneath his, weaving our fingers together. "I love you."

He looked almost afraid.

But I was not afraid. I received the young, muscular energy of his body, yet it was not passive. It was a great, intentional, rejoicing *yes*.

Since my run the night before, a plan had been taking form. But I let it grow and settle in and waited for Lizzie. I had invited her, and she arrived spot on time, eager to meet Isaac before he disappeared again.

She hugged me when I let her in. "Where is he?"

"He's coming. I hear you had a chat with Sharon."

"Fucking bitch. I can't believe her." She turned her head toward the stairs and yelled, "Isaac, hurry up. I'm getting old down here."

Lizzie could get away with stuff like that.

"Come on. I made breakfast." I beckoned her back to the kitchen. "Isaac's nervous, and we don't need to be watching him come down the stairs like it's prom night."

She sighed with faux impatience and followed. In the kitchen, she looked me up and down. "You, my dear, have been getting laid."

I laughed and blushed and nodded.

"Suits you." She whipped her head around at the sound of footsteps. "Finally!"

He wanted so much for her to like him. To approve. She alone was what qualified as meeting the family. And poor Isaac, he was painfully nervous. His limp pronounced, posture terrible, rubbing his beard.

But Lizzie did what I knew she would do. She walked right up to him, arms out.

"May I?"

"Uh, okay."

She rose up on her toes and wrapped him in a hug.

"It's so good to finally meet you," she all but squealed. Then she held him by the shoulders at arm's length and looked at me. "I approve." Then back at Isaac. "You can relax now."

If this was how our odd little family worked, I would take it.

We sat down to eggs and toast and fresh coffee, morning sun beaming through the windows of the breakfast nook.

"So your grandfather was a blacksmith?" Lizzie said.

"Great-uncle."

As forks clinked on plates and mugs knocked against the tabletop, Lizzie drew him out and got him talking. She was a pro, and before we were halfway through breakfast, he told her all about Kimmo's smithy and the summer he spent there, and how he hoped he could relearn and fire up the forge, "When I'm...done with everything."

The novelty was so entertaining. Aside from Kate, I hadn't heard Isaac talk to another human being in a very long time. At last they slowed down, and I found an opening.

Deep breath. "I'm going to go to my dad's presentation."

All eyes turned to me.

"Hear me out. Lizzie, you don't know this yet, but there's an error in the proof. I figured it out the day before yesterday at the cabin. I was trying and trying to reconstruct it from memory, and I couldn't get past this one spot, and then I figured out why—and it's because it was wrong. I was wrong."

Lizzie's eyes took on a vengeful gleam. "And your dad doesn't know."

"Unless he figured it out himself, which I seriously doubt, then no."

Isaac, on my other side, looked stricken. "It's next weekend. I can't be there."

"I know." I reached for his hand, more anxious than I expected. But summoned my courage for him. "It'll be okay. I'll be okay."

He looked plaintively at Lizzie.

"When, exactly?" She took her phone out of her pocket.

"Saturday afternoon. Two o'clock."

She tapped open her calendar, then looked up. "I'll be there."

"And I'm going to move out of this house and take Sharon's money."

Isaac knew about this part, but Lizzie's expression changed to concern and a bit of sadness. She put down her fork.

"You are? Where are you going to live?"

"North Carolina." I held Isaac's hand tighter.

"At the cabin?" Lizzie said.

"No. Somewhere near a town called Blind Fork. But not too near. Probably just rent something by the month."

"Is that—?"

"Near where I'll be in jail." Isaac's voice dropped low. "I tried to talk her out of it."

"I've got more tutoring applicants than I can even take. I can work wherever I want," I said. "I don't need all this space. I don't even want it. It only makes me sad now."

A little brown bird alighted on the windowsill and tapped at the glass before flying off.

"I know." Lizzie looked out into the garden. "It makes me sad too."

Isaac groaned and leaned his head on the table.

"What's the matter?" Lizzie said.

"I'm sorry. I believe in you. I know you can do it, but it's going to fucking kill me not to be there. God, I mean practically the hardest thing you've ever done in your life."

I took a deep breath. "I've done a lot of hard things, and yes, this will be one of them. But it's different now. Everything is different."

23

Kate awaited us in the parking lot at the police station in Blind Fork. I had paid for the truck to be delivered by flatbed, per Erin's instructions. The less disruption to its condition, the better. Kate hugged us nervously and told us the detectives had already taken it.

Erin arrived five minutes before the arranged time. What I was paying for her travel was not to be believed, but I didn't care. This was not something on which I felt any desire to economize.

Erin both was and wasn't what I expected in person. She pulled up in a black Tesla—the expensive kind. Tall, broad-shouldered, blonde, with a nasty-looking scar on her cheek, she looked in some ways the part of the high-powered defense attorney. But she exuded warmth and a slightly eccentric earthiness. Her clothes were understated. Light makeup, flaking a little around the eyes. The whole laid-back look could have been, and probably was, intentional. Designed to lull the small-town detectives into a false sense of security. I could easily imagine her dressed to kill in a DC courtroom.

She knew us immediately and walked over, shaking first Isaac's hand, then mine.

"You ready for this?" she asked him.

"Yes, ma'am."

"Any questions?"

"No, ma'am."

She smiled. "Then, *sir*, let's go get it done."

Isaac turned and held me tight. He kissed my lips and my hair.

"We just have to get through it," I said, as much to myself as to him.

He gripped me tightly and whispered in my ear. "I hate this. You guys have to get out of this shithole town. Don't even stay here tonight. Dustin DeVries is an idiot, but he's a dangerous idiot. As soon as he finds out I'm back—who knows what's going to happen."

And I whispered back, "Okay. I know. We will. And you do whatever Erin tells you to do."

He kissed me again and went to face justice.

The detectives had a few questions for me, and I stuttered and sweated my way through the answers. Not because they were not true but because the whole situation had me teetering on the edge of a panic attack. I told them this, and they gave me a glass of water.

Erin knew the whole truth—I wasn't taking any chances—but she advised me to keep to the latter part of the story where I hired her for Isaac and persuaded him to turn himself in. All in all, it was straightforward, though one of the detectives kept staring in a way that made me nervous. I almost told him to cut it out but was guided by both my anxiety and my better judgment to keep my mouth shut.

I was done in an hour. Kate was at the station all day. And Isaac, of course, did not come out.

Kate and I stayed that night at a hotel in the next town over. A bigger town, down the mountain, where one might come and go with more anonymity. We ordered pizza, and while we waited for it to arrive, we walked out to the convenience store across the parking lot for a six-pack.

"Our mom lives a mile past Blind Fork." Kate pointed up toward the mountain. "Same house we grew up in."

She was less than two miles from where her own son sat in a jail cell, yet she did not even know her children were here.

We walked back toward the hotel, away from the bright convenience store into the deep mountain darkness.

"When he was little," she said, "Isaac used to come into my room and sleep on the floor. He didn't like to be alone." A cold breeze blew her hair across her face. "He got the worst of it, I think. It was easier for me to tell our grandmother to fuck off. He had the softer heart, in a way, but me and my hard-heartedness didn't wind up doing me that good in the long run."

"It's not your fault," I said. "You guys were both kind of screwed either way."

"I know." She brushed her hair from her eyes and looked up the mountain again. "There was this meadow out in back of our house that never got mowed. We used to go up there and make hideouts and stuff. One time, we found these three field mice that had gotten abandoned, or maybe a cat got their mother or something. Isaac watched over them while I went and got a shoebox."

She stopped where the parking lot was still dark, before confronting the brightness of the hotel. Her cheeks glistened with tears, and she wiped them away.

"I'm fucking forty years old, and still… We didn't know what we were doing, but we figured out how to care for them, and we figured out how to care for each other. And he's going to figure out how to care for you."

I took her hand. "What happened to the mice?"

"We nursed them with an eyedropper, and they survived."

That was Monday. Then came Tuesday. I drove back to Lila's. Then Wednesday. Then Thursday, and the days strung out like beads on a wire, definite in themselves, but so far between one and the next. Erin called me each afternoon with updates. They were checking out the truck. They were interviewing some local people. They'd brought Kate back.

I felt for her. That was a long drive.

Erin's updates took up fifteen minutes of each day. Isaac could not call me those first few days. It took all the mental discipline I had built up of nearly a lifetime to focus the rest of my time on work. Mornings were for preparation. Going through the proof, making notes, practicing speaking out loud. I made videos of myself, and as much as it made me cringe, I watched them, and I learned. My plan was to isolate the part of the proof with the error and, in approximately a minute and a half, demolish the foundation that held up everything that came after. If I went on much longer than that, I figured someone would try to stop me.

In the afternoon I went running, right before my calls with Erin when I was at the peak of anxiety. Evenings were for tutoring. And I began making math videos again. Interesting things would come up with my students, and I would talk about them into the universe of TikTok. There was no more public crying.

Three or four students per day put a small but not insignificant amount of money back in my checking account, and given that the cost of living would be much lower after I moved, even if I had to empty my account to pay Erin, I could still get by.

My therapist referred me to someone ninety minutes' drive from where they were holding Isaac. My psychiatrist said I was too reliant on the Klonopin and recommended an anti-depressant. I couldn't afford to start a new med right before my father's presentation—the side effects being unknown— but I got it filled. Once Saturday was behind me, it would be all about the future.

The nights, though—those nights were hard.

Isaac was able to call only once that week. Jail wasn't as bad as he'd thought, he said, but I wasn't sure I believed him. He sounded nervous and spoke faster than usual but seemed to make an effort to stay upbeat, which I knew was not his normal setting, and which made me love him harder than ever.

The night before my father's presentation, I locked the doors and windows, warmed up my dinner and took it upstairs. My neck felt stiff, in spite of a four-mile run, knees creaking like they were made of wood. Self-doubt fixed its big clamps around my chest, but I worked to maintain my confidence and they didn't tighten down. Not yet. But I could feel them, and I knew what they could do.

Underlying it all, gnawing a hole in my core was the big void of nothing coming from Blind Fork. No news. Investigation proceeding. Hold tight, Erin said, this is normal.

But nothing was normal. My world felt like a flat disk, supported by three legs, but the legs kept changing length and the disk wobbled and slipped.

I passed my bedroom, where all my small objects were

packed into ordinary brown boxes, ready to be moved. I didn't
sleep in there anymore.

Daylight faded as I sat looking out the front windows of my
study. The yard at the house across the street was all cleaned
up, and landscapers had planted small trees and laid down sod.
I longed for Isaac to call. The ache to hear his voice was so
strong, I felt like I could reach through space and grab him by
the shirt and say *Call me. Call me, damn it.* But I knew even if
he could hear me, he could only call when they let him. And
that wouldn't be nine on a Friday night.

I was ready. My outfit hung from the molding above the
balcony door. Not armor this time. Just clothes. My notes
lay in a neat stack on the desk. I got up and turned the first
few pages over. Frieholdt's was clear and set and hardened in
my mind. Any more rehearsal would be like saying a word
so many times it loses its meaning. I reordered the stack and
looked over at my board.

It was time.

A child's board can be cleaned with a washcloth, but to
properly clean a board seven feet tall and twelve feet wide required the bucket and squeegee which had waited, unused,
in the hall closet.

First I took a picture. Then I stood on a wooden box to
reach the top and drew the sponge down in a straight line.
Deep black wiped out all trace of the chalky contents of my
mind. I reached and drew the sponge down again. The clean,
blank edge butted up against fragments of shape and symbol,
the powder of earlier erasures. A rolled-up towel caught the
milky water that dripped down to the ledge.

We would unmount the three big panels. Two would be
stored in Lizzie's basement, and one would come with me, but

not the chalk rail, carved by Isaac when he was twenty years old. There was no other wall it would fit, and so it would stay behind. A little mystery for whatever stranger next found their way up to this high room.

The board dried as I went, the shine and depth of the wet surface fading to matte black. By the time I cleaned the right-most section, the left was ready for new work.

I left the hall light on and the door cracked. As I climbed into my nest of blankets on the sofa, the big house around me disappeared, and this one room alone became my entire world. I lay restless and exhausted.

If I made it through tomorrow—If Isaac went free—If I failed—If DeVries's brother found Isaac—or Kate—or me—If I lost my life's work—If I lost Isaac—If I won everything back—If—If—If.

Staring at the black expanse of my board, I cradled my only certainty. That it would take chalk again.

24

We drove to the university, Kate, Lizzie, and I. They chatted softly and discussed directions, then Kate dropped Lizzie and me off and went to park the car. Walking toward the hall, the grounds around us looked like a college from a movie set. Autumn leaves fluttering down from stately rows of trees. Stone buildings rising over the grassy quad. Being Saturday, it was quiet, only a few students crossing on the footpaths. It was only the second time I had been on a university campus since I'd left Halberstam. I had forgotten how beautiful they could be and how some, like this one, were built so intentionally to express power and authority. All that stone. The arches. The carved names over doors. Designed to impress, not to welcome.

The metal heart in my pocket felt heavy against my leg. I wore a deep green silk shirt tucked into black dress pants. Well-worn leather oxfords. Hair smoothed back in a low bun. I had looked at my face in the mirror a long time that morning, considering my skin, and decided that I would not be hiding it today, or ever. I would no longer wear the mask.

Of course, that was in the safety of my own bathroom. Now, walking across the quad toward Healy Hall, the moments ticking down, I wanted to hide from everything. I wanted to walk down into the earth as if descending stairs and be swallowed up in the cool darkness. The sunlight stung my eyes.

Lizzie took my hand. "You okay?"

I squeezed her hand, longing for Isaac. One moment of contact with his body, his hand on my waist, the way it loosened the spaces between my joints. Thinking of him grounded me, but only a little, and I felt simultaneously heavy and unbearably light, as if I might blow away. So I held on to Lizzie's hand, clutching the leather bag that held my notes, and summoning every bit of my focus on the single task ahead.

When we came to the top of the stone steps to the lecture hall, Lizzie stopped.

"You can do this," she said.

I forced myself to speak. "I can do this."

We pushed open the heavy doors.

I was twelve years old. Henry sat in the front row, alone in the echoing classroom.

"Where is the error?"

I stood, back turned to my father, face turned to the blackboard. First I took it in in total, like a picture. All the figures arranged as a single system. Then I took it in in steps. This condition, leading to the next, and the two together leading to a third. I looked at it in halves—the same? Different? Or could it be broken up into more than two pieces. I arranged it every possible way in my mind.

Where? Where?

"I don't see it."

"You're not looking hard enough."

I had always seen patterns, as early as I could remember. Symmetry, fractals, things that were alike and not alike.

My father had a heavy hand with chalk, and the proof he had laid out looked starkly back at me in black and white. Where was the error? He had sent me as if on a treasure hunt— only, the treasure was the thing which collapsed the proof. He told me it was there. We had been through this exercise any number of times, and any number of times I had found it.

"You'll never move forward unless you can open your mind, Meg." Henry leaned back in his chair.

And I tried. While my friends were having sleepovers and trying press-on nails and false eyelashes, I was searching for the error in this proof. I was where I wanted to be. I didn't want the false eyelashes. I wanted my father to see me.

Maybe if there had been a Mrs. Brightwood that year— maybe then I would have cared about other things. Regular girl things. But Mrs. Brightwood was now Mrs. Alter half a world away, who visited every other Christmas.

Where was it? A failure of diffeomorphism? No. Where?

I would not fail him the way Mrs. Brightwood had. And if I did not fail, he would not leave.

I looked and thought and looked and thought. We were used to long silences, but slowly a knot built up in my throat. I could not see it. The treasure hunt had become a test, and I was failing.

"I can't."

"Tell me your conclusion, Margaret Brightwood. Is the proof correct?"

"No?"

"Explain."

I swallowed and crossed my arms. It felt good to pull myself in tight and small. The symbols on the chalkboard were right on the edge of what I could understand.

"I can't. I don't know."

Henry stood and walked up to the board. "There is no error in this proof."

Gravity shifted beneath me, almost like the earth itself was swaying.

My father looked at me, his eyes cool. "You knew, didn't you? You should have believed your own eyes. You've got to be able to defend your own conclusions."

I clenched my teeth. *No.*

I did *not* know. I had searched and searched and worked as hard as I could, but I did not know that the proof was right because he had told me there was an error, and I had believed him.

Fuck him. Fuck his clever little manipulation.

No more. Now, when it came to the work of my mind, I trusted myself and myself alone. And today, I would show Henry Brightwood that I understood perfectly where the error was.

As the outside doors fell closed, the vestibule echoed around us, passages opening to the left and right. Straight ahead, across twenty feet of marble floor, stood a set of smaller doors which led into the lecture hall. My eyes adjusted to the low light as I walked, and my heart began its familiar irregularity. Beat-beat-lurch-pause-beat. The metal claw around my chest tightened.

Physiological response to stress, I told myself and walked faster because I could tell that a large part of me wasn't listening.

By the door stood a young man, dark-haired and round-cheeked with an incomplete beard. Must be the grad student assigned to assist at the event. He looked at me, squinted for a moment, then flushed bright pink. He looked to his side, opened his mouth, closed it, and stepped forward.

"Ma'am?" He bowed slightly and waved a hand. "Are you here for the lecture?"

I drew myself up. I was taller than him. "Yes."

"Um, I'm sorry. Are you Margaret Brightwood?"

I scrutinized his face. This small man was in considerable torment.

"Dr. Brightwood," I said. "Yes."

"Um, I'm sorry, Dr. Brightwood." He was sweating. "I've been asked to...um. They said... I'm not supposed to let you in."

An electric flash went off low in my chest. Once I got this deep in the well of anxiety, things didn't have clear names anymore. Just feelings. And never good ones.

Lizzie stepped forward. "Excuse me?"

"Um, I'm sorry. I just... Let me call someone."

"Did you not expect her to come?" Lizzie said. "It's the crowning accomplishment of her own father's career. Why on earth would *they* say she couldn't attend?"

Lizzie, for all her good humor, gave a command performance in aggrieved hauteur. She held up her hand.

"No, we see how it is. You don't have to call *someone*."

She turned away, nodding for me to follow. For a moment I saw relief flood the man's face. A kid, really. Maybe not even a grad student.

I whispered at her. "What—?"

"*Shh.*" She had her phone in her hands, then up to her ear. After a moment's pause, I realized she was calling Kate, whispering, "When you come in the doors, make a disturbance.

Like something's happening outside. They don't want to let Meg in, and we've got to get this ridiculous little troll away from the door."

"Lizzie, I don't know." I put a hand on her arm.

She whispered furiously at me. "You did not come this far to let some petty bureaucrat man-child tell you—Dr. Margaret Brightwood—to run along home." She stuffed her phone back in her purse. "The fucking nerve."

We took two more steps when the outside door burst open and light flooded into the hall.

"Help! Oh my god, help!" Kate looked around frantically. "This guy collapsed on the path. I think he's having a heart attack. I don't know what to do. I don't have my phone. Can someone please help?"

The man-child ran for the door, phone at the ready.

"Go. We'll keep him occupied. Go," Lizzie whispered. Then she ran toward Kate, looking back at the man-child and crying, "Oh my god, do you know CPR?"

The moment they were out the door, I turned and strode across the lobby and through the doors to the auditorium.

I can't do this. I can't do this.

The room was already three-quarters full. I was alone. No Lizzie. No Kate. Alone. This wasn't the way it was supposed to go. They were supposed to sit with me, but now I was alone. Sweat prickled along my hairline, and the claw tightened around my chest. This was not how it was supposed to go.

Turn back. Escape. Run.

But what will Lizzie think if I run away?

Lizzie loves you. She won't care.

But Kate?

She won't care either. You can turn around and leave.

This was what happened when it really got bad. I had both the sweet coaxing and the siren screaming in my head. *It's okay, honey* and *Danger. Run.* I slipped my hand in my pocket and felt for the single Klonopin I had brought along in case of emergency. I had even practiced my statements after taking this medication. Just in case. But instead of taking it, I wrapped my hand around the heart and felt its little sharp tip against my finger. Between this talisman and those two brave and inventive women who had gotten me into the hall, I had just enough confidence that this was enough.

I didn't want to be recognized, but I soon realized there was little chance of that. I had been out of the public eye for so long—three generations of PhD students—there were probably less than half a dozen out of the nearly one hundred people in the room that would know me by sight.

I skirted the wall of the auditorium. One step. Another step. Forward, not backward. Just stay in the room.

I found a seat at the far right of a row. It had a terrible, extreme angle view of the board, but that didn't matter. I didn't need to see. I already knew what Henry Brightwood would say.

I sat down. Stood up again and forced myself back down. Just stay in the room.

"Excuse me."

The voice next to me was so small and shy, but it startled me nonetheless. I looked up toward the aisle. A girl of around fourteen looked down at me with big hazel eyes and a brown ponytail, dyed pink at the ends. Her cheeks aflame. Behind her stood a woman who had to be her mother. Same eyes. The girl looked familiar, but in my rattled state I couldn't place her. The room hummed with conversation, people shifting in their seats.

"Dr. Brightwood?" Her eyes got even bigger, if that was possible. "It's Samira."

Samira.

"Samira." My student. She'd just started last week. Very bright.

"I didn't know you would be here." She fussed with her jacket. "I guess I should have figured. I mean, it's your dad, right?"

There were several empty seats to my left. "It's nice to meet you in person. Would you like to sit with me?"

She broke into a toothy smile, and they immediately shuffled past, Samira whispering something to her mother and bouncing into her seat.

Maybe I could do this.

"Meg, what are you doing here?"

Again, I looked up to the aisle on my right, but this time it was not a face as glad and welcome as Samira's. This time it was Mike Antonovsky, one of my father's oldest friends, looking nothing like the jolly uncle figure he had played at Lizzie's wedding.

My face hardened into a mask. "Hello, Dr. Antonovsky."

He was an imposing figure, standing above me, so at ease in this space. He spoke in a low voice, trying not to be heard by those around us. "I believe you were informed that your father asked you not to attend."

The claw tightened, but I pressed the sharp point of the heart in my pocket again. The cage that was trying to close in around me loosened.

"I was not informed of any such thing." I looked up, feeling flat around the eyes. "I was only informed by the gentleman at the door that he was not supposed to let me in. If my father didn't want me here, he should have told me himself."

Antonovsky frowned, and his eyes twitched. He was annoyed. Good. I was anxious and on the verge of a panic attack, but I would be damned if I was going to let Mike Antonovsky talk down to me. Mike Antonovsky, a mediocre scientist at best, who had gotten tenure and done little more than hold department meetings ever since.

"Meg," he said, "I am asking you to leave."

"Mike," I replied, "is this a private event? Is everyone else in this room an invited guest? Was this lecture not specifically advertised and promoted to the public?"

"You know what I mean." He leaned closer. "You're not welcome here."

"Why? Is my father afraid of me? Am I going to rattle his poor nerves? And I thought *I* was the nervous one."

If I had been really angry at Antonovsky, that would have made it worse. But this pompous man, in spite of his influence in this world, was too ridiculous a figure to rouse more than an irritable disdain.

"This isn't a joke," he said, looking around to see who was listening. "Will you just leave and not make a scene?"

"Who's making a scene? I'm not making a scene." I leaned in and whispered, "Unless you are planning to pick me up and carry me out, I plan to sit right here, quiet as a mouse."

He scowled at me, deep lines running from the corners of his mouth all the way to his jaw. But he walked away.

Samira stared.

"I'm sorry," I said. "My father and I aren't getting along."

"It's all right," she said, bobbing her narrow shoulder. "My dad and I don't get along either."

Her mother frowned, eyes fixed forward.

The room settled to a hush. A woman I didn't recognize stepped up to the podium and began an introduction.

I could do it. I belonged in this room.

She went through my father's bio, which would satisfy the snobbiest elite with its catalog of big-name universities, professorships, and grants, which concealed the absence of any real breakthrough work.

Then she finished, stepped aside, and out came Dr. Henry Brightwood. The room greeted him with polite applause.

No. No, I can't do it.

The deep muscles in my core tried to propel me upward, to get up and leave. It was all I could do to fight it. My heart raced and skipped. My fingers went numb. A very tall man sat in front of me and to my left, and I leaned so that his head obscured the view of my father's face. If I couldn't see him, he couldn't see me.

He started into the proof with an introduction. The same introduction I had used in the spring. It was incredible how sure of himself he sounded. As if he had solved it himself, written it himself. As if he were somehow not lying.

His voice mingled with the tapping of chalk against the board. "As we know, most fluids are Newtonian under normal conditions…"

A primal drive said *Run. Escape.*

But what about Isaac? How could I tell him I failed?

This thought stopped me, and I almost laughed at the funhouse version of my mind that would consider for one second that Isaac Wells gave a shit whether I laid claim to Frieholdt's Conjecture. Of course he cared, but only because I cared. Whether I succeeded or failed or decided to dance the tango up and down the aisle made no difference to him, as long as I was happy.

Anxiety still hovered close to the surface. I felt it. I feared it. But at long, long last—like the pieces of a proof finally stringing together, forming themselves into something intelligible—I understood. It wasn't fear of failure, or of crowds, or speaking in public that caused the irrational sense of danger. Those lesser fears, though present, could be looked at by the rational mind and understood for the disruptive fictions that they were.

What haunted and tormented me, the root of my suffering, was to be shut out from love. It had been too much to bear, because for a child love is life. It is survival itself. To have love be dependent on my performance, my success, and then to fail at that performance and see the sun extinguish itself from the sky. To be lost in the coldness of space, and to know it was my fault. It's no wonder I was afraid.

It was not love from Isaac that released me. It was finally, finally feeling my own whole and complete love for him. It created a bridge for that frightened child to cross and finally become a woman who could exist in the world. Because if I saw Isaac exactly as he was, baggage, scars, faults, and all— if I knew he could fuck up and fuck up again, and if in full knowledge of everything I found him worthy of love, then simple logic dictated that I was worthy too. It gave me permission at last to love myself.

It also gave me permission to get up and walk out. I didn't have to do this just to do it. Just to succeed. If I decided it was the right thing, I could get up and leave. Nothing changed.

My father's back was perhaps more familiar to me than his face. I had spent so many hours watching him at the board. His chalk tapped like sleet against a windowpane in neat, looping script.

"In this part of the equation, the tensor is symmetric. However, we run into trouble with the velocity gradient..."

I couldn't believe this man could stand in front of a room

of the great and grand in the field, in the center of this bastion of legitimacy, and without any apparent strain or struggle, he could lie. And cheat. If I didn't already know, I would never have dreamed I was watching a person commit blatant plagiarism in plain view.

He looked out at the room for a minute, and he spotted me. One would have to know him well to see the shift in his bearing. But it was not shock on his face, or even fear. It was hostility. I gripped my hands together in my lap to stop the shaking.

Samira glanced at me. I managed a smile, and she turned her eyes forward again. This material was so far over her head, but I recognized that look. That fierce urge toward comprehension.

I couldn't leave. I wouldn't leave. I didn't come here to buy myself love or approval or even happiness. I came here for the truth.

Of all the things I could teach a girl like Samira, there was none more important than this. Authority, prestige, even so-called legitimacy were meaningless. What other people said didn't matter. Only truth mattered. Clear, provable, mathematical truth.

It took more than an hour for my father to finish. The room hung on every word, every symbol, every breath. This was the Impossible after all. Mathematics had waited lifetimes for this day. I looked to the back of the room about halfway through, and there were Lizzie and Kate, standing against the back wall. They gave me strength, those two savvy warriors. Who better to literally have my back at that moment than Lizzie, looking darkly at my father, and Kate, looking worriedly at me. I gave her a nod and mouthed, *I'm okay.*

I recognized as he was coming near the end and took my notes from my bag. Of course, as I had expected, all the symptoms came rushing back. The rigid spine, the burning gut, the numbness. My time was coming.

The notes I had so carefully prepared swam in my vision. The physical exercises I had practiced succeeded in keeping me conscious and upright but could not clear my mind. All my rehearsal had come to nothing.

He was nearly done.

I tried desperately to understand my own notes, my own plan, but my mind would not comply.

He set down his chalk and turned to the room. Applause. People stood. My father looked around, feigning diffidence, but smiling.

I can't do nothing. I can't walk out. He was about to leave the floor. People were gathering their coats. I had to do something. Anything.

I stood. "Dr. Brightwood?" My voice came out faint and high. I took a breath and pushed the words lower in my chest. "Dr. Brightwood?"

My father looked up. Now there was fear in his eyes.

Antonovsky walked out onto the stage, waving his pink hands. "As stated at the beginning, there will be no discussion."

Samira stared. Her mother stared. Lizzie, Kate, everyone, the whole room.

With ever so careful steps, I descended the side aisle, eyes fixed on the board.

A board. I could always understand a board. I found the section of proof I was looking for and forced myself forward, never looking away. My father tried to intercept.

"What are you doing? You can't—"

"Excuse me." I dodged around him without meeting his eyes, reached the front of the room and picked up a nub of chalk.

Slowly regaining feeling in my fingers, I blew a breath out through pursed lips. A board. Chalk. My back to the room. Maybe, just maybe.

The shuffling of coats and bags ceased. People whispered my name. Then silence fell.

Reaching up, I slid a section of board down, and around a group of figures I drew a large square.

I tapped the chalk against the board twice, hard, and my head turned only slightly, able to see the crowd through the corner of my eye, I managed as much of a voice as there was in me.

"Here is the error. A fatal error. When this proof is reviewed, you'll see that I'm right. And you will ask yourselves—you should ask, how did she know?" I turned to face the room, to face Lizzie and Kate. I spoke directly to them, which of course made it possible for me to speak to everyone. "I know, because this proof is mine. Not Henry Brightwood's, not ours together. Mine alone. The result of twenty years of research." My breath was failing fast. "The only way I could identify this error in this moment is because I made it. This mistake is mine. This proof is mine. And to present it otherwise is fraud."

My father said something—*crazy, lost your mind*. I lost sight of Lizzie and Kate. Antonovsky got in my face. Then Lizzie blazed onto the stage all crackling sparks and fire.

"Get away from her. Back off."

She wedged herself between me and Antonovsky, got an arm around my waist and steered me toward the lower side door. Behind us I heard Kate's low chuckle.

"You should see yourselves," she said, presumably to my father and Mike. "Fucking cheaters."

Then she followed us, still laughing.

The side door led to a long hall with a linoleum floor and tile walls. Gray-green and cold. A door at the end let in a white square of sunlight. We were halfway there when I grabbed Lizzie's arm and lowered myself to the floor.

"I think I'm going to throw up."

"Shit," Lizzie hissed. She dropped down next to me and dumped out the contents of her purse. "Here."

"What? No." I pushed it away. "I'm not going to puke in your purse. I'll just…" I leaned against the wall, knees to chest. "No, I think I'm okay. Just give me a second."

She scooped her scattered bits back into the bag.

Kate's voice down the hall was diplomatic but firm. "No. I'm so sorry, she's not feeling well. We need to give her some space." She was standing in the door, blocking the way. "Yes, she'll post a statement… Yes, she'll be okay. Thank you… I'll tell her. Thank you… No." She twisted to see us. "Go. Call me. I'll meet you wherever."

Lizzie helped me up and got me through the hall and out the door. My eyes pinched in the bright afternoon light. It was cool, and sweat chilled on my skin as Lizzie walked me as fast as she could down a dirt path away from the hall. As much as I felt like I was about to pass out, I also felt like I could fly.

"Excuse me." A woman behind us.

Lizzie turned around. "Oh, for god's sake. No. She's done. Can't you see that?"

"It's okay, Liz," I said.

It was Anne MacFaull. Dressed in the same anonymous way she had been when I first met her, I wasn't surprised I hadn't seen her in the room, especially since I had been vigorously avoiding anyone I might know.

She joined us as we walked. Lizzie placed herself protectively in the middle. I shivered and crossed my arms.

"I'll be brief," Anne said. "I believe you. I believe the proof is yours, and if you say it's wrong, I believe it's wrong."

"Thank you."

"I have to admit, it's not what I was expecting, but it will get reviewed, and I have every reason to think you will be vindicated. Did you not bring a jacket?"

"I left it in the room."

"Here." Anne shrugged off a light fleece and handed it to me. "Do you remember when Schenck plagiarized Alvarez?"

"Of course I do."

"The lawyer who represented Alvarez is named Howard Trask. He now works with me at Nautilus. If it's okay with you, I'd like to have him initiate a suit for theft of intellectual property."

"But—"

"I'm going to explain." She had natural charisma, this woman, and I was grateful for her fleece, so I waited for her to continue. "There will be no cost to you, and you won't have any obligation to me or Nautilus. I would write you a check and send you to find your own lawyer, but that's a lot of work. And Howard will pin Henry Brightwood down and remove his spleen with tweezers if he tries anything. If it were me, I'd hire him no matter who he worked for."

She took her wallet from her back pocket and slid out two cards. Her own and Howard Trask's.

"Why are you carrying his card?" Lizzie eyed her sharply.

"The kind of work my group does, you'd be surprised how often I need it. And it was pretty clear after you called me that something was fishy about this whole situation." Anne smiled. "Hold on to the jacket. Good to see you again."

She turned away and walked back to the hall. Lizzie craned her head around to watch her go.

"Who was that?"

"I'll explain later," I said. "Can we just sit down a minute?"

"Oh shit, you look pale." She steered me to a bench, and we both sat. "No, lie down. Head at heart level, legs up. There. Now you won't pass out. I hope."

I rested my head in her lap, face toward the sky.

25

The night after the lecture I slept, if it could be called sleep, as I had all week, with my phone next to my ear. And in the morning, it rang. I shot upright and snatched it.

"Are you there?" Isaac said.

Of course, I burst into tears.

"What's the matter?" His words were quick and urgent. "What happened?"

"No, nothing. Nothing's the matter. I'm just so relieved."

He sighed. "I'm sorry, baby. It's so early. You probably haven't had your coffee yet."

Crying turned to laughing, then to crying again, and I curled into my sofa nest, phone clutched to my ear, loving him so much I could barely stay within my own body.

"Are you okay?" I said. "Are you eating? Are you sleeping? I've been so worried."

"Yes, I'm fine. But I have to tell you something—but you have to tell me about yesterday. Fuck. I just don't know how long we have on the phone."

"I did it. I almost didn't, but I did—"

"That's amazing. You're amazing. Was it—"

"I'll tell you all about it, but what do you have to tell me?"

"They arrested Dustin DeVries."

"Oh my god." I couldn't take this pitch of anxiety much longer. "On what? How?"

"He found out I was back, and he fucked up. He went to a bar and got drunk and started going on and on like 'I'm gonna kill that motherfucker Wells the second he walks out of jail.' So the bartender called the police, and they had him on the security cameras, and they arrested him and searched his house and busted his whole operation, and now he's fucked." His accent always got stronger when he was excited. "Erin told me all about it. She was like, 'Yeah, you weren't wrong. That guy was bad news.' But she said half the department down here is acting like she did them a big goddamn favor bringing me in because, you know, they don't like me that much, but now they got Dustin, and they fucking hate his guts."

He laughed. I laughed. The utter relief of it.

"If I get out of here, we're leaving this place for good," he said. "I am never, ever coming back. You have to call Kate and tell her the whole story, okay?"

"Yes, okay. But it won't sound as good coming from me."

"Oh, she'll get it. She knows exactly what that motherfucker had coming to him. God, sorry—okay—tell me about yesterday. Tell me everything."

The story tumbled out of me, bouncing forward and back like a ball in a box. The kid at the door, Kate's ruse, Samira, Antonovsky, how Lizzie almost let me throw up in her purse, and finally the unexpected coda of Anne MacFaull.

I shifted onto my back. "I fell asleep at eight yesterday, and I've barely moved since. I'm so drained."

"I wish I was there," he said. "I would fucking spoon-feed you, and you could stay in bed for a week. A month."

I could have stayed on the phone all day, but the jail only gave him fifteen minutes.

"We'll be there tomorrow," I said. "Ten o'clock. I'll be there. How long do they give you to visit?"

"I don't know. I'll take anything I can get. Now, go get some coffee. Or go back to sleep. You sound exhausted."

"I am. I feel so drained. But we're almost through this. We're almost on the other side."

"Meg Brightwood," he said, "you are the strongest person I've ever known."

Monday morning met me far earlier than usual, though this time instead of going back to sleep, then dragging myself out of bed at a more reasonable hour, I jumped up and got dressed before it was light. We were going to get an early start for Blind Fork.

Coffee and breakfast helped only slightly. I was still physically weak. Lucky for me I had two capable and energetic friends to do the heavy lifting. Lizzie called her husband, James, who brought a drill and some packing blankets, and between the three of them, they unmounted the panels of my board and carried them out. They were heavy. Four feet by five, and the edges were not kind on the hands. Two went in Lizzie's SUV, headed for storage in her basement, along with a few rugs, pictures, and boxes. The last panel they slid into the back seat of my car.

As we carried out the last boxes, a cold drizzle started, and Sharon pulled up in her creamy-white Lexus. Stepping out, she stopped a moment on the walk and looked up at the house. She seemed wistful—an emotion I hadn't seen on her before—and she looked as if it pained her. But in true Sharon style, she rallied and climbed the steps to the shelter of the porch. Lizzie's face hardened. Kate eyed her shrewdly as I introduced them.

"I transferred the money to your account," Sharon said. "Have you got everything you need out?"

"Yes, I think so."

"We'll put everything else in storage, so in case you missed anything—" Her eyes softened and she nodded toward the door. "Can I...could we talk in private a minute?"

We walked together through the old house to the dining room, where she stopped, looking through the French doors out to the garden.

"That was brave, what you did," she said.

I looked at her, confused.

"The lecture is on YouTube already, including your part at the end." She turned her gaze back to the room. "You're probably going to miss this house."

"Yes and no."

"For what it's worth, Meg, I'm sorry." Creases appeared around her eyes. She looked older in the dim light. "I think I was jealous of all the attention you got, and it never occurred to me it might not be good for you. That it was harmful for you, all that pressure. Especially after Mom left."

Perhaps it was the softness of fatigue, or maybe the unusual look of regret in her eyes, but I reached out and hugged her. She responded, awkward and rigid, but strong.

"I'll miss it," she said. "I've always loved this house."

We walked slowly back to the porch through the parlor with its grand fireplace and window seat.

"With any luck, the money will eventually come to us," she said.

"We could be old ladies by then."

"I certainly will be. And you never know. Dad has been known to do some stupid things. And Uncle Stuart—I mean, he's just strange."

"Amazing someone as normal as Lizzie came from that family."

She nodded and hitched her purse higher on her shoulder, ready to head to work. She had always gone in ridiculously early.

"Good luck." She squeezed my shoulder. "If you need help—you know, getting on your feet—let me know."

The drizzle continued to fall, dripping from the gutters and the leaves. I started my car to let it warm up and said goodbye to Sharon, to Lizzie and James. Kate waved to me as she drove off. I would see her in a few hours in Blind Fork.

Then I gathered my purse and my coat and took one more walk around the house, footsteps echoing in the empty rooms, damp cold creeping into the wood and plaster. I locked up the doors and windows and said a silent goodbye to the grand, gray edifice which had for so many years been my sanctuary.

My gas tank was full, the rain had stopped, no wrecks or roadwork snarled my progress, and remarkably I did not need to pee or get pulled over for speeding. In less than five hours, I took the exit to Blind Fork. The Great Smoky Mountains lived up to their name that day, with mist from the morning's rain swirling among the trees and hovering over the foothills and hollows. I took the turn to the main street and drove up past the dollar store and the post office.

The mountain rose not far beyond, steep and wooded with dark evergreens. I would be getting to know this place, I figured. Isaac once told me there was a library on a side street.

An old one, he said, built back when people cared about making buildings beautiful.

I leaned over the steering wheel, heart racing. Only minutes remaining until I could see him. The moment I had longed for through all the trials of the last week.

The sky felt low and gloomy over this nook of the mountain. The roadside littered with debris, curbs chipped and crumbling. I turned down a side street, drove to the very end, and there it was. A plain brown building with a plain brown sign. Erin had told me not to worry. Just announce yourself at the gate when you drive in and go to the front desk, she said. They'll tell you exactly what to do. I checked my phone. There were two missed calls. One an unknown number, and one from Erin, but my momentum could not be checked at that point. I was about to see Isaac. The calls could wait.

It smelled of disinfectant inside, and the fluorescent lights buzzed, but where I had expected chaos and danger, I found a kind of ponderous quiet instead. Three people sat, spaced apart in a single row of plastic chairs, seemingly settled in for a long wait. They barely looked up as I entered.

The woman at the counter peered down at me from behind a scratched pane of Plexiglas.

"I'm here to see Isaac Wells," I said. "His lawyer said—"

She removed the reading glasses from her deep brown eyes, and her face suddenly opened.

"Wells?" She might have been suppressing a smile. It was hard to tell.

"Yes. Isaac Wells."

"Are you Margaret Brightwood?" I started to fish out my driver's license, but she said, "It's okay, honey. He's waiting for you."

I looked at her, expecting more. Instructions. Anything.

"Right over there." She pointed. "Down the hall and through the glass door."

This was such foreign territory. "Um, okay. Thank you."

A narrow hall led to the right where she had directed me. It was poorly lit and appeared to lead to an outside door. I walked halfway down, past a couple of closed office doors. This couldn't be right. I turned around and walked back the way I'd come, then turned around again, so frustrated. I was missing minutes with him.

Fine. Okay, fine. If I wind up outside and have to go around the front again, I'll just do it.

Through the glass door I saw another parking lot. I stepped out. Looked right.

Isaac stood, and I threw my arms around him. We held on tight, standing solid and still as if we could hardly bear to move.

"You didn't answer your phone," he said, his voice wavering, face buried in my hair.

"I was driving like ninety miles an hour. Why are you outside?"

"They're letting me go."

He looked in my eyes, only for a second, then he kissed me. I could have stood there in front of the jail kissing Isaac Wells forever. Not a glamorous way to spend forever, but I didn't care.

With a quiet groan he leaned his head on my shoulder. "You have no idea how happy I am to see you."

The air smelled of pine. His jacket felt rough on my cheek, and a cold wind chilled my back.

"Is this why Erin tried to call me?" I tried to reach in my pocket.

"Fuck the phone." He pulled me closer until I could feel his heart beating. "It happened so fast. Once the DA decided it was self-defense, they just wrapped it up. Erin is a fucking miracle worker. She got me a year probation. One year. I can't leave the state, and I have to be home by nine."

I pulled my head back to look in his eyes. "One year? *One year?*"

"That's all. I don't know how she did it," he said and laughed. "They practically apologized when they put the GPS thing on my ankle."

Shifting in his tight embrace, I draped my arms around his neck, gazed into those sparkling cinnamon eyes, and the rigid strain of the last few days, the last weeks, my whole damned life, fell away.

26

Winter at the cabin was the perfect balance for a life of intense thinking. Four months of splitting wood, breaking ice off the pump handle and bringing up water, clearing snow from the path, and a hundred other ways I learned to use my hands. Four months of decent sleep, excellent sex, daily human contact, and at last the right antidepressant. We put in an electrical line, so it was a little less like camping, but it was mainly for light and internet. The hearth got warm and stayed warm, like a great, sleeping beast in the center of our world.

As soon as it became known that the fearsome Howard Trask was going after my father, the math world grew considerably friendlier to me. A university four hours to the east offered me a research fellowship. I made clear to them I would not teach. Office hours once a month. No meetings. And they said yes, yes, and yes. They were lucky to be affiliated with me, and they knew it. I may have been wrong about this particular attempt at the Impossible, but my application of the Loading Hypothesis portended a major breakthrough.

Anne and I stayed in regular contact, and she found a way

to pay me a standing fee for consulting. We would spend hours online together, going into deep, nerd-level detail about both my research and hers.

As lovely and snug as winter had been, though, I had never been so happy to see spring. It advanced up the mountain, little white flowers arriving before the last snow melted. When the ground thawed, Isaac built me a new room to work in, extending from the kitchen where the ground was level. He taught me to use the circular saw and pound nails, and we raised walls and rafters together.

When the redbud and dogwood shook out their pink and white skirts under the tall bare poplars and oaks, the new room was finished and smelled of fresh sawdust and caulk. A big window in front looked out over the meadow and the ridge. My one section of board leaned against the solid wall in back.

On a bright blue day in April, Lizzie and her husband came to visit. They arrived when the sun was high, warming the damp earth with all the smells of roots and buds and growing things.

From my spot on the porch, I listened to Isaac and James as they advanced up the path, carrying the remaining two sections of my board. Their words weren't intelligible, but I felt the exertion in their voices.

Lizzie stood next to me, hands on hips. "You have gone full pioneer woman here."

"Only, with internet and a grocery store."

Her hair gleamed white-gold in the sun. Solomon's seal and foamflower speckled the meadow. Tall pillars of galax bloomed in the shade along the wood's edge.

Isaac and James tromped across the grass, breaking the mountain silence as they climbed the porch stairs and brought my boards inside.

Isaac shucked off his jacket. "Jesus. Fucking thing is heavy."

I had already marked off where I wanted it, and Isaac had installed the mounting hardware, so attaching it to the wall was the work of only a few minutes. I stood, hands clasped and bouncing on my toes like a little girl on her birthday as the men screwed the new chalk ledge to the wall. When they were done, I put my arms around Isaac's waist and murmured, "Thank you."

I had my board back. Home was complete.

He kissed my temple. "I need to close up the smithy. I'll be back in a little bit."

He took the grassy path toward the far side of the meadow. Unsurprisingly, his knee hadn't healed quite right, and it left him with a limp. It couldn't be helped, but it didn't hurt.

I offered to help start the cooking, but Lizzie shooed me away. "Go admire your board, Miss Little-House-on-the-Prairie. I'll do dinner. It's warm enough we could eat outside."

I stepped into my room and curled my toes into the old red rug.

The Heisenberg uncertainty principle states, more or less, that we cannot know all things at all times. We may know exact velocity but not exact position. Or the converse, but not both. In essence, we may know where we are but not where we're going. Or we may know our trajectory forward but not exactly where we are on it. As much as mathematicians love the concrete certainty of logic, we understand the power in ambiguity—those places that seem uncertain, even danger-ous, where what is known, or believed to be known, falls into a healthy, fertile doubt.

Two hundred years strong, Frieholdt's still stood unbeaten. I rested my shoulder on the hand-hewn timbers where my new room met the original wall. Built from trees that grew slow and hardy from that very mountainside, this place was as much a part of the mountain as anything could be that wasn't deposited by geology or grown from a seed. It would shake off winter ice and summer storms. The roof would not leak and the iron door hinges would hold for generations.

I opened my box of chalk. There were a lot of years ahead. Seemed a fitting place to begin.

★ ★ ★ ★ ★

ACKNOWLEDGMENTS

Before I thank the many amazing people who contributed to bringing this book into being, I want to say a word or two about math. Serious mathematicians will look at the mathematical language in this book and see that most, if not all of it, is complete nonsense. I, of course, do not understand the tiniest fraction of how that level of math really works. What I was exploring as I wrote this story and this character was the mind and heart of a researcher.

As a creative person, I have been fascinated to find many parallels between the practice of art and the practice of science: the struggle with the unknown, existing in ambiguity, self-doubt, exultation. I also find the language of mathematics beautiful and mysterious. It's incomprehensible to me yet reads like avant-garde poetry. Because I love this language, and to create some verisimilitude, I threw some of it into the story. Frieholdt's Conjecture is loosely based on the Navier-Stokes existence and smoothness problem. Karvonen, Wang-Hickman, Gault, and the Loading Hypothesis are made-up, as is Bonnie Fenty.

Doctor Sally Collins, a researcher in something called low-dimensional topology, specifically Heegaard Floer homology and knot theory, graciously answered a bunch of my questions about what it's really like to have a mind like hers, and what it's really like to be a woman in mathematics. I am so grateful for the time she took to share her insight. But I want to be perfectly clear here: all errors and math nonsense are mine alone.

Now on to the thanks.

An author writes in solitude, but a book is built by a whole community of people. It's a remarkable thing: all these marvelous people with their various skills—creative, business-smart, strategic—getting behind this story to fledge it into the world and into the hands of readers. I am regularly astounded by my luck for the following…

My editor at Graydon House Books, Cat Clyne, who takes what I wrote and brings it ever closer to what I really *meant* to write, and in doing so makes me a better writer.

Susan Swinwood, Loriana Sacilotto, Diane LaVoie, and the whole team at Graydon House. There are so many people working on this book whose faces I don't see, and I am grateful for all of them.

Erin Craig, art director, and Suzanne Washington, cover designer, for bringing Meg Brightwood to life on the cover of this book. I love the sly tilt of her shoulder and her intelligent side-eye.

My agent, Laura Bradford, without whom I would be but a babe wandering in the wilderness. I am so fortunate that this frank, funny, and wise person has my back.

Flannery Buchanan, bookseller and co-owner of Bluebird & Co. in Crozet, Virginia, who has been my advocate, cheerleader, and event planner extraordinaire from day one.

My kids, Morgan and Mia, who have really kept things reasonably chill through the teenage years. Keep it up!

Aaron Nisenson and Annie Nisenson, my brother and sister, who are on 24/7 call for various expert consults. I feel like we're not even really three people. We're one person with three different lives.

And my husband, Bobby Read, who is currently making brilliant, experimental, ambient analogue-synth music for me to listen to while I write. You all should hear this shit. It would blow your mind.

Jessica Payne, my author-wife. Thriller writer, mom, literary therapist (with one client—me), and dear friend. She does me the great service of telling me exactly what she thinks of my writing. She also writes amazing books. You should read them.

Author Elle Cosimano for her generous support and cheerleading despite the massive pile of work she has on her plate.

Kristie Smeltzer for reading an early version of this book and saying wise things that totally fixed it. And Tes Slominski for putting my butt in the chair and keeping me accountable. Jenny Cox for listening to me vent.

Kate Brauning, author, editor, and wise counselor, who once or twice a year uses her massively creative book-brain to help me out of whatever hole I have dug myself into.

Adi Banavage and Keith Fritz and all the staff at the UVA Emily Couric Clinical Cancer Center's Infusion Center, where I worked while writing this book. They just did their usual thing, but it's not usual at all to have such a supportive and healthy work environment as a nurse.

And last, my gratitude to everyone who labors in obscurity—scientists, artists, caregivers—perhaps not knowing if their work will ever see the light of day or be recognized and appreciated. Your work *is* important, and I see you.

In this novel, *The Blacksmith's Companion* is based on *The Complete Library of Metal Working, Blacksmithing & Soldering* by Oscar Almeida (Drake Publishers, 1976).

DISCUSSION GUIDE

1. Has someone ever taken credit for your work or your idea? How did you deal with it?

2. If you have a spouse, partner, or close loved one, is there something about your work or life that they can't possibly understand? How does that work in your relationship?

3. Through Isaac, Meg learns the names of plants. Through Meg, Isaac learns that math is everywhere, even when he isn't aware of it. What is something that you learned from someone you were close to? Was there something you hardly knew existed until they showed it to you?

4. Meg grew up with a highly conditional form of love that her father used to drive her to greater heights in her mathematical abilities. What are the pitfalls of using love and approval to influence behavior? What might be healthier ways to motivate young people?

5. Meg deals with sexism and misogyny in her field. What are some ways that you have had to deal with individual

or structural sexism in your life? What are ways that people have, or could have, supported you as allies in combating sexism?

6. As a high-level researcher, Meg contends with a lot of ambiguity before things become clear. What are some ways that ambiguity operates in your work or your life? How does it make you feel to contend with something that is highly uncertain or unknown?

7. The concept of a "gifted child" is a complicated one. Have you had any experience with programs for "gifted" children? If so, what was it like? What are your thoughts about these types of programs in a school environment?